TIME OF THE OAK

AN AUTOBIOGRAPHICAL FANTASY NOVEL

Sak

Dedicated

to

Jim Hodges

English/Latin Master Dauntsey's School 1954-1990

For Jenny,

Number 1 Book for Number 1 Fan

Love

SAK

Nov 2020

HELGE: AN ENIGMATIC VIKING

The Valkyries had left; Odin and Thor, father and son, had spoken and were ready to deliver their verdict, and seal Helge's fate. He trembled as Odin recounted the events that had barred his automatic entry into Valhalla, but now he stood proud and unashamed at those same memories.

Hordaland AD 769 840

Though his family, like most Vikings, were primarily farmers, the fjords and woods had always been Helge's greatest love; almost before he could walk he had been playing about with the skeletons of the boats rotting on the banks of the water. To him these derelict hulks were still the beautiful graceful boats he saw sailing up and down the fjords. Some were leaving on new adventures, their high prows glistening in the sunlight, almost leaping over the waves, eager to be on their way. Some were under sail and others, when the wind was lacking, displayed long oars protruding from between the colourful shields of the proud seafaring warriors. Helge longed to be on one of those boats, yearned for adventure, and, when the storm clouds gathered and the wind from the forest gusted across the lake, he would stand proud in one of those remains, letting the spray whip into his face as he embarked on his own imaginary voyages.

And so it was that in 789 three long ships prepared for sea and leading them was Helge, chosen because of his proven ability to navigate. He was an imposing sight; a true Viking, just over six feet tall, long blond hair; the beginnings of a beard; limbs that resembled the trunks of trees from the forests. At other times he could be found playing in the woods; alone, and armed with the stoutest of sticks, he became the fiercest of warriors slashing at the undergrowth, defeating the most stubborn of enemies. He always seemed to know where he was in the woods, always able to find his way home. The elders marvelled at this uncanny ability, even when taken blindfolded to a part of the forest he had never been to before he could find his way back.. Later, when he was old enough to sail in the boats he had admired as a boy, he found he could use this talent to navigate at sea.

In Hordaland at that time villages were very rare; most people living in isolated Long Houses with their animals, something that Helge found quite comforting. Sometimes cold and wet from his boyhood adventures the warmth, even the smell of the animals living in the Long House, lifted his spirits. And at night Floki, his Norwegian Buhund, slept on his bed.

Although isolated, communal spirit had grown up between different Long Houses and stories and tales were carried from place to place. Several of these stories were that there were treasures in Britain that would be easy pickings. The rumours were that these treasures were to be found in and around the great monasteries and were often poorly guarded. To a pagan, war like people, this was difficult to understand and many were sceptical, but such an opportunity, if true, should not to be missed.

And so it was that in 789 three long ships prepared for sea and leading them was Helge, chosen because of his proven ability in navigation. He was an imposing sight; a true Viking, just over six feet tall, long blond hair; the beginnings of a beard; limbs that resembled the trunks of trees from the forests he had played in not many years before, and skin toughened by his outdoor life. Fearless, cunning, soon to be master of the sea, he was, many believed, already at twenty three, destined to join the Gods and warriors of old in Valhalla when his time eventually came.

With no cabins or other forms of shelter, the three longboats needed little preparation other than checking their sea worthiness and loading provisions. Each of the sixty man crew had a small sea-chest containing the bare essentials and used as seats when it became necessary to use the oars to power the boat through the seas.

The last action before embarkation had been the slaughtering of animals whose blood was used as a sacrifice to the gods in the hopes of a safe and successful voyage. A great feast was prepared and eaten on the shore; there was much happiness and singing; a common feeling that this was what Helge and his comrades had been born to do; this was their destiny. If any of the one hundred and eighty men now boarding the boats had any fear or doubt, they did not let it show.

The wind was light as Helge and his men hauled their boat into the water, so the first thirty men took their positions and readied to row. Helge knew that rowing these great boats would be no easy task, despite the fitness of his men. Bearing in mind that his crew were also his warriors, he was determined to give them as much rest as possible. He ordered that each of the oarsmen would be at their rowing station for one thousand strokes, before resting as best they could in a cold open boat. Experience had taught him that each of these watches would take about two hours and would cover about two nautical miles. He himself would take the helm. Helge hoped that the wind would pick up once they had left the shelter of the Fjord and the sail could be set allowing more rapid progress to be made. The speed of the sea voyage was not essential to the success of the mission, but he needed to preserve the energy of his men. The constant battering of the sea; the cold winds blowing, and the constant dampness could sap the energy of even the hardiest of these seafarers.

After three days of sailing, damp, cold and weary sailors rested for just a moment, when land was sighted, to give a rousing cheer and offer thanks to the gods for bringing them safely to their destination. Though his eyes were weary, bloodshot, sore, though they stung from the salt laden spray that had incessantly battered his face, Helge had been the first to spot land; it was as if fate had intervened to enhance his image; it seemed to those men he commanded, and those in the other boats, that he had led them unerringly to their destination, Portland, a small island off the southern tip of Wessex. To his men his legend was further enhanced; they did not know of his doubts, the uncertainty he had felt of making landfall at all. Throughout the journey, armed with only the sketchiest information, and with a rudimentary knowledge of astral navigation, he alone knew what a stroke of luck it had been.

As the ships drew closer to the shores of Britain the voyagers could see quite clearly the outlines of a settlement at the centre of which was a great Monastery. Helge now steered his small fleet of ships away from the settlement and made landfall on the eastern edge of the island, as far from the settlement as he could. It was a relief to be on dry land again, to be able to light fires, to feel the heat coursing through their bodies once more. Helge's fingertips and toes had been almost frozen with cold and he had doubted his ability to fight under such conditions. Others must feel the same, and looking after the welfare of his men was to become a hallmark of his leadership. Not until their bodies had been warmed, did Helge send out a small hunting party, who soon came back with some wild boar, and the men were able to enjoy a welcome hot meal, rest and find their land legs.

But Helge's eyes were not the only alert ones that morning; a young monk in Portland noted three small ships on the horizon. So unusual was this that he watched for some time to ensure they were indeed headed in his direction. Once satisfied, he rushed to tell his Abbot, who in turn dispatched three men to the mainland to inform the authorities in Dorchester of the sightings. They had no inkling that the boats might constitute part of an invasion or raiding party, there were no thoughts that the three ships constituted a threat. No form of defence was even contemplated; instead the Royal Reeve, the local magistrate, was sent to investigate.

Dunstan Haynesworth was essentially a man of peace, from good farming stock. Not a nobleman in the accepted sense, (he maintained his family was just one step away from earldom,) he was a noble man in nature and thought, fair and a trusted emissary.

To some of the monks it appeared that the ships had simply sailed around the island to head for the mainland shore of Wessex. Had it been a clearer day, smoke from their fires might have given the lie to this thought, but here yet again Helge's luck held; a heavy sea mist had made the possible sightings of smoke unlikely. Though the Monks were untroubled, Dunstan was ill at ease; though he knew not why, this uncertainty caused him more anxiety. He did not have the power to take action; his role was more one of detection, observation and recording. He resolved to return to Dorking the following morning with his report.

A favourable easterly breeze, allied with a cloudless late evening sky and high tide, determined Helge's next move. His men, now well rested, re boarded their boats and keeping about one hundred and fifty metres offshore, followed the coastline until once again the settlement came into view. It was near four in the morning as they silently secured their boats on the beach. With only one hundred and eighty men Helge had to plan carefully. He chose five to go and reconnoitre the settlement and check the defences to see what hurdles had to be overcome. The five returned remarkably quickly; they had found, to their utter amazement, that there were no defences of any sort, no sentries or lookouts. All seemed quiet; a community seemingly at peace with itself and the world.

But Helge was troubled; surely this had to be a trap? They must have seen his boats; they must know he was there. He talked to his men at length, consulted with those who had more experience and while they all agreed it seemed to be a trick or a deception, they could not see or decipher what it might be.

It would soon be dawn; the scouts had reported a small wooded area just north of the settlement that could easily conceal the party, and from where Helge could observe the settlement, to watch and see if indeed a trap had been set.

So they watched as the settlement gradually came to life; before dawn the first cock crowed, followed by the dawn chorus, the birdsong of sunrise, then farm animals, mooing, neighing, scratching, and dogs barking. Helge and his men were now on full alert, fearful, their adrenalin pumping. Helge, sword and shield in hand, his blonde hair wafting in the dawn wind, held back his men, who were spoiling for a fight.

Ever vigilant, he watched and waited. A young shepherd boy was first to leave the settlement, he seemed in no hurry, strolling along, chewing on a hunk of bread. Then, suddenly it seemed, he caught sight of the empty boats on the shore; for a moment he stood there motionless, then with surprising speed, ran back to the monastery. The great bell was soon tolling and there was chaos as the settlement, woken so rudely, was galvanized into frenzied activity. Still Helge waited, feeling this was not yet the moment. Below, doors were thrown open and a mass of people streamed out, and headed towards the beach and the boats. At their head was Dunstan on his great black horse, followed by the monks, and then men, women and children from the small homes roundabout joined the throng. Helge still held off, staring at this mass of people in disbelief; none of them appeared armed in any way other than Dunstan but even his sword was still safely in its scabbard. Though the crowds below vastly outnumbered Helge and his men, he nonetheless lifted his sword and charged, his screaming men behind him, following with unbridled savagery, roaring and shouting as they ran.

The fight, if indeed such a massacre could be called a fight, was mercifully short. Helge made straight towards Dunstan, who in a state of shock, had no fight in him and Helge fatally felled him with one blow from his sword. He looked around him to see how the fight was going. It was going well, but he was horrified and sickened by what he saw. This surely, was not how it was meant to be? There was no glory here that he could see; his men, his warriors were behaving like animals, slaughtering all before them, men, women, children, all were being put to the sword. Buildings burning, women were being abused. What had he expected? He had given his men no instructions, it was valorous to fight, all his training told him so. But there was no valour here, it must be stopped, this must be stopped!. But by the time he had managed to establish some kind of order, it was too late for most. Not one of his men was much injured, just a bruise here or there, and one broken finger. As quickly as possible, and with little joy in his heart, he had ransacked the monastery, looted its treasures, gold, silver, fine fabrics, jewels, food and ale and loaded them on to their boats. After all, it was he had come for. It was what was expected of him!

On the homeward journey there was much rejoicing, merriment and happiness, the satisfaction of a job well done; of them all only Helge seemed to have any misgivings. Alone at the helm, he felt ill at ease, there had been nothing noble, nothing glorious, about their victory. What was victorious about the indiscriminate slaughtering of unarmed men, women and children? His solemn thoughts were interrupted by his men, breaking into song:

Drink, for the wind blows cold and
Drink for The Wolf runs free.
Drink to the ships with the sails like wings and
Drink to the storm-tossed seas.

Drink to the lasting nights
and those who warm our beds.
Drink to the mead that warms our hearts
and the cold that clears our head.

Drink to the All father's Eye
for Odin's sons are we.
Drink to the World-Tree where he hung
and the Runes of Mystery.

Drink to the truth of steel
and blood that falls like rain.
Drink to Valhalla's golden walls
and to our kinsmen, slain.

Drink to the Glory-field
where a man embraces death, and
thank the gods that we live at all
with our joyous dying breath!

Drink for the wind blows cold and
Drink for the Wolf runs free
Drink to the ships with the sails like wings
for Odin's sons are we! - *[Karen Unrein Kahan]*

The words mocked him. He had never felt less like a son of Odin; indeed, he felt that he had betrayed everything that Odin and Valhalla truly represented.

On their return there was more rejoicing, more sacrifices to the gods were offered and there was the usual feasting and drinking. Helge was feted as a hero and exaggerated tales and songs were being written and sung telling how he, Helge, was a worthy successor to all those warrior heroes that had gone before. Plans were made for more raids along the coast of Ireland and Scotland. Helge smiled and nodded and it was assumed that Helge would lead these skirmishes and achieve more successes. He seemingly acquiesced but there was no joy in his heart and his blood ran cold. For perhaps the first time he really noticed the women and children of his community, observing their gentleness, innocence and trust; he was much troubled to think he was being lauded for the slaughter of similar guileless victims.

As stories spread from Long House to Long House, any truth

there might have been at the beginning had long given way to pure fiction as his deeds and exploits were told, retold and enhanced. With the speed of a Thor thunderbolt he was acquiring a god like status and this carried consequences. Young, attractive and eligible in his own right, his new found notoriety seemingly attracted the attention of every father across the land who had a marriageable daughter and all of whom, it seemed, desired him for a son in law.

They streamed in from all corners, and Helge was obligated by tradition to meet them all, feast with them, discuss their marriage proposals and make excuses, or give credible reasons why the desired union could not take place. He was attracted to many of the young women, but in every case felt there was something missing, an indefinable something that made him draw back when a final decision was sought. Disappointment, disillusionment, arguments and pleadings, frustration and even anger was swamping him and it appeared there would be no end until he came to a decision.

Although at the time he was unaware of it, that missing ingredient was love; whilst he had been taught to fight, fish, hunt and farm, love had never even been mentioned, indeed unions were made principally to procreate; the men were brought up to provide and the women expected to look after family. Sometimes love would grow from these relationships, but it stayed private and was not talked about.

But love is like the worst enemy, it can strike anywhere, any time without warning. Love knows no boundaries, recognizes no class, no race and follows no rules and against love there is no defence - love, in the end, will defeat all even the bravest Viking! And so it was for Helge.

Sigrun had lived in the same long house as Helge for the last twenty three summers, but she was somehow unassuming, and so unnoticed by most, including Helge. She had manufactured her own invisibility, swayed by her feeling that she was different from the others, a misfit. She was self-conscious about her appearance, dark haired, skinny, angular of face, with a figure more akin to a teenage boy. She did not meet the Viking ideal of women, blonde, full figured and blue eyed. She went quietly about her tasks and blending into the background allowed her to observe all she saw around her, and notice things missed by others too absorbed in their own interests. She had seen the comings and goings of the would be suitors, had listened to the tales of Helge's great deeds, but she alone had watched Helge closely; had noticed how he seemed to get more ill at ease as the stories grew longer and more elaborate. She noticed also how his usually clear blue eyes lost their clarity, became dull and flat, but above all she noticed that he never once looked the speaker in the eye but rather stared steadfastly at the ground.

Sigrun pondered this in her mind and it disturbed her deeply, and it was her sudden awareness that maybe she was not the only person with a troubled soul that gave her the courage one evening to follow Helge down to the edge of the fjord.

"What really happened over there, Helge? Was it really not as they say it was?"

Helge turned swiftly, a look of anger on his face; who was this interloper, who dared intrude on his solitude and question him? When he realized the slight figure was Sigrun, his anger turned first to amusement, then to puzzlement. He turned his gaze on her, and when she did not turn away, almost without thinking, he began telling about the battle, as he had told no one else.

"No, no, it wasn't as they say. At least, not to me". He told her of the unnecessary slaughter, the blood lust that had appalled him, and his own cupidity, his responsibility, which he had not met. He opened his heart, not really to her, but to himself, saying what he felt, the revulsion at what he had done, how he felt so undeserving of all the adulation he had been given.

Sigrun listened quietly, aware he wasn't talking to her but was unburdening himself. But when he halted to draw breath, she asked softly "Is that not what you should do, isn't that what we are taught is noble, and the most to be desired?" Then, before he could answer, she shrugged slightly and said, "Well, it is what we are taught, but I myself have always wondered. We live on such a lovely earth, there seems room for everyone, why must we fight and take what others have. We don't go hungry, we have food and drink, what we need is all around us. Helge, I am so sorry for you. Again, he felt stirred to anger, but as he looked into her eyes it was quickly quenched. Instead he said simply "Thank you, you cannot know what that means to me." And so they continued to talk. They talked as the sun went down, they talked at the rising of the moon, they talked throughout the night and as dawn broke they were still sitting there on a bare rock, holding hands, gazing into each other's eyes.

When the next raiding party left to attack the monastic communities on the shores of Ireland and Scotland Helge was not there. He and Sigrun were celebrating their wedding.

Even without Helge, the raid was successful but along with the success came disturbing information. One of the British Kings, Offa, had formed a fighting force to keep all invading forces out of his kingdom of Mercia. He was so determined he had constructed a hundred and forty mile long ditch, to protect the western border of his realm from the Welsh. Offa had also made an alliance with Beorthric, who ruled Wessex, giving Offa almost total control of Southern Britain. His was a fearsome reputation, a tough, uncompromising man, it was rumoured that he had ordered the beheading of a suitor of his daughter, King Aethelberth the second, of East Anglia.

Unlike the other Vikings, Helge, unlike many others welcomed this news; here surely was an adversary, cunning, strong and brutal, an enemy on whom he could at last test his mettle, warrior against warrior, to fight for what he felt was right, a chance to vindicate what others saw in him, to live up to his reputation. Long before he said anything to Sigrun she knew his feelings, she had watched how his eyes had at last come alive again, how his body seemed to straighten; he held his head high, he was ready.

So Helge once again took the helm, to return to Britain to do battle against a strong and determined foce. Fierce winds were blowing an icy cold sea in his face but he was oblivious to the cold. On this voyage he was at one with his men, had enjoyed the pre voyage revelry, had wholeheartedly embraced the sacrifices made to the gods, he had joined in the singing with joy and laughter. This, he thought, is my destiny; this is what I was born to do. He would bring success, glory and treasures for his men, his community, the gods and most of all for his beloved Sigrun. He had no fear as he made his farewells but Sigrun, though she had little doubt that he would return in triumph, worried that he had lost what it was that had drawn them together. And yet, she told herself, he has been so happy lately, it must be right.

For the next three years Helge led many raids to Britain but the triumph and satisfaction that he sought and expected always eluded him. To those around him he was successful, riches and status came his way. His men worshipped him, felt safe with him; none knew of his fear, and wouldn't have believed it if they did. But Helge knew, he knew his actions were those of a man preserving his life, and the illusions of others, but with no heart for it. He had seen friends die, heard the agonies of wounded colleagues, he did not want to experience their indignities and it was this fear that drove him; he was only too well aware that he was no hero but rather a coward, simply fighting for survival. More and more he thought back to what Sigrun had said that long ago evening, and saw his enemies as human beings, men who shared, lived, breathed and thought much the same as him; he did not want to see them suffer any more than his own men and yet this made him more ruthless, to ensure he killed them quickly, cleanly minimizing their suffering.

In the halls of Valhalla, the gods were not happy. Arguments echoed around the walls, who was the real Helge, was he the heroic man his deeds suggested worthy of his place in that most hallowed place, or was he the man he saw himself to be?

Unaware of the discord in the halls of Valhalla, Helge continued going through the motions of battle, but still he hated the sight, the sounds and the smell of war and death. He was tired of losing friends, of killing, of being scared. Driven, he resolved to seek a way out.

It was Sigrun who saw a way forward. As he talked she realised that Helge had developed a love of Britain, of the concept of village life, and she saw the hurt in his eyes as he talked of the sacking and pillaging of small hamlets and villages, the suffering of the innocents. She listened as he told her of the changing face of Britain he had seen; how after the summer months had passed, leaves changed from green to yellow, golds and brown, changing the complexion of the woods and forests, and as the days grew shorter, the leaves fell away completely and the floors of the woodland were covered with wonderful hues, glowing warmly as the sunlight danced through the now bare branches. So different from the pine forests of his homeland where the thick canopy denied the sun access, so the forests remained dark, cold, wet and damp throughout the year. She was spellbound as he described the end of winter and the colours of spring, the ground now a mass of blue, white, yellow and greens blooms, the leaves on the trees a lighter, cleaner green he had not witnessed before. She saw into his heart and saw his dream, and was glad to share it.

Winter came to an end and plans were laid for another raid on

Britain. New crews were being recruited to make up for the many losses of the previous year, and the new, young looking boy boarding Helge's boat drew no particular attention, though some did wonder what use such a weak and pallid looking boy would be. But at the beginning, as the days passed, the men wondered. Helge appeared to have no patience with this young boy. It seemed out of character and no one else suffered from the rough side of his tongue. Very early on in the voyage he scathingly castigated the boy's rowing ability, then belittled him, banning him from all rowing duties, and demanding that should he learn navigation and helmsmanship, but still the boy couldn't please him, his temper was short and it seemed he was always shouting and berating the lad, giving him no peace nor rest.

Little did his men know how his heart ached, how he wished to reach out; to hug and protect his beloved Sigrun from the cold and damp, keep her warm as well as dry but he felt there was no other way of keeping her safe; a smile, kind word or intimate gesture of any kind might betray them both and put their lives in danger. But some of his men worried, it was not Helga's way. Some of them spoke to the boy, kindly, almost apologetically. Sigrun, unable to reply, found an opportunity to let Helge know that his odd behavior seemed just as likely to put her in jeopardy as loving kindness might. Helge was appalled by his stupidity, and gradually ameliorated his behavior, and in time, it was forgotten by the men.

The days passed, the ships landed and Helge's final battle took place on the edge of Savernake Forest. The Vikings were able to take advantage of the high ground, having made camp almost undetected on a small hill. The Saxons however were soon informed of their presence, and they were far superior in number, and due in no small measure to King Offa's reforms, were more organized than hitherto. Unable to make the surprise attack they had hoped for, there was little option other than a full frontal assault.

At dawn the Saxons heard the final preparations of the Vikings on the hill above them, as they made their final offering to the gods before charging downwards, Helge in the lead. In the confusion and noise of the battle, nobody saw the young lad hang back and slip silently into the woods. After one of the toughest fights any of them could remember, the Saxons were finally put to flight, but any celebration and rejoicing was cut short when they realised Helge was missing.

Not one of them it would seem had seen what had happened; his men searched diligently among the dead and the wounded. Soon, one man gave a cry and held up Helge's distinctive shield, another found his sword and helmet and finally, most disturbingly, some of his clothing was found.

But further searching failed to find any other trace of him. Bewildered, they questioned each other; surely the Saxons had not managed to capture their leader? But what other explanation could there be? With heavy hearts they set out to carry their wounded to the ships and prepare the dead for their funeral pyre.

Hidden in the woods bordering the shore, Sigrun, no longer in the clothes of a boy, but dressed as a Saxon woman, and Helge, also in Saxon garb, watched as their former comrades went about their tasks, watched as sacrifices were made to the gods; and watched as Helge's belongings were carried reverently aboard the ship. They watched as the ships departed for their homeland, the men with sadness in their hearts, although they felt Helge was now in Valhalla, the hall of heroes, with Odin.

But the gods were far from happy; they had witnessed the betrayal and watched as Helge had first feigned death, and then as the battle moved forward, had dropped his weapons, taken off his own clothes to reveal the Saxon apparel beneath, looted from an earlier raid, and watched him move stealthily towards the woods to join Sigrun. Their anger blinded them to his sorrow and sadness at seeing his friends depart, knowing that he would never see them or his homeland again; they could not understand his revulsion at war, killing and death.

The sky above grew black, thunder roared such as they had never heard before; Thor in his fury was hurling thunderbolts and lightning all around them. Helge and Sigrun crouched in a hole made by the torn up roots of an old tree while the fury raged overhead. At last it abated, damp and cramped they emerged from their shelter. The grey clouds passed, and the sun showed its face. "Well, we're still here" Helge said, somewhat ruefully, and clasped Sigurd to him. They began their journey to a new life.

Where they were headed they did not know, but they walked for many days; seeking shelter where they could at night. They hunted for food, built fires for warmth. They walked through forests, over fields, hills and dales. Helge had never been so far from the sea. One day they saw in the distance a great hill, topped by a plain, rising up from an otherwise flat landscape. The side of this great plain had been sculptured out like a great shell; there were woods nearby and to Helge's delight, a small river. Instinctively they looked at each other, and each began to smile. They felt in their bones this would be their new home. They were disturbed then, to find there was already an established settlement. For a few days they hid in the nearby woods, discussing the best way forward. Through his many raids Helge had picked up a smattering of the local language and hoped he could be understood. They decided to say that they were from Mercia, fleeing the excesses of King Offa and having discussed the details, walked somewhat fearfully into the settlement.

In time, the couple with an odd way of speaking was accepted. And for the next fifty three years Helge and Sigrun lived happily; without expectations, without the pressure of having to lead men into war, mixing with their neighbours. Helge settled down to life as a farmer. But his building skills were much in demand as was his boat building expertise. His odd arrival in the village had been long forgotten. His love for Sigrun had never wavered; she had borne him five sons; he was happy and content.

He lay on his bed surrounded by his family; his body wasted, his legs, once like the trunks of an oak tree, were now no more than thin sticks.. Sigrun held his hand as he smiled at her. "You have indeed been my Sigrun, my secret victory, thank you, my love." "Sigrun smiled through her tears, but did not speak, confident he knew her heart.

As death came to him Helge became the Viking he had once been. His body grew strong again as The Valkyries came to bear him away; He smiled at the thought of being with the heroes of old, to share stories with the gods. The Valkyries carried him to the underground and now he stood in front of Odin. But there was no welcome on Odin's countenance. He stood tall, barring Helge's entrance to that hallowed place.

"Helge you were a favoured son, your place here seemed secure; we thought you a brave, fearless, much loved warrior. But you betrayed us all, shamed all who loved and respected you. Worst of all, you have caused dissension in this place of heroes. This Hall cannot agree what should be your fate."

Helge stared, he trembled, he found nothing to say.

"It has been determined that you will be imprisoned"

"Imprisoned? For how long? For all eternity? Where will I be imprisoned?"

"In our mercy it has been decreed that the length of your imprisonment will be determined by yourself. The location will be revealed when the time is right"

Even as Odin spoke these words, Helge felt himself shrinking, down and down, smaller and smaller. He peered upwards, and realised he was looking at the underside of Thor's big toe; then he saw no more, complete blackness.

Thor bent down and picked up the small pod and with all the force he could muster, threw it far from him, where it landed on the earth Helge had loved. Such was the force of Thor's passion induced throw, the missile was buried deep within the fertile plain that Helge had farmed for so long.

To Helge in the darkness, most of the time he slept, and like a trauma victim, the passing of time to him was confusion. He awoke, not knowing how long he had been asleep, and then he slept again. In a waking moment he counted the times he had been conscious, and estimated he had been in his prison for five days.

But those five days had been a thousand years! When Helge next woke he sensed that his prison was getting larger, very slowly it was expanding. There was noise from above his head, not loud but like sand falling on an egg shell; he also sensed it was lighter outside though he still could not see.

Another thousand years passed and Helge awoke to a sound he had not heard in a long, long time.......a child was sobbing.

CHRIS

(Autobiography 1)

Chris sat sobbing beneath the tall oak. How had things come to this? Was it something he'd done? What next in his life?

Despite the bullying and mental cruelty he suffered at the hands of his Father, Chris had not considered himself an unhappy child; indeed had you asked him he would have said he was happy. This was his life and he didn't realise others lived differently with fathers who were proud of them, and told happy stories of their sons' achievements.. His father seemed to love his three daughters and enjoy showing them off, but it was not so with Chtis, was it somehow his fault. These thoughts didn't help, Chris gulped, and his tears increased.

When he looked back in later years Chris considered that he had been a cheerful and caring child, but the stories his sisters told didn't bear this out... ' But' thought Chris, 'In infant school I learnt to read and write quite well, I was even asked to take and read that essay on St Francis of Assisi to all the classes. It was me that was asked to let each class know of the death of King George VI.". But at home things were different! His father was always comparing him unfavorably with his cousins, never giving him any sort of encouragement or praise, was quick to criticize and punish anything he did wrong. Chris, eager to please his father, found he was unable to either read or write or even tell the time in his presence - which infuriated his father and reinforced the low opinion he had of him. However hard he tried, nothing was ever good enough and with his father's temper seemingly always directed at Chris, life was becoming increasingly intolerable. Chris began to dread his father's homecoming each evening. Bed was no refuge, as he could hear his father berating his Mother over the uselessness of 'her' son. Never once did he hear her come to his defence or protest at the treatment meted out to him.

His inability to perform existed in front of the whole of his paternal family, and consequently his Grandmother, aunts, uncles, and cousins were all of much the same opinion as his father, a dark haired, big eyed, frail, nervous child, polite but ignorant, with a seemingly perpetual silly grin on his face.

Chris came to think that he was of little worth; he withdrew into a world of his own. Finding it difficult to make friends in his own right, he clung to his sisters and their friends. He didn't have the courage to formulate his own opinions, preferring instead to repeat what he heard others say, especially those that made people laugh when he repeated them, often without understanding what he was saying.

And yet, despite the fear of his father, it never occurred to him to feel sorry for himself. He was a caring child, always on the lookout for others. Instead of his mother comforting and consoling him after his father's outbursts it was him who would climb on to his mother's knees and say;

"You look sad, why are you sad?"

"I am not sad" but expressionless eyes and lack of even a hint of a smile told a different story;

"You are sad, I know you are sad; why are you sad?" but she would only repeat her initial statement, without warmth, without any form of intimacy and this too enhanced his feeling of inadequacy.

At school there was a girl, Brenda, one of those people who no one likes, unwashed, dirty, smelly with a permanently runny nose, rough skin pitted with blackheads. Even the teachers held her at arm's length whilst the children shunned her. There was a school party to celebrate the Coronation of Queen Elizabeth and Chris invited Brenda. His friends and family were horrified but when his sisters questioned his motives he said:

"Well if I didn't invite her, nobody else would."

That was the true nature of the boy most people seemed to think a waste of space.

Then, out of the blue, his life changed.

His Uncle Beram and Auntie Vera had no children. But in all other aspects of Beram's life he was an outstanding success, Managing Director by day, principle of the Working Mans College by night, artist, amateur archeologist, poet, linguist, author. All these things Chris had learnt from family conversations, but the best bit about his uncle, in Chriss eyes, was his dark green 1926 Rolls Royce. Chris truly loved this 30 year old vehicle.

But not its owner. Uncle Beram was, to this frail nervous child, fearsome looking and though he was always kind to him and despite the fact that he enjoyed visiting him, Chris was more in awe of him than he was of his father. It was Auntie Vera who made these visits so happy. She was tall and dark haired, Chris considered her the most beautiful woman he had ever seen. He always looked forward to their visits, so it was with great joy when one day, from his bedroom window, he saw their wonderful car pull up outside the front door.

His parents, aunt and uncle were seated round the kitchen table sipping cups of tea when Chris was called down; his father looked happier than he could ever remember seeing him, but his mother appeared sad and edgy. Beram seemed his usual fearsome self but Vera seemed worried.

His father spoke:"Christopher you are going for a holiday with your Uncle Beram and Auntie Vera......................."

He heard no more; his mind was a blur, he alone was going for a holiday? He was the special one? And it was so, for the first time he was in the front seat of that wonderful car, between his Aunt and Uncle, waving farewell to his parents and sisters, but in his moment of joy his abiding memory was a strange, almost triumphant look on his father's face, the sad smile of his mother and was it a look of envy he detected in his sisters expressions? At that moment he neither knew nor cared.

THE JUDGE'S PROTEST

THE OLD BAILEY, FEBRUARY 18th 2016

Lord Chief Justice Keslsey had been practicing law for almost fifty years. Still mentally sharp and considered one of the finest legal brains in the country, he had now decided it was time for him to retire, his present case would be his last. He sat down in his chambers to consider the approach his summing up should take. When he thought back to his appointment to the Bench he remembered how he had been troubled by the thought that the higher you reached in a profession, the more remote you became from the core of your vocation.

He remembered the first case he had heard as a judge, he was worried as he saw the jury being swayed by the eloquence and charm of the defence rather than weighing up the evidence. In his summing up must be neutral yet on the side of justice, a difficult juggling act. but he felt always an urgent need to be certain of the innocence or guilt of the accused.

Today, he still felt that same need. This case was high-profile and seemed to have been going on for a long time. The accused, a known gangster, quite full of himself, had a very able defence team, who had, albeit with a velvet glove, destroyed those giving evidence against him; the leading barrister had made the jurors laugh, made them like him personally, so much so that the evidence against his client seemed of almost secondary importance. Keslsey had been aware that this was prejudicing him against the accused, the client might be innocent and it was his job to determine the truth, make the judgement and then guide the jury; an inflection here, a raised eyebrow there, a touch of sarcasm or irony always helped. Judge Kelsey closed his eyes;

it seemed to him that he slept. When he opened his eyes, the clock still showed the same time, but somehow he now seemed to know exactly what had occurred and so began to write his summary:

His reputation as a defence lawyer had been built on this ability, not because his was the best record in terms of the percentage of acquittals he obtained, it wasn't!. But from the outset of his career he felt strongly that the legal profession should be about truth, fairness and justice. He loathed the use of legal loopholes, abhorred the practice of bullying obviously nervous witnesses, where they would be judged on their performance in the witness box, rather than on the evidence they gave. He believed that every accused person deserved the best defence possible but that defence had to be based on the truth, even if that meant admitting their guilt; only with the truth could a proper defence begin and thereby justice could be served. Though his clients reacted in many ways from anger to resignation, frequently the reaction was one of incredulity, 'it was if you were there' or 'how did you know that!'

When he became a judge, jurors were often fascinated by the accused's reactions to his summations; surprise, anger, relief, smiles, disbelief, all gave the jurors a strong indication of innocence or guilt. Prosecutors and defence teams alike would leave the court shaken as the verdicts appeared contrary to expectations, but there were very few appeals made from the cases over which he presided.

As he took up his fountain pen to start his summary; his eye fell upon an item in the latest edition of his old school magazine, lying open on his desk. In the fifty three years he had been receiving this publication it had never so affected him as what he was now reading did. An oak tree had been discovered in a part of the school woods, whose existence up to this point in time had somehow remained unknown and unexplored. There was great excitement in as much as the tree was thought to be more than two thousand years old but sadness and anger after health and safety Inspectors from the Department of Education deemed it to be a danger to the pupils of the school. *"It could fall at any moment!"*

Judge Kesley thought this was a ridiculous ruling as it stood, with no evidence to support it, but this was not his major concern; he was swept with an absolute certainty that this tree must be saved, though he could not identify why, or what was so important about this tree. His immediate response was to ring the chairman of the Board. Unusually for him ,he tried to use his position and influence to urge that the tree deserved a reprieve but all his entreaties came to nothing, for he was unable to say just why the fate of the tree was so important to him. At a loss to know what to do next, and in effort to save the tree, he closed his eyes in the expectation that the solution would be forthcoming, but he simply fell asleep. When he awoke all he felt was a deep loneliness and unease.

The case came to an end, and after clearing his office he went home for a convivial evening and a well-deserved sleep.

Next morning he set out on a journey to revisit the past. Some time later, having driven for miles, he checked into the Clyffe Hall Hotel in Market Lavington. He still had no clear plan as to his next course of action, he had tried to sort it out in his head on his way down, but nothing had come to him, just this need to do something! He walked slowly up the short driveway, his mind filled with memories of the hundreds, possibly thousands, of times he had done so before.

He gazed across the road and beyond the old playing fields, making out the outlines of the Manor House. Almost without thinking he crossed both the road and the playing fields and found himself at the edge of the Manor Woods. The article in the Dauntsean had mentioned that the oak tree was discovered in a previously unknown part of the woods, but how could there remain a part of the woods unknown, with all those boys, and later boys and girls, wandering the woods, practising their woodcraft skills, it didn't make sense. He felt some strange force driving him forward and suddenly he was there; standing in front of a mighty oak, reaching high into the sky, overarching the woods below. Still standing tall at well over a hundred feet, this once proud tree looked strangely vulnerable; it was the height of Summer yet the leaves were turning brown and dropping off, the boughs seemed to be hanging limply, covered in moss and cobwebs, as if a living being had given up on life. To Kelsey it was as if the very soul had been ripped from the heart of the tree. Then a voice interrupted his thoughts'

"I knew you'd come, I just didn't know when."

A somewhat dishevelled, unkempt old man, with long straggly white hair and an emaciated body round which was wrapped in a tattered old cloak, supported by a tall wooden staff, stood before him. In a funny way, thought Keslsey, he resembles the old oak.

"Err, sorry. I'm not sure... do I know you? Were we contemporaries here? Are you too here to save the oak?"

The old man simply smiled, held out his hand and said; "once more, for the last time."

Keslsey stood rooted to the ground, unable to answer, or even understand, this odd appeal.

A little more impatiently, "climb up on my shoulders."

"What! I am 72 and you must be at least that and........'

"Oh, I am far, far older than that, but that is not the point" and again he held out his hand and as he did so, he appeared to grow taller, younger; his saggy skin became taut, muscles appeared and his head was crowned by thick, long blond hair. Keslsey, not knowing why, or even quit how, found himself doing as he had been bidden and as he did so, he remembered.

INTERREGNUM

(Autobiography 2)

(Nothing lasts forever).

Chris was now enjoying a happiness he had not even imagined. The drive that changed his life so dramatically, he scarcely remembered once it was over. At the time he knew only that he was happy to be in the front of the beloved car, the long green bonnet bouncing up and down in front of him on the bumpy roads, the wind blowing in his face because Uncle Beram drove with the canvas hood down whenever the weather allowed. Even when it rained, the side screens weren't used, in fact, come what may, rain, sleet or snow, the side screens were never used. The large three quarter steering wheel fascinated chris. When he asked why part of the steering wheel was missing, his uncle explained that it wasn't missing, it was designed to allow the driver to see through to the windscreen, unobstructed by a top arc on a fully circular wheel. But above all, he remembered he was so happy to be with these two people, his favourite Aunt, and his Uncle, who had chosen him over and above his siblings and cousins, to holiday with them.

But he vividly remembered his arrival at Lissendon Mansions; the car turned left, off Highgate Road into Lissendon Gardens and stopped in front of a heavy white barrier, flag shaped. It was the biggest gate Chris had ever seen. Vera stepped out of the car to unlock a huge padlock, and as Uncle Beram eased the car gently into the large empty yard, Vera closed the gate and relocked it.

Next to the Rolls was a large silver Humber Hawk of the type much favoured by the top brass of the British Military; the only other car in the courtyard, its bonnet seemingly longer even than that of the Rolls but to Chris's eyes it was nowhere as beautiful. Standing, staring in the courtyard, he was puzzled by a loud humming noise but he didn't like to ask what it was. Perhaps he ought to know, and would be shouted at.

In front of him were the sights that were to become so familiar to him, in their familiarity and comfort. Directly in front was Lissendon Gardens itself, neatly manicured lawns, neat colourful garden beds and a zig-zag path that was swept clean of dust, leaves and rubbish every day. These gardens were protected by green iron railings just inside which were two magnificent Horse Chestnut trees whose branches overhung the courtyard and were to be a rich source of conkers over the years. Beyond the gardens was Highgate Road, overhung by high wires that were used to power the trolley buses that ran quietly up and down the road. Chris found these large, almost silent machines enchanting; to him they were like great prehistoric monsters with long large antlers reaching to the sky for energy. He enjoyed it when the antlers sometimes fell away as if the creature had died, until it was resurrected by men with huge poles, who managed to re connect it to its life force.

Now he saw to his right there was a large house of brownish yellowy bricks. built in the Georgian style. There was a large, somewhat unkempt garden in front, surrounded by heavy duty iron railings. Where a back garden might have been expected there were two gates even larger than the one into the courtyard, so large that they were supported on cast iron wheels. Behind these gates was a long building built of the same bricks as the house but with huge art deco windows of multi-coloured glass between strips of green iron work, laid out so that each window resembled a giant fan. Through the open entrance Chris saw row upon row of green machinery, all sporting coloured lights. This was the source of the humming ; this was the local power station.

While he was trying to take in the beauty of his new surroundings, so different from the plain, rather drab and dull Victorian street where he had lived with his family, his aunt and uncle were trying to shepherd him towards the majestic building where he would be spending the rest of his summer holiday. Inside, he was disappointed. The entrance was dark, as was the entrance hall beyond, everything was constructed of dark, blackish wood. Once through the black front door the entrance hall was also dark, narrow and unfriendly; even the kitchen, which would over time become his haven and refuge from the world, seemed tiny, sunless and depressing. But his spirits rose when he was shown into a room, the last on the right of the hallway. The late afternoon sun streamed in through the large single window, a large divan bed dominated the room, the head set back into a shallow alcove. Was this where his aunt and uncle slept, it was so grand, and yet friendly.

'This will be your room'. He stared open mouthed at his Auntie Vera. His room! He thought back to his erstwhile home where he had never even had his own bed, let alone a room of his own.

Most of that first afternoon and evening were now lost in time but four things remained etched in his memory. The kitchen which had seemed so small and unfriendly when he first saw it, came alive as both his Aunt and Uncle prepared the evening meal. His father had never set foot in their kitchen at home and it had never occurred to him that men could cook. Then his Auntie Vera asked him to help set the table for dinner, again something he had never done. He marvelled at the crisp white table cloth, loved the matching cutlery which glistened, housed in a free standing oak canteen; then the laying of the table itself, from side plates and the white linen serviettes in silver napkin rings. Chris loved it all but most of all was enjoying being the sole recipient of his aunt's attention; her smile, her laughter and gentleness.

Halfway through dinner his Uncle brought out an atlas and

opened it at a double page spread 'Do you know what country that is?'

And without warning his old insecurities returned; instead of reading some of the names, as he was well capable of doing, he panicked. If it took up two whole pages, soit must be a large country.

"America" he stammered; and the look on his Uncle's face said it all, though unlike his father he did not shout, did not mock him, but patiently explained it was a map of the British Isles, explaining that it was made up of England, Ireland, Scotland and Wales and said; "You can always tell Wales because the shape of it is like a pig's head"

"Oh" said Chris thinking of his new teacher; "When I get back to school next week I will tell Miss Bellamy that she comes from the land of the pig"

And then the first time fhe slept in his new bedroom, maybe the best memory of all. At home he was used to just saying goodnight to his parents downstairs and occasionally getting a kiss from his Mother before trudging up a cold, carpet-less flight of stairs to a cheerless bedroom at the top of the house, to share a bed with his three sisters. Now he had his own pleasantly decorated warm room, a comfortable bed of his own and his pyjamas had been laid neatly on his pillows. As he climbed into his bed he noticed for the first time, on the opposite wall, a painting of his uncle. Chris, who was still quite nervous of him, thought the portrait made his uncle look somewhat grim and a little scary. Settling into his bed the noise from the power station seemed very loud and Chris wondered he would find it difficult to sleep, but from his bed he had a view of the colourful art deco windows, which combined with the hum, he found weirdly comforting.

A few minutes later his aunt had come into the room, while his uncle hovered in the doorway. His aunt lent over the bed to kiss him good night and Chris, without thought, threw his arms around her and clung to her as if his life depended on it, his kiss lasting almost as long as the hug which he was reluctant to release. This set the pattern for the future. Whether his aunt and uncle were having a quiet evening, or had friends over, or were entertaining business colleagues, this routine never varied. Even when they had to go out in the evenings the ritual was the same. Chris would stay awake until he heard the front door opening, knowing that his aunt's first action would be to check on him. Many memories of childhood would get lost in the mists of time but these meaningful moments were to remain with and be a source of comfort, well into Chris's adulthood.

The next three years were to be a totally different life. On the first day of this new life he met the Scottish family who lived next door, their daughter Elizabeth was the same age as him, and their son Ian a few years older. The two families were very close because of the closeness of their kitchen windows, through which many conversations were held and many invitations to visit were issued - and accepted. Elizabeth was to become an important part of his life.

Then there was the short five minute walk to see his paternal Grandmother who lived in the same complex with her youngest daughter Sehri. They had a first floor flat overlooking Parliament Hill Fields, which led on to Hampstead Heath. He had always been very timid around his Grandmother, whom he found quite fearsome, and usually sought refuge with Aunt Sehri, but in this new life, he clung to his Auntie Vera. After a while Sehri coaxed him away, settling him in a chair in the corner, with a drink and a book to look at. For a while he forgot his surroundings, but he pricked up his ears on hearing his name.

"Do you remember, when she was pregnant with Chris, and none of us knew? Beram had asked his brother why she was so moody and he said 'because she's pregnant of course' and that's the first we knew.."

"Yes" said his grandmother, "and it was me that saved his life when they first brought him to show us. Do you remember, like a bundle of rags it was, and we kept unwrapping them, until we reached this poor little stick thin child, with huge eyes. What was it the doctor said Sehri?"

"He was so weak he couldn't be allowed to cry, or expend any energy until he had recovered his strength, that's why he stayed with us for the next few months."

"You have to wonder why," said Vera, casting a quick eye at Chris, who seemed to be absorbed in his book. "She wasn't like that with the girls, not even Linda, who was born later."

Chris suddenly sneezed, and the conversation was left there, but though Chris had heard every word he had no idea of the import, and wondered what it meant.

Although he genuinely loved Beram he was also frightened a little in awe of him and still tended to be nervous in his company, scared of making a mistake and rarely spoke unless he was asked a question. This led to some problems.

Because his nervousness around his father had affected his ability to read in front of him, it was assumed that he could not read at all, and Beram took it upon himself to teach him. They would take trolley bus rides and Beram would use the names of shops as an aid to reading. Chris could read the names with ease, but he did not want to upset his Uncle. He went along with these lessons and in a few weeks his Uncle was taking the credit for having taught Chris to read! But there were positive results for Chris as well. A small bookcase was bought for his room and his first book was purchased, Robinson Crusoe; Chris liked the bright yellow cover. Not long afterwards his uncle bought home two old musty volumes, The Outline of History by H.G. Wells Chris instantly fell in love with the brown and gold cover as well as the musty smell, but most especially he was fascinated by the large sepia print of the Giant Gigantosaurus dinosaur. A few days later, in appreciation of his supposedly new found ability to read, a complete set of Robert Louis Stevenson's works appeared on the bookshelf in his room, courtesy of his Aunt Sehri and Grandma.

One Monday Vera told him they were going to the West End to buy him a new school uniform. But the uniform the man in the shop bought was not the one for Romilly Lodge, the school he had expected he would be attending, but, Vera told him, for a different school, near where they lived, Gospel Oak Primary school. Any apprehension he felt disappeared when he fell in love at his first sight of the blazer; dark brown with gold trim around the lapels and on the breast pocket a golden cembroidered acorn.

The school itself did not disappoint either; unlike the unfriendly and somewhat forbidding turn of the century building that had been his old school, Gospel Oak was practically brand new. A bright, white, two story building with clean lines. No more of the rickety exterior fire escape stairs to the classrooms that he used to dread. In place of the gloss painted brown brick walls of his old school, the side walls of each classroom were almost entirely of glass, with fresh white Venetian blinds.

Perhaps his only disappointment was Miss Bartholomew, the headmistress, who, compared to the young, vibrant Miss Rawlings at his previous school, seemed old and stern.

Thus began an idyllic period for Chris, at the heart of which were Beram and Vera, whom he adored, loved and admired; in his eyes they could do no wrong. The flat was full of warmth, wisdom and seemingly endless laughter. He had never heard his father sing, but Beram would sing as he shaved in the morning, would sing as he cooked or did bits of DIY around the flat.

His initial fears of his Uncle had, as he came to know him better, been replaced by love and respect. Whether Chris was in the sitting room, or playing cricket with Ian and friends in the yard, where they used the gate post of the power station on which to chalk a wicket, his joy at seeing the Rolls coming through the large white gate always gave him joy, as he knew his uncle was home. Chris wasn't aware at this point what his father did for a living, but not only did he know that Beram was Managing Director of Tata Iron and Steel Ltd. Chris had actually been to his office in Hyde Park overlooking the gardens of Buckingham Palace. He had been feted by those who worked there and particularly by Charles, the office Chauffeur. This was, on one occasion, the cause of a falling out with Vera. After Charles had driven Beram to Heathrow, he and Chris were alone in the company Daimler-(another car Chris came to love) and Chris admired a coronation pen that Charles had been given, it was shiny gold, with a replica of the crown on top. Charles gave it to him, much to his joy, a joy which turned to disappointment when Vera made him give back.

As Principal of the Working Man's College in North London Beram would spend two or three evenings a week there, often taking Chris with him, where again he enjoyed the reflected glory and attention.

.One evening, he was summoned to see Beram, who was working at his desk in the dining room. Beram showed him an article in the local paper and explained it was about him, Chris, asking the question 'would he be the next lawyer in the family'? Chris smiled somewhat inanely, as he was wont to do when embarrassed or did not understand what was being said to him. He was naturally unaware that the article was mainly about his paternal Grandfather, who had entered Lincoln's Inn, but left before qualifying. He was bemused and had nothing to say, but the memory lingered with him, and he would ponder it, and wonder why his uncle had thought it important enough to bring to his attention.

On another occasion Beram took him shopping to buy a birthday present for Vera. They chose a rather beautiful, delicate jewelled watch. On the card Beram had written "Love from Beram and Chris." Vera opened it with delight. She thanked them both and gave Chris a big hug and a kiss. He was embarrassed; he found himself blushing and said "It's not really from me; Uncle Beram bought it." Vera and Beram smiled at each other, but Chris still felt somehow guilty that he had received thanks for a present to which he hadn't contributed,

While he had come to love and respect Beram, it hadn't changed the fear he sometimes felt around him. It was nothing like that with his aunt, in fact it was the complete opposite. He found pleasure in her company and was totally at his ease. He treasured the moments when it was just the two of them. For the first few months she walked with him to the school. When his wheezing and sneezing and runny eyes were found to be due to hay fever and he had to go to the hospital every week for an injection he so enjoyed the long walk with Vera from the flat to the Whittington hospital that he scarcely thought about the injection.

At home he followed her around the flat, talking incessantly. What he had at first sight thought a small, dark, unfriendly kitchen became the centre of his universe. Watching Verar go about everyday life, ironing, cooking, washing, or sitting down having a cigarette and coffee, he asked nothing more than to be in her company and she imbued in him a confidence and warmth that he had not known before.

So it came as a shock when it was Vera, and not Beram, who first lost patience with him. The school didn't set homework, so Beram would set some for him to do, which usually Vera had to oversee and mark. During one somewhat tedious session Chris was idly tapping his pencil on the desk as his aunt tried to explain some mathematical theory; she asked him to stop but rather mischievously, as a joke, he gave it one more tap. To his amazement and horror she slammed down the book, snatched the pencil from his grasp, and glaring at him, snapped it in two. A shocked Chris was mortified that he had upset his aunt so, and blushingly and cringingly, tried to apologise for his thoughtless action.

But Beram had his moment too! Painting in oils was yet another of his talents. He had been painting a scene of a wheat field as Chris watched. Chris was intrigued and mesmerised as the painting took form and when Beram paused to clean a brush, he pointed at a bit of the painting that he particularly liked. Whack!! The back of Chris's hand stung from the blow from Beram's.

"Never, never touch a painting when it is wet" Beram yelled. Chris ran from the room in floods of tears. As in the incident with Vera, he was angry at himself for upsetting his Uncle but at the same time was incensed, because he had not actually touched the painting. Confused and unable to explain, he threw himself onto his bed and wept. Was-there something wrong with him that made him upset people so? But he learnt from his mistakes, and never repeated them.

Coming home from school one winter evening, it started to snow and by the time Chris reached the white gate, the snow was quite thick on the ground. Children from the flats were playing snowballs , others were building a snowman and still others an ice slide. Chris really did not want to go inside and do his homework so he pretended not to notice his aunt at their sitting room window as he joined in the snow fight. Though he was soon cold and somewhat damp he was having such a fun time - until he heard a tapping on the window. He glanced up and saw his aunt beckoning him inside. With a sad heart he said goodbye to his friends, saying he had to go and do his homework. But his aunt met him at the front door with his winter overcoat, a pair of gloves and the woolen bobble hat his grandmother had knitted and sent him back out to play into the snow. What a joyous time that was.

Life continued smoothly; he was enjoying school and his ever expanding group of friends. This could be said to be indirectly down to Beram. Two popular school hobbies were the collecting of book matches and of cigarette cards. Both Beram and Vera were smokers and Chris's collection of cigarette cards grew very rapidly as did his hoard of book matches but they were nothing special, no better and no worse than those his friends had collected, until Beram went away overseas for work.. He went to parts of India, Africa and the USA. On his return Chris had his collections not only enlarged, but with an international flavour that nobody else could match. All the boys seemed to want to be his friend and to swap cards and matches with him. This led to him talking incessantly about his Uncle. As his confidence grew he would, after having lunch at school, take boys 'home' with him, to see the flat, to let them see and handle Beram's display of Roman antiquities and show off all the books that lined a whole wall in the sitting room. His delight was a little undermined when he was made to apologise when Vera overheard him boasting "......and he has read every one, some of them even twice!!" It wasn't so much the apology that upset him, he genuinely felt a little deflated at the realisation that some of the books remained unread.

With new friendships and having more faith in his own abilities, his social and academic skills slowly began to improve. He enjoyed being popular with both his contemporaries and his teachers. Miss Bartholomew had one day, accompanied by two ladies, approached the table where he and his friends were lunching, and singled him out to pose on the front wall of the school, for the cover of Woman's Own magazine. He could not get back to Vera fast enough to tell her the news but alas, after months of looking, that particular cover had not appeared!!

On another occasion, during afternoon playtime Miss Bartholomew called him to her office;

"Chris there are some silly boys downstairs playing kiss chase do you think you can go and stop them?"

"Yes Miss Bartholomew" said a dutiful Chris not daring to tell her that he was not only an eager participant in this game, but was the instigator. She thanked him for getting the boys to stop.

To Chris the most beautiful woman in the world was his beloved Aunt Vera; nobody could, or would ever, match her. Beram was an avid amateur archaeologist specialising in Roman Britain. He took Chris with him on a tour of the amphitheatre in St Alban's which was conducted by the famous archaeologist, Sir Mortimer Wheeler. To the amusement of many, the skinny little boy stared open mouthed and wide eyed, following every move of Lady Mortimer! Even the great man himself was amused. Chris himself was not aware of his actions, and when his uncle told the story at home he said 'sorry' to his aunt, worried that she would be hurt.

Chris's life seemed to go from better to even better, with many new and exciting experiences, going on archaeological digs, exploring many of London's markets. In Portabello Road market Beram bought him a naval cutlass dating from the reign of William 1V; Chris loved it for the curved blade, brass guard and shark skin hilt. He was also given a fret saw and a plentiful supply of plywood and soon became adept at cutting out quite intricate patterns; he enjoyed everything about it and found the smell of newly cut timber warm and comforting. One of his proudest moments was when Beram asked him to make a new cabinet for a small, old radio he had bought. It was not the most difficult of tasks, just a simple box with two large rectangular holes for the dials and controls, with beading around the edges. Chris glowed with pride when it was given a prominent spot on top of the fridge in the kitchen.

Then there was the holiday in Ramsgate. When he was woken at six in the morning, Chris thought he had never been up so early. It was still dark as they climbed into the Rolls and, as usual, the hood was down. Warm in his bomber jacket and bobble hat and squeezed between Vera and Beram on the front seat, Chris was as happy as it was possible to be. After about an hour and a half they pulled into the car park of a transport café for breakfast. Theirs was the only car and though it was dwarfed by the lorries and vans it seemed it was an object of great interest. After enjoying a full English breakfast, (which up until then Chris knew as a Saturday morning breakfast; that first Saturday Chris had been surprised when he had been asked to lay the dining table for breakfast, rather than the kitchen table, and when he and his aunt were seated Beram had come in, bearing a huge china charger loaded with fried eggs, bacon, sausages, mushrooms fried tomatoes and black-pudding, along with a toast rack filled to overflowing.)

Before they left to continue the trip to Ramsgate, Chris was advised to go the lavatory, and as he was walking to the washroom a group of drivers were of the same mind;

'Is that your Dad's car?'

"No it's my Uncle's and we are going on holiday and we had to get up at 6 O'clock this morning!" This caused much amusement amongst the group of men and Chris was left with the feeling that 6 o'clock was perhaps not so early after all. All he would remember of the rest of the journey was the feeling of total happiness and safety, the car full of much laughter and his aunt's rendition of 'We're of to see the Wizard', which his Uncle followed with ' Follow the Yellow Brick Road'. Excitement nullified his tiredness as they at last pulled up outside the Stellamaris Bed & Breakfast on the sea front. It was unremarkable, except for the slim dark haired lady who served the breakfasts and on whom he developed a secret crush.

There followed a week of pure bliss; long rides in the car, visits to the Roman remains at Richborough Castle; walks along the quaint horseshoe shaped harbour wall and along the beach at Pegwell Bay, where steep chalk cliffs created a majestic backdrop to the sandy beach, though they had to be careful not to be trapped when the tide came in. They swam, picnicked and had competitions as to who could fly his rubber band powered aeroplane the furthest.

Back home again and at school it was exam time and Chris's results were good, as was his report, and the school got ready for Prize Giving Day. To his surprise and to the delight of his Aunt and Uncle, Chris was presented with the prize for 'Most Improvement' From a selection of books he chose 'Captain Scott of the Antarctic' as his prize, and in a packed school hall in front of all his teachers and friends he beamed widely as he was presented with it by Dame Ninette de Valois. Walking away with his prize, he reflected how his life had changed and improved since he'd come to live with Vera and Beram.

Alas, he was still prone to cower and stammer the few times his father came to visit and as hard as he tried, he was unable please him. He always felt a great sense of relief when his father left. But apart from this, life continued to be interesting and secure. Oddly, in all that time neither his Mother or sisters came to see him, neither did he think to ask about them.

On the morning of the Eleven Plus exam (which determined the type of secondary school he would attend) Vera lent him her prized Parker 51 fountain pen which Chris had not been allowed to use before. There was a belief that multi users would ruin the nib; this privilege heightened the importance, and for Chris, the tension of the day.

A few weeks later the results came through and Chris was relieved to learn that he passed. He assumed he would be going to the local Grammar school, William Ellis, which pleased him greatly as it was close by, indeed it could be seen from their sitting room window. He was more than a little surprised when he was told he had an interview at Holloway County Grammar school.

It became clear that the reasoning behind this choice was because both his Uncle and his Father had attended this school, and his interview was with the Headmaster, a rather kindly older man, who had taught them both. Chris felt it was more a reminiscence of their time there than an assessment of his own capabilities. It seemed no surprise when he was accepted. At first he was a little apprehensive as this school was nearer to his parents' home than it was to the flat he now viewed as his home, so he was relieved to be told he would be staying put. His wonderful life would continue.

Then one morning Vera again handed him her Parker 51;

"Thank you, but why?" For a fleeting moment he thought it was a gift.

"Just another test" he was told.

He had all but forgotten about this test when a few weeks later he was called away from a game of cricket he had been enjoying in the yard. His Aunt and Uncle were seated at the kitchen table on which there was an opened letter. Beram looked at him and smiled;

"The last test you took was an entrance exam for a boarding school in Wiltshire and I am thrilled to tell you that you have passed and you have been accepted as a pupil..........."

Chris heard or remembered no more of that conversation. Boarding school, Wiltshire, kept repeating in his head. Wiltshire; away from the flat, away from his friends and of course, away from his beloved aunt. Gradually his anxieties were cast aside as over the following days his Uncle, a great story teller, romanticised about the joys and advantages of boarding school life and how much Chris would enjoy it. Then there was the excitement of being taken to the West End to be fitted out with his new uniform, which this time apparently included every item of clothing imaginable. There was another visit to Portabello Road Market to purchase an old travelling trunk and an old army knapsack to act as an overnight bag.

Chris was unprepared for what came next -

"Until you start your new school you will be going back home."

Home!! Home? The realisation or rather facing the reality, that the flat, the place he loved, the place where he felt comfortable and happy, where he was most secure, was not, after all home, hit him very hard and though he said nothing, showed no cct the change was within him and that he was viewing his old home as an outsider. The neglected front garden where once he had played with his sisters, now seemed devoid of any charm, the drab Victorian exterior of the house was cheerless and unwelcoming. Inside the only room that had been redecorated was his parents' bedroom, other than that the house was exactly as it had been when he left; even the blown light bulbs in the hall and on the top landing had not been changed, or had blown again and not been replaced.

Chris was saddened and depressed by what he saw; before it had been acceptable, because it was all he knew. Now he was missing the cleanliness and order of the flat; missing the warmth and homeliness of the kitchen which held so many cherished moments. The kitchen here could have been lovely; it was larger and lighter than the kitchen at the flat, with plenty of storage space but the stove was smelly and thick with grease; there was always a mass of unwashed crockery in the dirty sink and the silver cutlery that he remembered lovingly polishing every week obviously hadn't seen a polishing cloth since he left, lay carelessly in a blackened pile on the draining board. This was no place to sit and chat; this was just a place where his Mother cooked without enthusiasm, joy or imagination.

Whilst the 'grown ups' were deep in conversation Chris and his sisters were getting reacquainted, he hadn't seen them for three years, and he didn't know them anymore. Used to being the centre of attention, he was full of his own importance, felt his news was more important, he wanted to show off his new possessions and talk about the new school he would be going to; they on the other hand had much they wanted to show and tell him. It was quite a relief to be called downstairs into the sitting room;

"Say goodbye to Uncle Beram and Auntie Vera."

It was, he felt, a very cold goodbye and his Aunt felt oddly distant, his Uncle unusually formal; there were tears in his eyes as he watched the Rolls disappear from sight. He turned to his parents but his father had already turned his attention back to the racing on the television and his mother apparently had nothing to say. He felt very alone.

Going to bed the first night back was the worst of all, no loving goodnight, no embrace, just trudging up a darkened staircase to a bedroom and bed he had again to share. The bed had not been made, the sheets were torn and as he cried himself to sleep; he missed his room and he missed his beloved auntie Vera.

The summer holidays dragged on. Chris felt a stranger in his own home; his father was as distant as ever and if he spoke it was to criticise, his sisters had their own friends, the two eldest had started new schools and were involved in their new lives. Where Vera had been hard working, and yet involved Chris in her everyday life his Mother was in her own world, didn't seem to worry about cleanliness and had little to say except clichés she kept repeating ad nauseum

"Remember when you are at school that manners maketh the man"

She seemed to sit around the house smoking, listening to the radio and then about an hour before his father was due home, she would do a quick clean and start cooking the tea. Yet when his father came home she would complain how hard it was to keep house and how tired she was.

So Chris was relieved when the day at last came that he dressed in his new school uniform for the first time, packed his rucksack and waited for his beloved Rolls, Aunt, Uncle and Grandmother arrived to take him to Paddington station.

THE SQUARE PEG

(Autobiography 3)

The noise, the confusion! It seemed to Chris like a scene from Dante's Inferno that greeted him at Paddington Station. The snorting of steam, the smell of smoke, the hot metally smell of boiling water, the blowing of whistles and the slamming of train doors, the grunting of the engines themselves - great green and brass monsters, sporting exotic names as they strained, creaked and slowly moved forward, lines of carriages moving with them like great, red and cream serpents. All around him were hoards of people running, walking, jostling for position, whilst others stood idly by, simply waiting; how on earth was he to find a Major Wigmore, a man whom he had never met but who was supposed to shepherd the new boys on to the right train.

But there were, in amongst the throng of people, groups of boys, of varying ages dressed, as he was, in the fawn uniform of Dauntsey's school, and Beram led the small party to a group of boys of similar age whom he seemed to think looked as if they knew what they were doing. To Chris's embarrassment he foisted him on to them, unaware of an unspoken divide between 'old boys' and the 'new bugs'.

Settled in a compartment, Chris sank back in his seat, hoping it would engulf him, somehow make him invisible to the other boys. Not that they had been overtly nasty or unfriendly on the platform, but he himself had winced at his mother's attentions; licking the corner of her handkerchief and wiping a spot from his face, and rather too loudly trotting out her favourite phrase yet again "now don't forget, manners maketh the man!" Blushing, he looked towards his aunt for comfort and her reassuring smile made him feel more at ease; a firm handshake from his Uncle, who produced a £1 pound note, the maximum amount of pocket money allowed and the most Chris had ever held, gave him something else to think about..

Then one of the boys asked his name.

"Chris"

"Funny rname; sounds more like a Christian name..."

Blushing yet again, Chris found himself apologising, as he stuttered out "Saklatvala". Nobody had bothered to tell him that at this school everyone was known by their surnames. None of the boys could pronounce his name and after an awkward silence one said well we'll just call you Sak, more laughter. But Sak he became. Things didn't get any better when another boy asked what prep school he had gone to. Chris had never heard of a prep school and assuming it was just another name for a primary school, blurted out "Gospel Oak". The other boys looked puzzled and in unison, or so it seemed to Chris "never heard of it". It transpired they had all been to a prep school called Purton Stoke.

An awkward moment was avoided when the carriage door slid open and a short but erect gentleman entered the compartment and after addressing each boy by name turned to face Chris

"And who do we have here then"

"Chr......... Saklatvala Sir"

Major Wigmore formally welcomed him to Dauntsey's School

Back on the platform his family and the parents of his travelling companions seemed to be getting on well with each other. As the train began to pull out of the station his final moment of his former life was the sound of his uncle's deep throated laughter.

All the self confidence he had gained during his time with Beram and Vera seemed to have deserted him and so for the next two and a half hours he stayed mainly silent and if he felt other eyes upon him, he closed his eyes, feigning sleep but in reality he was wide awake and listening to conversations that were alien to him. The others spoke of exotic holidays abroad; of their parents' new cars; of their family owned farms or businesses, Not one of their families, it appeared. worked for anybody else.

Uncomfortably aware that he did not fit in, but unable to understand the reasons why, he concentrated on the journey itself, repeating to himself the names of the stations they stopped at, Reading, Newbury, Savernake Forest, and Hungerford. Between these stops he was deep in thought. He was aware at some point he would be asked more about himself, his background and his family and he was not only self conscious about the truth, he was also ashamed; ashamed of his own family and ashamed of himself.

He was jolted out of this misery by the shrill whistle of the train, mingled with the hissing of steam being released and screeching of brakes as the train shuddered to a halt. Grabbing his khaki webbing knapsack, he joined the throng of fawn clad boys amassing on the platform. Already the old hands were heading off ,whilst the new boys waited for further instructions from Major Wigmore. He formed them into a loose crocodile before herding them down a gentle slope from the station and across a busy main road. As he looked around him, Sak marvelled at the high, long viaduct that they had just crossed on the train. It spanned a great valley, the once red bricks, now grimy, dark and foreboding; the legacy of a hundred years of smoke belching steam engines; yet to Chris there was something mystical about this great structure, the blackened, long slender legs seemed to belong to a great long legged monster, dominating the countryside around it as if to say, this is my realm - beware!

But those around him seemed unaware of the majesty that lay before them and he was pulled from his reverie by the instructions of the Major to join the small group of boys in front of a of a red and black bricked cottage, (the gatehouse). They were ushered between two rather forlorn and derelict pillars of what had once been a grand and imposing gate; "Just follow me" said the Major as he set off at, Sak thought, quite a brisk paced.

He was began to enjoy himself; the driveway wound its way through wonderful and magical woodland of great and varied species of tree, elms, oaks, aged pines and silver birch, shared with shrubs, rhododendrons, bracken and ferns, moss and stinging nettles. The smell of the woods were evocative of another place, another time, and momentarily he was back with his beloved aunt and uncle walking through a similar wood on the way to an archaeology dig at a Roman Villa. He remembered the shock and pain of being stung for the first time and of Vera quickly finding dock leaves to heal his pain. The afternoon sun was warm on his back and there was laughter all around.

But gradually his happiness gave way to unhappiness and the feeling of ill ease on the train became worse as he became aware that he was the object of the boys' mirth. They were laughing at his cheap and tatty knapsack, taunting him, asking him why he did not have a decent suit case like the rest of them. In vain he tried to recall the reasons why Beram thought a knapsack would be more appropriate but his reasoning now seemed weak and unconvincing, as deep in his heart he came to the realisation that the real reason Beram liked it was because it had been cheap.

'Can you only afford Army surplus then......' In less than half a day Sak was a figure of fun even before he had reached the school.

He now wished the woods that just a few moments ago had given him so much pleasure would swallow him up; he was different ; he was alone, there was no one to turn to.

His knapsack seemed to get heavier with every stride, his back ached, his new shoes began to pinch and rub at his heels despite the thick woollen school socks; his heels began to blister and the drive seemed never ending. He wanted to stop, to sit down but knew that he couldn't. He longed for the comfort and warmth of his aunt but she was far away. Yet another bend, surely this would be the last one, but no, the driveway, if that is what it was, continued on. His misery was compounded by those boys who, arriving by car, stopped to pick up friends along the way.

Mercifully, the walk up the driveway, which in reality was no more than a mile and a half, came to an end. His first glimpse of the Manor was marred by his misery, pain and tiredness; it's magnificence was completely lost on him. He blindly followed the boys inside, the 'new bugs' shepherded into the main reception rooms to be welcomed by the Manor Housemaster.

MAKING THE SQUARE PEG ROUND

(Autobiography 5)

Sak's first letter home betrayed none of the anxieties he really felt, but rather concentrated on such positives of those first few days that he could summon up, and both Uncle and Aunt and his parents could be forgiven for thinking he was happy and had settled in well.

He did not tell of how the Master's inability to pronounce his surname caused laughter and embarrassment, a process repeated many times when they were taken to the main school and introduced to each subject Master, another first for him. Major Wigmore had made matters worse by saying "It's not English is it?"

"No Sir"

"Where does it come from"

"India, Sir"

"Well you speak very good English"

More laughter and Sak was too mortified to say anything different.

Rather he wrote about the beauty of the Manor House, of the ivy clad exterior, the panelled walls of the two main reception rooms and the well manicured lawns.

He hadn't lived in the countryside before and when, on that first Saturday evening they were marched in a crocodile to the main school to watch a feature film, (The Sound Barrier) he had been amazed by the brightness of the night sky and overwhelmed by the sheer number of stars.

He loved the walk to Market Lavington for service at the local Church, prior to returning to the Manor House where all the boys were required to write a letter home, which was inspected by the Masters prior to sending.

He had written nothing of the further humiliation of being given "30 words" and being labelled a sneak. It had all come about the first night in the dorm. The silence bell had gone, meaning no boy could talk until the getting up bell in the morning. After lights out Michelle was singing himself to sleep. A housemaster burst in and asked who had been talking. No one owned up and the whole dorm was to be punished. Sak, who tended to take things literally, piped up and said "No one was talking Sir, Michelle was singing" happy that he had resolved the problem. He was shocked when Michelle received a mild punishment and completely stunned when he received a harsher one - he simply did not understand. Sadly for him, he had alienated the rest of the small dorm.

Nor did he let on how ashamed he felt by Beram's frugality; the mocking of his knapsack on the walk from the station had been bad enough but how they scoffed at his old tin trunk with his name roughly painted on it. It stood out like a sore thumb from the almost uniformity of the other boys' trunks. They were the same shape, either green or blue, with black trimmings and brass corners; proper trunks with their names neatly stencilled on. the feelings he had first experienced on the train were solidified, he felt different and slightly inadequate as the boys talked about their families, their summer holidays, their cars. Sak prayed they would not ask him any personal question, but he could not put off the inevitable;

"What does your Father do, Sak?"

He mumbled, almost whispered "he works for Kodak"

"What" and before he could answer, somebody said "He is the

managing Director of Kodak", there were nods of approval and Sak stayed mum; in that moment he realised that if he were to keep his head above water, total honesty might not be the best policy. When the boys started to talk about their cars and asked him what car his family had, he simply, and all too easily, said "Rolls Royce". The boys were impressed; he was one of them after all, crisis averted and the square peg had had the sharp edges softened on the way to becoming round.

Of course, in his letters he did not admit to feeling lonely or confess to missing the comfort of his beloved aunt.

After Sunday lunch the boys were instructed to go for a Sunday walk of at least two hours duration and not to return to the Manor or its environs within that time. When they had walked from the station that first day he had loved the woods they passed through. Now, just before the main road linking Market and West Lavington they crossed a wide and fast flowing stream and Sak thought this would be a good place to play Cowboys and Indians. He and a couple of other new boys did just that. All the while they were playing an old black Daimler was parked on the other side of the road. Unbeknown to him within it were his aunt and uncle,who had driven down to his cousins' house in Salisbury, borrowed their car, and driven over to check on him. If only he had known.

Those new boys who had been to Prep school had no difficulty in the transition to Dauntseys; to them it was merely transferring to another boarding school with enough shared traditions and way of life to make a seamless change but for Sak a whole new way of life lay before him and everything had to be learned from scratch. It was not because the other boys were deliberately cruel or the Masters insensitive to his needs, it just did not occur to them that he was different to any other child, they assumed that his background and experiences were the same as all the other boys. At least, so it seemed to Sak.

His physical appearance did not help either. Showering after his first game of football his slightness at first shocked and then amused; they had never seen anyone as skinny as he was; one boy put his thumb and little finger around his ankles and called everybody to come and see, and laugh, and thus a new new nickname was born- and Spindleshanks he became. Of course he laughed along with them, he knew no other way of coping, but deep down he was hurt and wept silently in his bed at night. Much of the confidence he had gained with Beram and Vera was slipping away and events at the first art lesson did not help.

Mr Johnston, (known as Teddyboy because of his drainpipe trousers) was a young and very talented artist - much in demand in the commercial world of comics; he did the full cover pictures for many titles. In the art room a portrait of his beautiful wife had pride of place. In this first art class the boys were expected to paint a portrait. Sak was at first delighted to be chosen as the model and all started well. But Mr. Johnston asked the class what animal Sak most resembled. Many answers, more laughter, more blushing and embarrassment for him. Matters were made worse when Mr. Johnston said Sak resembled a baby lamb! There were hoots of laughter and for days afterwards the sounds of 'baah, baah' would follow him. But it seemed that Sak would have the last laugh. Mr Johnston said he wanted to paint Sak's portrait, and instead of going for the compulsory walk on Sunday would he, Sak, take tea with him and his wife and then sit while he painted his portrait. Sak was in seventh heaven; he felt important and the thought of being in the presence of Mr. Johnston's wife, who reminded him so much of his aunt, gave him great comfort.

Sunday came and Sak waited at the bottom of the school drive - and waited and waited, and waited some more. As the boys began to return from their compulsory two hour walk he was still there, still waiting. Those who knew why he was there teased him unmercifully and yet again he felt wretched, humiliated and more alone than ever. In his letter home that morning he had written with pride and joy of his forthcoming afternoon.

The next art lesson was not until Thursday and Sak was dreading it and if he could have found an excuse for missing it he would have, not out of anger or disappointment but more out of embarrassment, how to face the class and Mr Johnston. But Mr Johnston was full of apologies, all about family problems, the gist of which went right over Sak's head. Mr Johnston said they would do it this Sunday afternoon if that was alright. But it was a repeat performance, no Mr. Johnston. Sak again cried himself to sleep. If anyone heard, nothing was said. Yet he was still gullible enough to wait for a third week in succession and for a third week he was let down. That week's apology ended with the words "....but anyway I don't need you there to paint your picture". He sat there and grinned, his face growing redder and redder as he felt every eye upon him. But there was to be no happy ending, no portrait ever appeared.

Even 'the sheep' came back to mock him; In the first few weeks he began to realise that his primary school education had been somewhat different to those the other boys had received at their prep schools and it was oddly enough an early French lesson that showed him that he had not been taught English as a language; yes, he could read and write, knew about nouns, adjectives, verbs, adverbs etc but that was about it. The pluperfect. what the hell is that? When the French Master started to talk about phonetics he hadn't a clue what he was talking about and knew even less about phonetic punctuation.

When asked to read a sentence in French he stumbled over the pronunciation and Mr. McGregor said "Saklatvala, try pronouncing as a sheep might; he tried. - where do you live?" said Mr McGregor

"North London, Sir"

"Well they have funny sheep in North London "- he laughed, the class laughed and Sak went deeper into his shell. The deeper he withdrew into that shell the less able he was to ask questions about things he did not understand and so he didn't learn. The fear of being laughed at and humiliated overrode every other consideration and this inability to ask, this inability to stick up for himself, only made matters worse.

One subject he was determined to succeed in was Latin. The stories in Latin for Today, (Quia hodie Latine) were full of Roman history and mythology, something he loved and which somehow brought him closer to life back with Beram and Vera. Though no scholar, he was able to make a reasonable fist of it but again his insecurity was his downfall. Desperate for friendship, he was eager to please. There was a boy in his dorm, Bridgestone, who found himself a little out of his depth. His father was an Old Dauntsean, and this, allied with his wealth, made his son able to attend the school regardless of his attainments - no entrance exam for him.

When set Latin prep Bridgestone would come to him for help which, in his desire to be liked, Sak gave only too willingly - but this created its own problems. He knew that his work was not perfect and he needed to ensure that it didn't become evident he had done Bridgestone's work So in an effort to disguise this, he deliberately put in some incorrect answers in his own work. This resulted in Bridgestone getting good marks in class. When it came to exams he did very badly. For Sak it was the opposite. Somehow, Bridgestone got all the sympathy, the teachers suspecting he must suffer from exam nerves. Sak on the other hand, incurred the teacher's wrath, as it appeared he was lazy. Despite this, Sak could never refuse Bridgestone's requests for help; neither could he bring himself to tell anyone the truth.

Even near the end of term the Maths master still couldn't, or wouldn't, pronounce Saklatvala properly, and it seemed it was the only name with which he had any difficulty. After afternoon tea the Duty Master would read out the names of the boys who had received letters. On this occasion the Maths Master was on duty. He managed the first few names without a problem but then started to struggle, " Sak, Saaa, eventually managing Saklatfarta." An explosion of derisive laughter filled Sak's ears, he could feel himself blushing but could not bring himself to laugh with them. The boys of course loved it, shortened it and Farta became his yet another opprobrious nickname. Sak, not understanding that there was no malice intended, once again shut himself off from his fellows, but if he had given it a little thought he might have realised that it was just boys having fun, more so because it was a fun of which he himself was guilty at times.

One of the other new boys who shared his dorm came from farming stock; his father owned a racehorse named 'Reverend Prince' which was entered in the Grand National. Come the great day , all the Manor Boys and Masters gathered in the Quiet Room to listen (that's what it was called!) - some Masters had even placed bets. The boy in question was the centre of attention. Alas, 'Reverend Prince' fell at the first fence. Much laughter, mocking and derision, in which Sak joined as enthusiastically as anybody else. At that moment he did not notice, and wouldn't have cared, that the wretched boy had left the room in tears. Later, he felt ashamed, so remorseful he apologised for his behaviour.

Many may well have given up at this point and ask that they be removed from the school. Such an escape never occurred to Sak. Despite everything, he liked the school and what it had to offer - all his misgivings and insecurities stemmed from the fact that he felt he did not belong but he badly wanted to. The inadvertent lies on the first day had set the course; like a chameleon changing its colour to blend in with its environment so it was with Sak, listening to the other boys he altered his background to fit in and thus began the fiction that became the face of Sak.

Nonetheless there was one group of boys with whom he felt more at ease. On his first day in class, a new group of boys arrived - the Day Boys, invariably known as the Day Bugs. These boys were from the local village school, attending Dauntseys under the aegis of scholarships endowed by the Worshipful Guild of Mercers. The boys were mostly from the Council Estate. Sak found he had more in common with these boys, could understand their backgrounds, share their unease in the new environment, as well as their insecurities that echoed his own. Nonetheless, there was an unwritten divide between the two groups, friendships were difficult to forge.

So feeling academically lacking and socially inept he muddled his way through the first term, accepting the routine life that was boarding school and finding there was much that he enjoyed, events where he felt one of the crowd and not singled out for unwanted, often thoughtlessly cruel, attention The good times included Saturday night films or concerts and lining the touchline on Saturday afternoons to watch the 'First Fifteen' rugby team; enthusiastically taking up the chant of 2,4, 6, 8 who do we appreciate D-A-U-NTS-E-Y-'S, Dauntsey's! as he cheered on the school team.

He loved the Sunday Church Services which were held at either Market or West Lavington. Not only did he appreciate the architecture of both, and enjoyed the singing of hymns, it was also the one place where for 90 minutes he could relax and be himself, no fear of awkward questions, just time to truly be Chris again, at least in his own mind.

Most of all, right from the start with that first walk through the woods, he fell in love with the countryside, the school and the Manor Woods. The Manor House where the Juniors lived, and its grounds were on one side of a valley, at the bottom of which lay the school swimming pool, as well as a fast running stream. On the other side lay the Manor House playing fields and the School woods. Although the Manor House boys had to cross the stream and pass by the School woods they were 'out of bounds' for the Manor boys, as were the Manor Woods for the School House boys. Passing the school woods on his first walk to the main school he marvelled at the mass and beauty of the rhododendrons, the abundance of bracken and ferns; this was a whole new world for him and he loved it.

The main school was situated close to Salisbury Plain and as he walked up the short Poplar lined driveway to the main building he stopped in his tracks, strangely drawn to part of the plain that seemed at odds with the rest. In shape it was as if a huge windscreen wiper had swept along the side and carved out a huge concave feature in the form of a massive Roman amphitheatre. He felt drawn to it and many times when he was struggling with a lesson he would gaze at it in a dream like state until a piece of fast flying chalk, a shout or rap on the knuckles from the teacher, brought him back to reality; strangely whatever problem he had been struggling with seemed less difficult.

When Beram had first told him he was going to boarding school he had waxed lyrical about the game of rugby, and how you could bring opponents to the ground with a tackle and Sak had been keen to learn the game and perhaps be as proficient at it as his cousin Jeremy at a different public school, Bryanston. Alas, it seemed his puniness was against him. A French master who was also in charge of the first fifteen one day came into the classroom, saying for all to hear

“Took the team to Bryanston yesterday and saw the best Fly Half I have ever seen, quite brilliant - name of Saklatvala. Any relation?

Sak admitted he was his cousin and Mr Young went on to bemoan the fact that he had been left with a seven stone weakling. More of that derisive laughter. Hoping for some sympathy he had written of the incident in his next letter to Beram and Vera. Beram wrote a poem;

Poor little bugger
He'll never play rugger
And never grow big and strong.

Then Sak found a sport at which he excelled, fencing. Blessed with lightning fast reflexes, his slight frame was in this sport a distinct advantage. He loved the romance of it and he felt like a knight of old, fighting for his King. Major Wigmore was delighted and there was talk of him representing the school. Sak was proud and inwardly happy; he felt he was now on a par with his cousin Jeremy's sporting prowess. It was not to be!

About a third of the way through the term it was time for an 'Exeat Sunday' whereby the boys could be taken out by their parents for the whole day. He watched with envy as car after car came to pick up their boys, envious also as he watched other boys whose parents could not be there being taken out by other boys. Virtually alone in the Manor House he reached a new low and it did not get any better with the return of the boys chattering of the meals they had enjoyed, the gifts they had been given, films they had seen as well as new delights to refill their tuck boxes. All he had to offer was elaborate and exotic excuses as to why his parents could not be there. Yet again he cried himself to sleep that night. In class he was quiet, hardly daring to say anything for fear of making a fool of himself and being subject to more ridicule. He blushed whenever a question was directed at him. He barely spoke out of the classroom, on tenterhooks that he might betray himself and inadvertently let slip his true background. What had his Grandmother said; "Liars have to have good memories", he wished he had remembered that, on the first day.

He was not always unhappy; he enjoyed doing various jobs around the Manor House. When volunteers were called for to paint the toilet block, Sak was first in line, as he was when the call came for volunteers to mow or roll the grass. So whilst other boys busied themselves in the cellars pursuing various hobbies, building model aeroplanes and firing up the miniature diesel engines, he was doing things that he loved and which he could do well.

He looked forward to Sunday afternoon walks, and after that first weekend and the cowboys and Indians foray, he didn't seek out the company of others, preferring to be alone, free to explore and enjoy the beauty of the woods in his own way. As he walked, he would write stories in his head which he determined to write down, but when it came to putting pen to paper it was somehow not the same; sometimes he just sat under the trees enjoying the solitude; here there was no pressure, here he could totally relax and be himself at one with nature. This was his paradise.

The joy in his heart knew no bounds; it was half term and as he dressed that morning it was scarcely believable that in just a few hours the Rolls would be trundling down the drive with his Aunt and Uncle. More than two hours later the initial euphoria of the day had been taken on a somewhat sourer note. Due at eleven am they eventually arrived a little after one. Sak had waited, not daring to move; he had watched as car after car had arrived to pick up their sons. It seemed reminiscent of Mr Johnson, the art master. He despaired of their ever arriving; even the Masters seemed concerned and stopped in their cars to enquire if he was alright.He smiled and said he was.

After what seemed an eternity the Rolls appeared and Sak felt that the past seven weeks had never happened; here was his life, he asked for nothing more. As was his accustomed habit, he made straight for the front seat, to sit between his aunt and uncle but was surprised to see his Mother and Father sitting in the back. It had not occurred to him that they would be there. Although he had written home every week the regular letters he received in return were from Vera, with only the occasional letter from his Mother . Naturally, he was pleased to see them but in his mind they were not in his half term equation. After all, in the past three years they had had nothing to do with him apart from the short time he had spent "at home" prior to joining Dauntsey's.

Greetings over, he settled down in the front seat blissfully content. During the short drive to Devizes, Sak was happy; for a few hours he could be himself, no more pretence. If only! His happiness was short-lived. They were in Woolworths and Sak was standing next to Vera, when his Father pushed between them.

"Don't forget you have a Mother"

He looked up to his aunt before reluctantly leaving her side and joining his Mother. He didn't doubt he loved his Mother but it was a different sort of love that he felt for Vera, and in that moment he knew that things could never be the same. he Mother who had let him go, had not been to visit him in almost three years, who had seldom written, was resentful of the person who had given him unconditional love, who had brought out the best in him. Surely if she had wanted to she could have refused to let him go, and if not that she could have at least made the effort to contact him. So it seemed to him that responsibility for managing a delicate situation had fallen to an unfit 12 year old. From that moment on he hid his true emotions, faked emotions he didn't feel. He was drained, tired and disillusioned. This was not the Half Term he had expected.

Over lunch his Father lost his temper with his Mother and embarrassed everybody by shouting at the top of his voice, all because she had mistakenly diluted his fizzy drink. So much for the caring family man in Woolworths; Sak truly felt for his Mother. It came as a relief when Beram suggested they go to the Cinema in the afternoon. The film itself was immaterial; anyway they had to leave before the end of the main feature to get him back to school on time but he could be alone in the darkness, alone with his thoughts, alone again. Happy to be alone.

Things seemed to worsen when he returned to school that evening. The Rolls which he so loved and treasured was the object of ridicule. "We thought you said you had a Rolls Royce but it's nothing but an old banger...." He just didn't understand, but then, neither did they!

Along with many other parents the Saklatvalas attended the Morning service the next day. Beram drew attention to them with his loud singing. The Sunday was more relaxed than the day before as Sak had stumbled on a happy resolution of the tension between his Mother and Aunt. He understood because he realised that his Mother was resentful of the love that Sak had for his Aunt and he could feel his Aunt holding back just as he was doing. His Uncle's singing had put the spotlight on him and on his return to school he was quizzed. The boys wished to know who all the people were, which were his parents. Without thinking he answered truthfully,

"Well whose car is it then? " Too late to change his story

"My Father's"

"Well why does your Uncle drive it?"

He concocted an elaborate story that seemed to satisfy them; the square peg was getting rounder.

Mercifully that first term came to an end; he had been looking forward to his return to the flat and a life that he loved and was used to, but it wasn't to be. The joy of being met by his Aunt soon turned to disappointment when he realised they were headed not for the flat but towards his parents' house in Hornsey Rise. It was,he supposed his home too but he had not considered it as such for years. He was full of foreboding at the grim unfriendly exterior, the wild unkempt garden overrun with hollyhocks. His Mother's welcome was perfunctory and her dismissal of Vera bordered on the rude. Sak clung to her as long as possible but he sensed she was pushing him away and he understood why so he released his hold and he let go.

After a few days Chris began to realise that Dauntsey's had had more of an effect on him than he had realised and he was missing it. There was an order, a sense of security and though he had been unhappy the boys had seemed willing to believe the fiction that he had, half accidentally, created about himself and had accepted him as one of their own; they were not aware of his insecurities, his feelings of inferiority. In the time he had been away his sisters had been growing up, developed new friendships and interests, as had his former friends and they now had little in common with him. He realised he himself had changed, also that he felt different in himself and sinisterly he felt somehow superior.

His Mother, whilst saying she was pleased to have him home, did little to make him feel at home, took little interest in his school life and gave him no encouragement to initiate any conversation other than to deride what Vera and Beram had done for him,

"Well of course Miss Rawlins, (Headmistress of his first Primary school) always said you would do well"

She delighted in telling him of Vera's discomfort when Beram had mocked the Birthday present she had lovingly bought him. Aware of Beram's love of the Classical world and his attempts to translate Ovid's Love poems, she had bought him a deluxe Classical Greek/English Dictionary. Instead of thanking her, or acknowledging her thoughtfulness he had dismissed it with "Well, what do I want with this!"

Chris's Mother cackled with joy at the memory

He stared at her in disbelief. He did not understand her resentment and not for the first time wondered why, if she felt so strongly, did she let him go in the first place? He doubted that she ever made that sort of effort for his father.

Uninterested in his school life, she just left him to his own devices which were not up to much. All his books, all his possessions, all the things that interested him, were still at the flat. His sisters' schools were still in session; he was bored, cold and lonely.

His Father made no effort to welcome him back either; it was as if Sak, or Chris, as he now was once again, did not exist and if there had been no tasks for him to do his Father might not have spoken to him at all. But he was useful to have there, to do all the jobs his Father did not want to do himself but which most fathers saw as their parental role. The house was perpetually cold, the stairs remained uncarpeted, and the corridors, stairs and landing were devoid of any form of lighting. The coal cellar was located halfway along a dark corridor at the side of the house, the cellar itself also unlit because his Father refused to change the light bulb and his Mother showed no inclination to do it either. He could not recall a single time when his Father had collected the coal, it had always been him! Who had done it when he wasn't there? He hated the cold, was scared of the dark, fumbling around in trying to push the shovel into the pile of coal, struggling to get the coal to sit on the spade, as he tried to fill the scuttle in the blackness, only to be shouted at and sent back out when the scuttle was not filled to the brim. Never a word of thanks. His Father was wont to read on the toilet and invariably left the book on the floor when he was done and again it was Chris who was sent upstairs to fetch it for him, the ever pervading chill, the darkness of the unlit staircase and landing as scary as the coal cellar. He felt little better than a slave to his Father's will.

His sisters' school term ended a few days before Christmas so at least he now had some company; Jill, his eldest sister, had been responsible for the Christmas decorations for as long as he could remember and she set about her task with relish. Soon the siblings were cutting crepe paper, tinsel, and cardboard which Jill fashioned into the most delicate, beautiful decorations. She made the crib. Her creations always unique, tasteful and well made. Chris was allowed to help make the paper chains which entailed licking the ends of strips of coloured paper to make interlocking hoops creating long chains which she then hung. On Christmas Eve his father would take Jill out to pick a Christmas tree, which she alone would decorate and he would heap praises on her. Chris loved her decorations and was very proud of her but how he wished he could be more involved, how he wished to receive that sort of praise but he did not fit in any more, but then, had he ever? and there was nothing he could do about it, this particular square peg would never be rounded. He tried his best, put on a brave face to hide his misery. He felt cut off, bored and lonely, which was hardly surprising as he had nothing there, not even his own room. When at "home" he had to sleep in his younger sister's room with its girlish wall-paper, all her dolls, toys etc, her clothes in the wardrobe, nothing in that house could be identified as his. He didn't give much thought to the idea that maybe it was no better for her, forced to share with a more or less unknown brother.

Around that time his Father would come home laden with large boxes of chocolates which he had chosen with the greatest of care, not alas, for the family, but for the 'girls' in his office. Too lazy or disinclined to wrap them himself, he was lucky to be able to instruct his middle daughter Elizabeth to undertake the task. She was a perfectionist and did a beautiful job, wrapping each parcel with care and precision. He would ask Elizabeth to take special care with the largest one, which was not for his Mother, as Chris thought at the time. Years later he realised the special gifts over the years had been for his Father's long term mistress. This led him to further reflect that perhaps his pulling up Chris in Devizes for what might be seen as favouring his aunt over his Mother that first half term, had been in part to assuage his own guilt.

For Chris it had been an earth shattering bombshell; later he thought maybe it had been the most loving gesture he had seen his Father make to his Mother and in his innocence he had subconsciously seen it as the beginning of a new, gentler, deeper, caring relationship.

But alas that concern so apparent in Devizes had not stood the test of time and only a few months later his vicious and seemingly uncontrolled temper was as bad ever and aimed always at either himself or his Mother. Temper wise Christmas was always the worst and as this Christmas approached he began making it uncomfortable for all. He took almost no part in the build up to Christmas; wrote no Christmas cards except to his 'precious' office girls, totally ignored his wife's siblings when they came round bearing gifts and certainly did not reciprocate.

Christmas day itself was memorable for all the wrong reasons; it had started well enough with the opening and shared joy of their stockings. Helping prepare the Christmas lunch, laying the table including the crackers, the opening of the tree presents augured well but as they sat around the dining table and Mother started to bring in the food which she had been preparing since the early hours. As he sat down he his Father observed the tiniest of chips in his wine glass and went totally ballistic, screaming at his wife, accusing her of not washing up correctly, of putting everything in the sink at one time. Didn't she know how valuable crystal was etc etc. Chris had heard it all before, as had his sisters, and though he felt for his Mother he could not help to wonder why she had almost brought this upon herself because his Father was right. A glass of wine in a fresh glass might have helped soothe the situation but no corkscrew could be found! Off he went again. The Christmas mood was lost, it was a sombre family that ate the meal in almost total silence and the pulling of the crackers was quite joyless. What saddened Chris the most was that this could have all been avoided with a little more thought from his Mother, a little more/care from his Father; it differed very little over the years when he was at home, there was always something to set his Father off, and things his Mother could have done to avoid ructions. A story his older sister Jill told him years later suggested that his Mother was well aware of this, and deliberately created such situations!

Another unchanging Christmas ritual was that after lunch Jill was charged with taking the others for a walk of at least two hours duration. To be out of the house and away from his Father's sullen mood was a relief. They would return to find their parents asleep in their chairs in front of the fire, the table remained uncleared, the washing up still to be done but the mood seemed to have lightened.

If Christmas Day was the usual let down, Chris had reasons for looking forward to Boxing Boxing Day. The day after Christmas was traditionally spent with Beram and Vera. This would be the first time he had been back to the flat since he had been at Dauntsey's and here at last he would surely feel at home. Before they reached the flat they stopped off at his Grandmother's, a place Chris had grown to love. Auntie Sehri usually brought laughter and fun but not this time. Almost as soon as they arrived she steered him away from the others and took him to task.

"Why haven't you brought any Christmas presents home with you. Did not Beram give you £1 pound at the beginning of term? A little show of gratitude would not go amiss after all he has done for you"

He was dumbfounded. The one pound has been his pocket money, his to spend on bus fares to town when permitted, to spend in the tuck shop for occasional treats; besides, it had barely lasted half a term. He had been grateful, had not worried that most boys had at least five times that amount and had not minded that other boys had their funds replenished when he had not. He had no answer to her rebuke, he just blushed and remained silent and felt ashamed. All Sehri saw was a sullen and selfish boy and was not averse to letting him know.

The nervousness and uncertainty that had replaced his joy at being back at the flat proved baseless. The flat was warm and welcoming, as were Beram and Vera and the day was much as anticipated and Chris felt at home, he was back where he belonged. The day went well and his Father had been on his best behaviour. There had been more presents, Chris had been entrusted to lay the table, a task he had always enjoyed, and the food was delicious and everybody seemed happy. His Mother, a very good cake maker, possibly her only cooking skill, seemed happiest when she found fault with Vera's Christmas cake finding it

"....a little dry but then I quite like it dry..."

It was getting late and and as Vera gave him a farewell hug she said

"...we'll see you in a few days..." and in that way he learned all his holidays would in future be split between "home" and the flat.

A few days later Chris was on his way back to the flat, with Vera in her old Austin Seven. He was happy; conversation flowed effortlessly, she asked about school and he chatted about all the positive things, the Saturday night Subscription concerts and films, they talked of pop songs. He had talked about the end of term production of Twelfth Night; it had been his first experience of live theatre and he had marvelled at almost every aspect of it, the lighting giving depth to the sky, the exterior scenes so realistic. The costumes and makeup and above all the acting. He went into detail about the whole play remembering many of the lines, especially those of Sir Toby Belch and Sir Andrew Aguecheek. Vera laughed with him and was reminded of the time she had collected him from Salisbury after a short stay with his cousin Roger. The train journey back to London was almost two hours and Chris had kept the whole compartment enthralled with his re-playing of the entire film he had seen with his cousins. He felt alive, he felt wanted and appreciated

The first week back at the flat was all that Chris could have hoped for. Chris was totally happy, totally at ease, life was back to its best. Alone with Vera during the day, trips in her car, helping her shop, spending time in the kitchen watching and helping her cook and the late afternoon ritual of making her sit down while he brewed tea in the silver teapot he loved so much. Then there were weekly trips to Thornton Heath to visit her Mother, the daily walks to his Grandmother's flat, the smell and taste of her home made bread. When he collected coal for them it was in a place well lit and overlooked by the kitchens of both the flat, and that of friends next door, he felt secure.This was pre Dauntsey life back again.

He looked forward to Beram coming home each evening, when he took an interest in what Chris had been doing during the day, was kind and caring towards Vera, was witty, interesting to be around.

The second week arrived and so did his school report! As did the bill for the first term. Neither made good reading, he had not done very well at all, not even in his Latin, he had no idea why. The teachers seemed to find him pleasant enough, well behaved but just not very bright. Verta and Beram went through the report with Chris line by line, seeking reasons for his poor performance but he was unable to give any. He was distressed, not for himself but for the two people whom he felt he owed so much, for the two people whom he felt really cared, the two people who he loved the most. He was embarrassed, found himselfblushing and unable to say a word. He felt unable to explain and with his lame excuses just made a fool of himself, he had wanted so much to please, to do well and he had failed.

Failure in his son was anathema to his Father and Chris was half expecting Beram and Vera to react in a similar manner but there were no raised voices, no histrionics for which he was grateful; he looked to Vera for solace but could sense the disappointment in her eyes despite the kindly smile.

The bill for the school fees accompanied his report and Beram thought it prudent to go through it with him and so he relaxed a little, at least here there would be nothing to be embarrassed about but of course he was wrong, the fencing lessons!

“I see you took up fencing”

“Yes....” but before he could say anything else, before he could boast of his new found skills

“It costs one guinea a term. That's far too expensive, you will have to give up”

He was shattered, confused, angry. He wanted cry, he wanted to explain he was good at it, wanted to shout out “you said you wanted me to have the same start, the same advantages as my cousins, why are you taking this away from me”

He said nothing other than a muttered apology.

The lecture that followed made him feel worse, the tears welled up and he was on the verge of blurting out his real feeling, to tell of his unhappiness, his wish to live with them and go to Holloway County Grammar School but he hid the words. Quite simply he was too scared to speak up. Beram had made it clear in various ways that a top priority had been to help Chris to be more assertive and stressed the importance of being decisive. This message however wasn’t always clear. During his time at the flat Chris was introduced to a number of new culinary delights. One Saturday Beram had taken him to the butchers and said he could choose the meat for their Sunday lunch. He chose pork. Beram had not been best pleased and complained to Vera, to Chris’s grandmother as well as Sehri that Chris had chosen the most expensive. The embarrassment this caused him made him apprehensive when confronted with a choice, so, too afraid to voice his true thoughts he kept them hidden.

Imperceptibly the general dynamics in the flat shifted. Chris no longer looked forward to Beram’s return from work with the same joy, he was uncomfortable in his company and more guarded in his conversation, fearful that talk may lead back to school, his lack of success.

He began to notice subtle changes in the flat that did not help his confidence. “His” room had been changed round for no discernable reason, he was made aware that others, other nephews, had been using it as and when required. No room of his own at "home" and now no room to call his own in the flat. The local friends he made had moved on, formed new friendships and were that little bit more distant. The one constant in his life that made this bearable was Vera's acceptance of him as he was.

So it was not with a heavy heart that he returned to school but rather one of relief. The boys and masters had accepted the fiction of his home life and accepted him as one of their own and this place once so alien to him, was now where he felt most comfortable. His confidence grew whenTata made a deal with Mercedes to supply engines for the Tata trucks. Beram had designed the cabs and his bonus was a brand new Mercedes 220s and Sak returned that half term with the brochure for 'his' car, evidence that his transport was no longer a thing of fun, but a vehicle his classmates admired and envied.

This new found comfort did not extend to his academic or sporting endeavours especially when Major Wigmore found out he was no longer doing fencing. He wanted to know why but Sak felt unable to tell him why; it would not do to let the whole school know his family considered the one guinea fee excessive, (less than many boys' pocket money) so the Major formed the impression that Sak was too lazy to bother. Naturally, this soon went round the masters' Common Room and reinforced the view of the Latin master that Sak was a capable but lazy boy. When he showed promise on the cricket field both as a wicket keeper and batsman, it seemed to him that his talents were ignored. Effort was just not enough and he continued to fail and he was disgusted with himself for, as he saw it, letting Beram and Vera down yet again. He wondered if his father's assessment of him was the right one after all.

Nervous of making close friendships for fear of giving himself away he cut himself off from possible friendships and became even more of a loner, but now this was accepted as "just Sak!. He still looked forward to the cultural extras that Dauntey's had to offer; the films, the subscription concerts when he could be himself and just enjoy what was on offer but most of all he looked forward to the Sunday afternoon walks; as always, eschewing the company of others he found solace in the Manor Woods, the colour of the rhododendrons, the smell of damp moss,the sun shining through the tree canopy the fast flowing Manor stream at the bottom of the valley. He enjoyed everything about them, began to feel they were his woods, nobody appreciated them as much as he did. The trees were his friends and confidantes. Sakwas finding life tolerable, he had his own regular routine, holidays split between his 'home' and the flat;. But the fictional home life he portrayed at school was a constant effort to remember what he had said previously. 'Liars really do need good memories' he thought after he found himself in the middle of contradicting something he had said previously. Miraculously, to his imind, nobody seemed to notice. He was not aware of the strain he was putting on himself, did not realise that the work he put in on maintaining his fiction was holding him back and the longer it went on the worse it was becoming.

Sunday 19th October 1958 was to Sak just another Sunday; he had been at Dauntsey's for three years and was in his final year at the Manor and he was not really looking forward to moving into the main school, away from the intimacy of the Manor. The Latin master had been particularly hard on Sak, frustrated by his seemingly lack of effort. Sak was mulling over the prep he had to do that evening. He had already done the work for his Bridgestone and was pondering how he could modify his own so he would not look too foolish nor give away the subterfuge.. He wandered aimlessly in the woods, not following any of his usual paths, his mind on other matters; he wanted to break out of his perceived uselessness, yearned to be a success in something, anything, preferably Latin.

FROM LITTLE ACORNS

He looked up, and to his horror he realised he had no idea where he was, he was totally disorientated. He had hitherto believed he knew every inch of 'his' woods; they had been his security blanket, his comfort, his joy for the past three years but this was different, and he was scared. He stumbled on through thick undergrowth the like of which he had never seen before, but he kept going as if something was urging him on, compelling him forward. It was nonsense of course, but it was as if a hand was pushing him on, steering him through the undergrowth until he stumbled into a clearing. In the middle of the clearing stood the thickest, tallest oak tree he had ever seen.

He stood and stared in awe, he walked around it and it took him sixty steps to circumnavigate it; as to its height, he could only guess but to him it seemed to reach the sky. He was overcome by the majesty of this magnificent tree, this giant of nature, and though he knew not what force had brought him to it, he instinctively knew he was meant to be there. His fear dissipated, an inner peace swept through him as he embraced the tree and kissed the bark. As he sat at the foot of the tree, his back pressing hard against it as if he wanted it to swallow him up, all his frustrations filled his head. Suddenly the peace was gone, he could feel his pent up anger bursting through, he had simply had enough; he wanted it to change or things must end, he cared not which. He cried out, he screamed, he yelled, voicing anger at himself at his stupidities, and pleaded, pleaded to be a success in at least one thing; the tears were streaming down his face, he was sobbing, he was choking on his tears.

The sound of his sobbing awakened the sleeping Helga. Though the source of the sobbing was a mystery to him he was sure that he was meant to hear it. He recalled the words of Odin

"In our mercy it has been decreed that the length of your imprisonment will be determined by yourself"

Was this then his moment? He had taken Odin's words to mean some great task worthy of his warrior status awaited him, one final battle to prove his worthiness to sit with the heros of old, to at last enter the hallowed halls of Valhalla; so he hesitated, unsure of the right move to make, he did not want to anger the gods again. He was uncharacteristically hesitant and he was still wrestling with his conscience when he felt the presence of Sigrun; recalling the action they had taken which had so angered the gods he felt again the love they had shared, the life they had enjoyed, the happiness they had found after settling in Britain and the family they had raised. They, not the gods, had been right then, pushing all thoughts of the gods and the glory of Valhalla aside. He knew what he had to do and as he prepared to break out, his prison was suddenly filled with light and there before him stood Sigrun, smiling, nodding her encouragement. As her image faded and the darkness returned his sense of loss overwhelmed him, before he found himself filled with a renewed strength. He turned away from the sound of sobbing and with arms outstretched slowly moved forward until his hands touched the opposite side of his cell. He smiled, the walls were wood, then dropped to the floor laughing; he had not felt dead timber, this was alive, and growing; his prison was the inside of a tree! When he had felt himself shrinking Odin had picked him up, placed him an acorn which he had flung to earth, and as the acorn had grown into a mighty oak Helge had grown with it. Helge who had grown up in the forests of Scandinavia, who had deserted his country to settle in Britain, had been imprisoned in an Oak , the very essence of Britain. The irony was not lost on him, so with distressing tears outside and tears of laughter inside, Helge set about his release with renewed energy and joy in his heart.

Had he not been so self absorbed wallowing in self pity, Sak might have noticed movement from within the tree, might have heard the creaking timbers or heard the sound of snapping branches; he might have heard the tone of exultation as Helge inhaled his first breath of fresh air in nearly two thousand years. But he was oblivious to all extraneous sights and sounds.

Eventually he had nothing left, the effort of crying and the disgust at himself had drained him emotionally and physically; the tears dried and he sat with his eyes closed, dreading having to walk back to the Manor House, face the struggle with his Latin prep, the reprimand he would receive from the Master after it had been marked. He wished he could stay there forever....

"Well, why don't you?"

His eyes snapped open, but that confused him even more, for before him stood a giant of a man, dressed in animal furs, long blond unkempt hair flowing over his shoulders, with a matching beard and a broad sword hanging from a piece of rope around his middle. But the most striking thing about him was his clear blue eyes, a clarity which Sak was sure he had not seen in anyone before. He was transfixed, trying to rationalise what was before him. He was unaware of any school play in production which would account for the odd apparel.

"I ask again, why don't you? Why don't you just stay here forever "

"What....I mean how do you know, I am sure I didn't say anything out loud"

"You didn't. But I know more about you than you think..."

"But how?"

"That is not important right now, before I go any further I need you to answer the question, as of this moment your future, and note this, as well as mine depends on the next thing you say. What is it to be?"

He hesitated before answering; every time he had been asked to make a decision in the past he had been made to look foolish, his decision had always been wrong and here was a complete stranger telling him to make what was probably the most important decision of his life. Although in his heart he had his answer, he was for the moment incapable of articulating it.

He looked to Helge who now sat impassively on the floor of the glade, but could discern no clue as to what would be the right answer. He studied the face; those clear blue eyes gave nothing away, but he thought he could detect the beginning of a smile.

"No of course I don't but what I.........

"Shhh, you have no need to say a word, just listen to me" and listen he did, as he had never listened before. Mostly he listened in silence, but sometimes he laughed or momentarily crying and at times squirming in embarrassment for Helge recounted his whole life with unerring accuracy, not just the good and bad times, but his thoughts, his, hopes and dreams it was as if Helge was him, talking as if he was recalling his life to a stranger but with total honesty; he had been laid bare. He had seen the truth that was himself and he had been shocked; he was not as good as he thought, he had more to be thankful for than to regret, and he really had no cause to sink into the morass of self-pity that had consumed so much of his life.

A long silence followed that was eventually broken by Helge

" You want to succeed at something and you feel that Latin is the key. Would you like to be fluent in it?"

"Oh, yes please!"

"Well the easiest way to achieve that is to take you back to Roman Britain, let you live there until you have mastered it."

Sak laughed, but as Helge didn't respond, he realised he was serious

"But before I take you back, there are a number of things you must know. Do not be afraid for no real harm can befall you, you cannot be killed"

The thought chilled him, that was not something he had given thought to

"Why not"

"Think about it; how can you be killed before you were born?

The next thing to be aware of is that all the knowledge you now have will be retained but you must never use it to change history, alter events, if you try you will immediately be brought back to your own time."

"But how long will I be there? I am not the quickest to learn. The school will want to know where I am, Vera will be worried; it's just not practical"

"You will not be missed and while you are away in Roman times, time today will not move; you will return to this exact place at this exact time.

One last thing. When you return you will have no memory of me, you will have no memory of Roman Britain, but you will remember what you have learnt. Now,take my hand and close your eyes."

He did as he was bid. His eyes remained tight shut until a voice said

"You can open them now."

So he did. He looked around, who had spoken? He was alone; no longer in his school uniform he was wearing a simple tunic, belted at the waist, which came down to his knees and a cloak over his shoulders, which he immediately wrapped around himself for both warmth and comfort.

Then he looked around again. He knew exactly where he was yet he was totally lost. The landscape was familiar yet different; in front of him was Salisbury plain, the great scallop shaped depression that he gazed at from the classroom window was there but nothing else but fields and hills which were almost entirely covered in thick dense forests; there were no buildings, no roads or paths, there were simply no signs of civilisation. Panic began to set in. He had not really believed that the stranger had the ability to send him back in time and had closed his eyes to humour him; but here he was. He sat and tried to remember everything that had been said to him. In so far as he could recall everything that had been said had been the truth, so maybe the phrase that stood out must be too -

"Remember, no real harm can be done to you because you have not yet been born."

With this in mind and with renewed confidence he surveyed his surroundings more closely; in the far distance he thought he saw smoke and that he reasoned, is a sign of civilisation. He was on the verge of setting off towards the smoke but stopped and sat down. For much of his life he had reacted to situations without much thought; now he was in charge of his own destiny. Smoke might well be a sign of habitation but two things bothered him, there was no way he could judge how far away it was and two what if, after he had set off in its direction the smoke died down-he would be completely lost. He needed a more reliable landmark. Think Sak, think.

There were two constants; using the great cut out feature on the edge of the plain gave him his orientation and the movement of the sun could be his guide but where was the nearest Roman settlement?

There was the ancient fort at Old Sarum, just outside Salisbury but did that have any Roman connection? He was as unsure as he was to the direction in which it lay, other than it was easterly and roughly twenty miles distance.

Aquae Sulis came into his head, from whence he knew not, but he had his answer. Aquae Sulis, the Roman name for Bath. He knew that Devizes lay some six miles west of his present location, and Bath lay about twenty miles due west of Devizes; by following the setting sun he reckoned he could make that in about six hours.

The shadows were growing longer, and sensing it was early evening he determined to seek a safe place to sleep, and perhaps forage on the way for some berries or fruit and find a stream from which to drink. He would set off for Bath the following afternoon. So much was his faith in Helge's word he was unafraid.

BRITANNIA MAJOR

(Aquae Sulis)

His six hours had been a gross underestimation; His thinking had been locked in the twentieth century, envisaging roads and paths, which until he neared the town, simply did not exist. He found following the sun was relatively easy when it was visible, but when it was not he did have alternative landmarks, a prominent tree, or a peak to aim for in order to keep him on a more or less straight line. At times, when the undergrowth was thick, the stops were frequent and the going slow.

His pace only quickened when, as the woods thinned, there were grassy plains and as the sun broke through the clouds a great light seemed to be reflecting upward from the ground. He was startled for a moment, then he smiled; water, the sun's reflection was snaking its way along the ground;. A river, he had stumbled across a river. Euphoria swept over him; all major towns in the ancient world he knew were situated on the banks of great rivers. This must be the River Avon, follow it and surely he would reach Aquae Sulis.

His first action on reaching the river was to stoop down and, cupping his hands, gulp down as much of the cool fresh water as he could manage, a refreshing change from licking the dew off leaves and other foliage that had helped sustain him over the last few days. As he splashed water over his face he caught sight of his reflection, almost unrecognisable; dishevelled, tangled untidy hair, a grubby face covered in goodness knows what,- after every fall he had wiped his hands and invariably rubbed his face, he looked down at his hands, they were filthy and his nails as black as soot; his legs were scratched, sore and mucky.

He scanned the landscape for any sign of human habitation; there seemed none, he looked again at the river; its current was gentle and the water clear enough for him to see the river bed; it did not seem to present any real danger, so, with with a boldness he did not know he possessed, he stripped off, laid his clothes neatly on the the bank and ventured into the river. He was hit by the coldness of the water and for a moment all other senses were dulled, but as he became accustomed to the temperature his sores and scratches began to sting. He did not know whether the cold water acted as some sort of anaesthetic or if he was just getting used to the pain , but it seemed to subside and he began to relax. Using his hands he scrubbed himself clean, he splashed water over his face and scooped water over his hair- he had no idea what he looked like and nor did he care, he felt great.

Having thus refreshed himself and rested for a while in the morning sun, he set off on what he hoped would be the final leg of his journey. As he was now following the river downstream he made rapid progress and, imperceptibly at first, began to see signs of civilisation, flattened grass, broken tree branches, and then more substantial tracks made by man or beast, it did not really matter which. Tiring now, and a little apprehensive, he trudged on in the footsteps of the unknown who had made them. The tracks soon turned into recognisable paths and Sak's heart began to beat a little faster, a mixture of excitement tinged with fear urged him on, he picked up his pace.

Soon he could see ahead of him an encampment of some kind. Round wooden buildings with what looked like thatch reaching nearly to the ground. Coming closer he perceived it was not thatch, as he knew it, but grass or rushes. The thought that these must be the homes of the Britons brought him to a halt; he had no idea what language the ancient Britons spoke, so how was he to communicate. This thought was followed by a more worrisome one - he was dressed as a Roman, how did these people feel about the Roman invaders?. His heart pounded as a group of men clad in animal skins and carrying stout wooden staves approached him. They spoke.

The words they spoke were unlike any he had heard before, yet strangely he understood what was being said and more amazingly he found himself answering in the same language. They were curious to know what a Roman boy was doing so far from any Roman settlement, what was his name, how had he got there and where was he headed for. Where were the rest of his party, he surely wasa not alone?

He was overcome by an odd feeling. Uncannily, it was almost like his first day at the Manor House. Another persona manifested itself almost without thinking about it. He told them his name was Cicero. He had been travelling with his family from Londinium, had wandered off and couldn't find his way back. He had been wandering on his own now for five days, he was tired and hungry and lost. As before, this fiction had an element of truth; he had no thought of deception, was just seeking a way to survive in a new situation. As he hoped, this group had no knowledge of Londinium and no reason to disbelieve him. Sak stood and watched as they went into a huddle; they were obviously talking about him; as a Roman he was their sworn enemy; some were for killing him there and then, others who, believing him to be from a wealthy Roman family, were all for keeping him hostage and holding him to ransom not knowing that there was no one who would come looking for him, because no one was missing him. They turned and studied him more closely. These men, stout, well muscled and tanned from years of working the land, apparently took pity on this pale, scrawny, nervous, shabby looking boy, (for his smart Roman clothes were now torn and muddy from his journey), so out of place in this setting. He obviously posed no threat.

"How long since you last ate?"

"Six days since my last proper meal"

"Better follow us then."

They didn't point out the way to Londinium, they didn't know where it was. They knew something of Aquae Sulis, but saw no reason to mention this. He was taken into the home of one who seemed to be a chieftain of some kind, and fed, he neither knew nor cared on what, he was hungry and wolfed it down. It seemed his host was expecting him to stay. It became evident that he should help, collecting wood, trapping animals, foraging for food. At first he watched the other boys closely, but soon found that he didn't need to, he knew, as if by instinct, what was required of him.

Like a chameleon, he was blending into this new environment with ease. It surprised him how little it seemed he needed, to be content, if not happy. He found the simplicity of life where one had what one needed rather than what one wanted was satisfying in an odd sort of way. It took him some time to get accustomed to the darkness of the house, the smell of animals and man living together, the perpetual smell of cooking as well as the rudimentary sleeping arrangements but he felt at ease both with himself and those around him.

They had accepted him for what he was, they had no expectation and for the first time in a long while he sensed there was no pressure on him. He felt most at ease when in the company of the women in the house; to his surprise the 'Mother' of the house appeared closer in age to himself than the men folk. Without thinking he had asked her birthdate and of course she had no idea what he was talking about; year of birth confused her even more. His strange questions had aroused her curiosity and he quickly realised he had to be careful of the answers he gave to her. Having no idea of the year; whether it was BC or AD he could not relate anything to historical events such as the birth of Christ. But, he reasoned, they understood seasons and in the end found she had, according to her 'husband' just celebrated her fifteenth summer, and though a mere year older than him, she was more mature, more worldly, yet in many other ways, still a child.

Sak had been enjoying life in the camp for about a month, though he could not be sure how accurate his counting of the days were, when one night he awoke suddenly. Something had been troubling him for a few days but he had been unable to identify the source of his unease and now he knew and it had shocked, almost horrified him. In his sleep Helge stood before him, he said nothing, just stood there, shaking his head, before fading away into the darkness. Now fully awake, Sak realised that in the time he had been with this family he had not, even for one second, given his family a thought, had not even missed his Aunt and as for Dauntsey's, and Latin, it was as if they had never been. So complete was his contentment and happiness he had no thought for anyone else. It took the appearance of Helge to remind him he was there to learn, ostensibly Latin, but unbeknown to him he thought now, the gods through Helge were allowing him to learn so much more.

He roused himself from his bed of straw and as quietly as possible, so not to wake the household, he felt his way to the door and went out into the cold night. Pulling his cloak more tightly around him he sat on the wall, trying to make sense of things. The family he had been with had nothing in twentieth century terms and yet they had everything. The family acted as one for the benefit of all, they genuinely cared for one another and each was allocated the tasks most suited to their talents. They farmed, hunted, butchered and sowed seeds. They had no urge to travel or seek greener pastures. He thought about his own life at Ashley Road. Suppose the roles had been reversed; They would surely have considered the home that he so denigrated the epitome of luxury and comfort. Perhaps his assessment of his home and family had been too harsh; unlike the family who had offered him shelter and comfort, shared what little they had with him he had contributed nothing towards his own family or home. The possibility that he may have brought his misery upon himself was not something he had considered. In the same moment it also came to him that he was enjoying his sojourn here, not only because he had no responsibilities but also because he was a curiosity and the center of attention; was this also the reason he had enjoyed his time with Vera and Beram so much?

He needed to reach Aquae Sulis as rapidly as possible, complete the task he had set himself, or rather, that Helge had set him. There was much to be done at home.

Helge smiled

With a renewed sense of purpose he set off very early the following morning. The farewell had been simple, dignified and brief. They understood his reasons for wanting to find his family; he felt guilty that their understanding was based on a lie, but he could not tell them the truth they would not be able to comprehend it. He wanted to cry and hug them when they said he would be welcomed back at any time and if he did not find his family he could return. How could he tell them that would never happen, that they would never meet again. It would have eased his mind to know that just as he would never remember Helge when he returned to his own time, they would have no memory of him once he had left their sight.

It was with a renewed resolve and determination that he turned towards Aquae Sulis. Knowing now for certain that by following the river he would reach the town made the last part of his journe much easier and it also gave him time to think. What would he do when he got there? Who would pay attention to a stranger in a large city and how, if asked, would he explain his presence there. But fate intervened. So lost in thought was he that had not noticed that the terrain was changing, the ground was getting softer, his feet becoming damp. Once aware, he instinctively moved away from the river. On firmer ground he stopped to take stock of his position; he had wandered perilously close to a mass of reeds and bulrushes, a lucky escape he thought. Climbing up to the top of the river bank so that he could still follow the river,he was surprised to see the outline of a city in the middle distance, could it be Aqua Sulis already? Perhaps another two hours would see him at the gate of the city. What would life hold for him there? Regardless, he must continue. Overcoming his nervousness he began the final part of his journey

"Auxilium, Auxilium"

The faint and desperate voice stopped Sak dead in his tracks; someone was in trouble and was calling for help.

"Adiuva me"

They were calling to him for help.

"Ubi es" he shouted back.

Then the enormity of what had happened hit him. Somebody had shouted at him in Latin, he had understood and replied in the same language. What was happening? But puzzled as he was, there were more important things to attend to at this moment..

"Non possum venire ad vos ut et ululatum exercitus"

Guided by the continuous shouting, Sak headed down the bank he had so recently climbed, then felt the earth softening and trod more cautiously. He came to the river's edge. Both the source of the problem and the voice were immediately obvious. A boy he judged to be of about his own age was almost up to his waist in the soft mud of the river . In his despair not only was he shouting, he was also flailing his arms around like a windmill making matters worse for himself.

With an air of authority he did not know he possessed, Sak commanded him to be still and the boy fearful, of the stranger, did as he was bid.

Sak, unsure of what to do next, found himself thinking of old cowboy films he had enjoyed watching and how the baddies had been rescued from the quicksand by the goodies, usually the Lone Ranger or Cisco Kid. He laughed to himself.

"Animosus in armis stare expandes"

The boy, as commanded, bent forward as far as he could with his arms straight out before him. Sak explained that he would be safe in that position if he kept still and said that as it would be too dangerous for him to venture too close, he would find something with which to pull him out;. He looked around, but could see nothing suitable, now what was he going to do? Of course, take off his toga, roll it up as tightly as he could and tie a knot either end.. He flung one end towards the boy being careful not to release the hold he had on the other. Eagerly the boy reached forward and grabbed the cloth just above the knot

"Hold tight, relax your body and I will try to pull you out!"

Sak pulled as hard as he could but nothing seemed to be happening; the boy appeared to be stuck fast. Sak began to doubt himself and he heard in his head 'spindle shanks' followed by Beram's words ".....he'll never grow big and strong.." He would not let them win! He wouldn't give in; he pulled and tugged, found himself slipping, and dug down his heel then pulled again. Almost imperceptibly the boy was being pulled slowly towards him.The boy seemed too scared to move a muscle to help himself, but eventually Sak managed to drag him close enough to reach his hand and pull him onto the river bank. The boy lay there for some time, until Sak told him they should move before he caught his death of cold. He bestirred himself a little, then pulled himself to his feet with the aid of Sak's hand. Slowly Sak guided him up the bank to the top. The boy looked at him, smiled with some effort and said"Tibi gratias ago, tibi gratias ago". He embraced Sak briefly but a mixture of exhaustion and relief took hold and he dropped to the ground, oblivious to the world around.

Unsure what to do, Sak removed what garments remained on the boy and gathered up as many armfulls of autumn leaves from the downside of the bank, where, he now realised, there were trees which might have provided some sort of tool for rescue, and saved his tunic. He covered the boy in an effort to keep him warm, which made him think of the babes in the wood, a pantomime he had seen when he was much younger. He then set about laying both sets of clothing out to dry and sat down and waited. For what he was unsure.

He spent the time waiting for the boy to wake trying to figure out what had just happened, not the rescue, that had just been a natural reaction but the conversation that he had just had in Latin. If he could speak Latin already then he had no need to stay and he could return to his own time and continue with his life. He tried to recall the words he had spoken but none came to him, he was even more perplexed when he tried to have a conversation with himself out loud. No Latin words came to mind other than reciting the most elementary Latin declension -amo, amas, amatis amantis amant, and he was even unsure of that! He surmised that Helge or his Gods had given him the power to communicate enough to survive but that his actual learning had not yet started.

The boy stirred, for a moment looked disoriented and scared; he sat up from his bed of leaves, looked around and saw Vala.

"You saved my life"

"Nonsense I just pulled you from the water"

"I was stuck, I had been there a long time and it felt like I was sinking deeper into that morass."

He went on to tell his tale. He and two friends had left Aquae Sulis that morning to go fishing. He had ventured too near the river and got stuck. His two friends had lost their fishing poles in the river in their futile attempts to extricate him from the sludge. Having failed, it was decided they would make haste back for help. He had no idea how long they had been gone or how long it would be before they returned but with no way of ascertaining the time it seemed to him they had been gone for hours.

"Without you I am sure I would have sunk beneath the surface and been lost forever. Thank you again, I owe my life to you. By the way what is your name?

Feigning memory loss he said

"I cannot recall, I seem to have no memory of who I am or where I come from"

"But your family....

"I have no recollection of anything. The only thing I can remember is your cry for help"

There was a long thoughtful silence before the boy spoke again.

"Well my name is Marcus and my home is in the centre of Aquae Sulis where my father holds an important position. If anybody can help you, it will be him"

To Sak's relief ,before the conversation could go further they heard noises in the distance, of horses and men, the rattling of a cart, all headed in their direction. Marcus seemed oblivious to Sak, concentrating entirely on the group, straining his eyes then at last he turned back to him in triumph

"It's ok, It's my Father and my two friends with some of our servants. Everything will be alright now and my Father will be very grateful to you"

When the entourage got closer Marcus jumped up and ran towards them at remarkable speed, considering the sorry state he had been in not long before. Sak saw a man he assumed to be Marcus's Father, alight from his horse and embrace his son. They were talking animatedly with occasional glances in his direction. Had he been able to hear the conversation, he would have learned that it centred not on Marcus but on himself, his bravery and how he had saved Marcus from certain death. Marcus explained to his father that this boy who had come out of nowhere, had no recollection as to who he was.

Then Marcus turned and ran back to Sak

"I told you everything would be alright, my Father says you must come with us."

INTER PEREGRINO

(A Stranger in Their Midst)

To Sak it seemed that Marcus's Father embraced him with the same joy he had shown when hugging his own son.
"I am deeply indebted to you. Thank you"

Although Marcus had told him of his saviour's plight, his father still questioned Sak. He wanted to assess the boy for himself. As the local Magistrate he was used to dealing with all types, and able to disseminate the truth from the lies. He listened to the boy's answers, looked at his clothes and then took some time to study the boy himself. Sak felt somewhat uncomfortable under this scrutiny, but said nothing. His clothes, of the finest quality, were a strong indication that he came from a Roman family. He spoke the Latin of Rome, which suggested to the magistrate that he came from a high ranking military family. Finally the boy himself. True, he thought he was a bit pale, but his pure black hair and brown eyes bore all the hallmarks of a true Roman. This examination was enough to decide him the boy posed no danger.

After the boys had been dried and wrapped in heavy warm blankets they were settled onto a cart which then set off, for Sak knew not where, nor did he much care. He was mentally and physically drained, and try as he might he could not stay awake, neither the animated chatter around him nor the noise and bumpiness of the cart could arouse him. He only awoke when a servant was trying to lift him out of the cart. Startled and disorientated, he looked nervously about him

"It's alright my friend, we are home"

Home! The word did not sit easily with him but he was genuinely pleased for Marcus. Looking about him, he was disappointed. The villa was not at all as he had imagined it might be when he first saw the party sent out to recover Marcus, and, as it turned out, himself. It was big certainly, but the plain white weather worn walls were uninspiring, without character. The monotony was broken only by square openings that served as windows, and a single door. He did not then notice the bright and quite startling orange roof tiles. But this belied the grandeur, beauty and elegance that met him indoors.

There was much to assault his senses; he had fleeting glimpses of colourful mosaics and the warmth of the floors came as a surprise, but there was no time to take it all in as Marcus rushed him through large rooms, along corridors and finally ushered him into a large reception room, where two slaves hastened to exchange their rough coverings for something lighter and more suitable for wearing inside. Other slaves bought cooling drinks served in silver goblets. Sak was absorbing the sumptuousness of the room, the luxurious furnishings made from a multitude of fabrics, from animal hides, delicate silks, soft velvets, and gold coloured seats of every description. But what struck him most of all was the fact that the room opened out onto a pillared verandah which seemed to run along all four sides of the villa. There were pools, statues and all number of exotic plants; he was entranced. Then Sak's attention was drawn towards a lady who entered the room. She was tall, slender, with bejewelled hair piled high upon her head. Marcus ran to her and flung his arms around her'

"Mamma"

She embraced him warmly and was fussing over him when her attention was caught by the young stranger in her room.

"Mama this is the boy who saved my life....."

He was interrupted by his Father who entered at that moment. "Ona my dear, we owe this boy a debt of gratitude. Without his intervention we would almost certainly have lost our son" and he went on to relate what had occurred. Throughout this, Sak, somewhat embarrassed, sat staring at the floor, unaware that Ona was staring at him with curiosity. She was confused. How was it that he should appear out of nowhere just when her son needed him most. Had Sak been more aware he might have noticed the numerous shrines around the house to the many Roman gods. She was a believer and paid homage to her gods each day. Could this, she pondered, be another example of a god taking human form. If only it were so, it would mean their family had been truly blessed and her own son must, as she had always believed, be very special. At all costs this boy must stay with them; the gods would be angered if a gift was rejected and retribution could be harsh.

At first conversation between husband and wife was conducted in whispered tones but an argument seemed to be brewing and the voices got louder, with frequent glances at Sak. Marcus was frightened, he had never witnessed such animosity between his mother and father before and was at a loss as to what to do.

Sak was also distressed as he realised that the argument was about him and for a moment thought that this might be the time to return to his own time, back to his true home; if people were going to argue about him it might as well be in a time and place he was familiar with. But instead of covering his ears as he did at home, he listened; there was an essential difference. His presence, rather than he himself, was at the core of the argument., The magistrate, Cicero by name Sak came to realise, was convinced that he was just a lost boy who had lost his memory and he felt deeply it was his duty to try and find the boy's. true family.

Ona on the other hand really believed him to be either a gift from a deity if not a god in disguise, and it was their duty to honour whichever by treating him as one of their own. Both believed they were right. Sak wanted to help.

"Excuse me. I am just a boy, I am not a god."

There was silence; both studied him, Cicero was the first to speak

"So you are beginning to remember?"

"No"

"Then if you don't remember, how you know you are not" chimed in Ona.

He could not answer but he was mortified, a familiar feeling. For once, in a difficult situation, he had told the truth and had not been believed.

It occurred to him that he had been destined to meet Marcus which meant this was the family he was meant to be with so, taking advantage of the ensuing silence, and summoning up his courage, he spoke, "may I make a suggestion." They nodded their assent

"I believe, Sir, that you said you were a magistrate and an important man in the area. As such you have many contacts, much influence and I assume some power. May I suggest you institute a search of the city and surrounding villages and homesteads to see if I belong anywhere and if I do, I can be returned to my proper home. Failure to find my family might be an indication that your wife is right in her beliefs and therefore I belong here for a reason known only to the gods." In saying this he believed there would be no such claim and this is where he would stay.

They looked at each other, they were smiling;

"Eloquently put young man, you are wise beyond your years. I think perhaps there might be something in what my wife thinks. But enough, despite the early hour let us put it aside until the morrow and now join together in celebrating my son's lucky escape over lunch."

The glow of Ona's eyes and a smile on her lips showed she was in complete agreement.

"Might I suggest that after lunch you take these two young men to the Baths, I am sure taking the waters will prove restorative." Marcus clapped his hands in joy

This was not what he had expected. When Ona had first suggested they go to the baths Sak had envisaged a single pool, something like the Lido, an open air pool on Hampstead Heath or may be something similar to the Prince of Wales Public Baths, the indoor pool in Kentish town where he had learnt to swim. Had he not been with Marcus and Cicero he would have thought he had stumbled into an important religious complex, the buildings tall, grand and colonnaded were more in keeping with a temple than a municipal swimming pool. Then he mentally slapped his forehead. 'Idiot' he thought, 'you know about the baths, it's why it's called Bath'. He couldn't help laughing a little, and the others looked at him.

"Have you not been here before" enquired Cicero

He shook his head, still looking about him.

Well let's show you round before we indulge ourselves.

He marvelled at the magnitude of the "Great Bath" , a barrel shaped room of enormous proportions, whose richly frescoed walls echoed to the sounds of diving and splashing; it was a noisy, exuberant place. In adjacent rooms the masseurs were at work slapping and pummelling tired, weary men of all ages and physiques. In exercise rooms the huffing and puffing of the weightlifters added to the cacophony of sound as they showed off their physical form and prowess.

No space was wasted; the corridors and passageways were filled with loud voices and raucous laughter as jokes were told; others were talking in hushed tones, furtively looking around to ensure they were not being overheard and Sak could only guess and speculate as to the gossip and slander being shared.

In other rooms he heard the exhilarated cries of patrons as they emerged from the intense heat of the sauna into the cold plunge bath. Or was it, he mused, a cry of relief. In yet another room there were occasional groans as elderly men slowly immersing themselves in the warm water. These, Cicero explained, were old Legionnaires, trying to ease the effects of rheumatism and arthritis.

It was a relief to be shown the quieter rooms that were used for the conducting of business transactions, the playing of board games and other smaller bathrooms which he learnt were used for the essential rituals of daily bathing which were such a vital part of Roman life. He was pleased to learn that he would not have to use these rooms as Cicero's household, like many well-off households, had its own bathhouse.

Cicero was troubled. As he was showing Sak around the Baths he had been observing him. Aquae Sulis was unique within the whole Roman Empire. It was the only city built around a spa; it had no military, strategic importance. The warmth and healing properties of its waters were legend and people from all corners of the Empire made pilgrimages to the town, some to take the waters, others to make entreaties to the gods, to offer up prayers and it had a thriving tourist industry. Yet it seemed that Sak was seeing and hearing about it for the first time; everything seemed new to him. For a reason best known to himself, Cicero had kept the Temple Courtyard till last.

This courtyard was made up of many religious and ceremonial buildings dedicated to a plethora of gods' Bacchus, Jupiter, Apollo, Sol, and Luna. Thanks to the collection of miniature bronzes in Beram's sitting room, Sak recognised many and began a conversation around each of them, Cicero was both pleased and relieved.

Marcus was getting fidgety and bored with traipsing around a complex he knew so well. He was pleased when they at last made their way to the changing rooms.

To Sak's dismay,' changing room' proved to be something of a misnomer; To him it could be accurately described as a Disrobing Rom and he felt slightly uncomfortable as he made his way, naked, to the hot room. The heat hit him like a brick wall; steam rooms and saunas were not anything he had experienced before. He was guided to a marble bench. The heat was stifling and his nostrils began to sting. He tried sniffing but that just made matters worse. His hair was getting damp and he began to sweat as never before. There were many in that hot room, they all seemed to know Cicero and his son. They chatted away, mostly it was about Sak, and what he had done for Marcus. There was a round of applause. Thanks to the steam he was spared his blushes.

His relief when the session in the steam room came to an end was short lived. The second room was almost as hot but it seemed drier. A slave helped him to lie prone on a marble slab and proceeded to rid his body of the sweat and dirt from his skin using a metal scraper and olive oil. Still hot he followed Marcus into yet another pool for a swim; though the water was tepid, it felt cool to his newly cleansed but still hot body. Unbelievably there was still more to come. Cicero, Marcus and other men jumped into another pool, splashing about and seemingly enjoying themselves; Sak followed suit and thought he would die, it was bracingly cold. They did this for fun and relaxation? Once dressed Cicero took them again towards the Temple Courtyard but this time they did not enter. There was a large sacrificial altar in front of them but Cicero headed to one of the smaller altars scattered about. There were many people paying homage to the goddess Minerva, some seeking cures, others in anticipation of a divine favour, or in thanks for having received one. Cicero gave thanks for both the safety of his son and for the stranger in their midst. Then they headed home.

VALA

It was late, the boys had been abed for a considerable time, but Ona and Cicero were still up. It had been a long and stressful day for all of them; Marcus, stuck in the muddy waters fearing for his life, his Mother's concern when his friends had returned with the news of her son's predicament, his Father's concern as to what he might find on reaching the river. Then there was Sak. Who was this stranger? Ona had been curious as to how he had reacted at the Baths; she was still convinced he had some connection to the gods and was looking for a sign or indications that might vindicate her beliefs. Cicero's recollections of the afternoon's events were clear enough but as he spoke he began to see things in a slightly different setting.

"At first I took his reaction to the town and Baths was because of his memory loss; it was if he was seeing them for the first time, but it was more than that, it seemed he had never seen buildings like that before; He was awestruck and I accepted that at face value. But as we walked around he was muttering things like, I never expected… or, I didn't think it would be.., .I didn't know… , etc. I didn't question it at the time, but thinking about it now it seems as if he knew more than he was letting on. The only time the conversation flowed easily was in the Great Temple. He was drawn to the statues of the gods, talked about them with great knowledge and affection. I am puzzled."

Ona listened in silence, her heart was pounding and she trembled just a little.

"Oh my dear husband, don't you see I was right all along, he has been sent by the gods. I knew it." Clapping her hands in joy she summoned a slave to bring wine. "Let us give thanks for this blessing"

"My Dearest Ona, are we not getting ahead of ourselves. We have an agreement"

"I cannot stop you from conducting your search but I fear it will be fruitless. No one will lay claim to this boy. He belongs in this family. I shall name him Vala Est". Cicero laughed

"You can't call the boy Blessed One!"

"Indeed, and why not? His coming is a true blessing. Just think if he had not appeared we would now be in mourning for our son; all your hopes and aspirations as well as dreams for him would have been dashed. Is that not a blessing;? And how would Aelia be feeling at the loss of her younger brother? The only sunshine in her life would be in her name. No, it is a good and appropriate name. I will not be swayed."

Cicero loved his wife, her simple faith, her illogical logic. He smiled to himself and then, swayed by her. "A gift from the gods, a blessed one, would be brave and valorous, as this boy has been, why should we not call him Vala', that means strength and courage."

Ona, despite her resolution, thought this over. "Vala', yes it is a good name, it has a ring to it.

Over a breakfast of cold meats, bread and fresh fruits, washed down with spring water Sak learnt his new name. Although Marcus and Aelia had initially laughed, they approved the name, thinking it most appropriate.

"I really am not worthy of such a name" were the words that came from his mouth but deep inside he was glowing with pride.

"Today Vala', we have something special planned for you."

Marcus and Aelia departed to another part of the Villa for their lessons; two servants led Vala to one of the bath houses where he was washed from head to foot in the warm bath sunk into the marble floor. He was dried, oiled and perfumed, his hair combed and finally dressed in a pure white toga edged in a deep blue. There were leather sandals for his feet.

He was enjoying all the attention being lavished upon him, he felt good and was pretty sure he looked good too.

Led out to the central courtyard the reason for all the attention became apparent; an older man was setting up his easel, laying out his paints in preparation for painting his, Vala's portrait; a picture to be paraded around the City, to all the great Villas in the City and surrounding villages and compounds. For a moment he was transported to another time; he saw the tearful, skinny boy at the end of the school drive waiting in vain for his art teacher. He wanted to laugh aloud. The image faded but not the memory; this, he thought more than makes up for it.

He stood for what seemed like hours, hardly daring to move, occasionally the artist would emerge from behind the wooden panel on which he was painting to take sightings. Every now and then Ona or Cicero, sometimes both, would come and study the painting, nod their approval and call out encouragement to him.

Eventually the artist called out that he could relax and Ona and Cicero were summoned, as were Marcus and Aelia. They gathered around the painting.

At first glance Vala was pleased with the results, it was a good likeness, too good he thought, as it showed what he thought were all his imperfections, the teenage spots, tiny blackheads around the underside of his nose and a yellowhead on the corner of his lip. The spindle shank legs protruded from under his toga. However the others seemed impressed; Aelia looked at him

"If you do have any family they would be sure to recognise you"

Vala found himself blushing, he tried to hide the yellowhead from her.

There was still a problem for Cicero, Ona! She was becoming anxious, distracted, as she waited for the men to return, only relaxing when they returned each day with no news. Ona was Cicero's greatest love and concern. He worried what would happen if the boy were taken from her. With reluctance and with only Ona's welfare in mind, he called off the search. Secretly, Sak too was relieved; it had become more and more a worry that Cicero was spending time and money searching for something that did not exist.

TIMES PASSED

There came a day when Vala', to his surprise, awoke to find a new and rather splendid toga had been laid out for him to wear; not the usual white but a deep red edged with golden embroidery. Other than his under clothing, his everyday clothes were nowhere to be seen. He felt confused, but didn't like to question anyone as to what was going on. Once he had bathed, his personal slave, Pericles, came to dress him. Uneasy at the whole concept of slavery, Vala had done his best to treat the house slaves as equals insofar as social conventions would allow, but despite his best efforts, they had remained aloof and did their work silently. So why was this day different? Pericles asked how he was feeling, and as he dressed and groomed him he was smiling. Then he led him to the large room usually reserved for visiting dignitaries. The immense table, set for a banquet, was surrounded by not only the family but the entire household. As he entered they applauded. Vala paused in confusion, looking automatically towards Cicero at the head of the table

"In your honour" said Cicero"

"But why?"

It was Ona who answered, "A year has passed since our home was first blessed with your presence, we are here to give thanks and celebrate"

He stared at her, too stunned to say anything, he turned his back, tears came to his eyes, he was shaking. Instinctively Ona stepped forward to comfort him, but was restrained by Cicero

"Give him time" he murmured.

'A year?' Vala thought to himself; he had really had no idea. A year of real family life, a year of total acceptance and much,

much, so much, more.

He was still trembling when he eventually spoke. He did not want to lie to them but he could not tell the truth. He chose his words carefully

"I hardly know where to begin. Ona, although I am unable to tell you who I am I can say that I am nothing special, just an ordinary boy to whom you have shown great kindness. Cicero, you welcomed a stranger into your house simply because I happened to be in a place where I could help your son out of a difficult situation. Many would have thanked me, fed me, given me clean, dry clothes and sent me on my way. You gave me a family, a name and an identity. You treated me as your son and I feel I can truly say, you two are the best parents I have ever had........."

"Oh Vala Est. are you beginning to remember?" interjected an anxious Ona

"No, not remember exactly but sometimes at night I have vague impressions of cruel, uncaring parents, of rejection, of being made to feel worthless and I give thanks to you two ,who have been true parents to me, who demonstrated that being a parent is so much more than being the result of a physical union. You call me son and I have been privileged to address you as Mamma and Pappa. This time Cicero did not stop Ona as he watched her as she rushed forward to embrace him

"We are! We are proud to be your parents, by association if not by birth."

"When I arrived I was shy, nervous, mentally still a child with no self-worth and full of self-pity. That child no longer exists. Through your kindness, example, compassion, acceptance and wisdom a grateful young man stands before you ready to face the world with confidence. I hope all I may achieve will honour the memory of you both."

Ona was alarmed "Are you leaving us?"

Momentarily unnerved by his indiscretion, he paused, quick thinking helped him regain his composure,

"No I have no plans to leave yet, but the time will come when I have to leave, to make my own way in life, to have a wife and family. I can only hope I am lucky enough to find the happiness that you and Cicero have.

He then turned to address Marcus and Aelia

"It cannot have been easy for you either, having to accept another brother, one of a similar age, who seemed to get all the attention, a lot of the love, yet you both accepted me without question. Thank you, I love you all.

"But you saved my life"

"Yes, what would I have done without my brother?"

It was a teary eyed Cicero who gave thanks to the gods and the feast began.

There was chatter and laughter all around him but for Vala it was a little while before he felt he could join in. A year, a whole year, and what a year it had been.

Later, lazing beneath a vine covered trellis the reason he had lost all track of time was because the past year had been one of what seemed in retrospect, pure happiness. Supposedly reading a scroll from Cicero's library, he thought back over the past year. Initially his acceptance in the family seemed to be because of Ona's conviction that he was a deity in one form or another and had been sent to them, the rest of the family had accepted the fiction that he was a boy who had lost his memory. Their first impressions of him had been influenced by his actions in saving Marcus but that had soon faded into the background as he simply became a respected member of the family.

Vala, still to an extent self-effacing and somewhat reserved, had nonetheless enjoyed all the adulation that had been heaped on him for saving Marcus. Although he still felt uncomfortable, he wasn't quite sure why, about the afternoon trips to the Baths, when he was there he could not resist listening in to the gossip that murmured in the corridors, especially when in the early days it was about him. For the first time in his life people had been talking about him in positive ways and when they spoke to him it was as an equal, there was no derision but something new, respect. Respect for him.

The awareness of this respect had given him the confidence to settle into his new life more easily than he might otherwise have done. Beram had given him a taste for Roman history, he had loved the stories of Roman heroes and heroic tales found in his Latin texts books but the real Roman life had surprised him in its ordinariness. The routine and order of daily life was much as it was in his own time. Nonetheless, there was much to marvel at. in this new life. For a boy who had grown up in a semi-detached house and then a small London flat, it had taken time to become accustomed to the size of the villa which seemed more of a small self contained village; everything they could possibly require was at hand. They were almost completely self-sufficient. The wide variety of food at hand had surprised him and he thought back now to his naive question:

" You have varieties of fruit only found overseas, where does it all come from?"

"Well our Empire does encompass the entire world, our trade routes cover both land and sea!"

He had been ashamed, he must think before he spoke, he had known that, just hadn't put it into context. He had made a vow to think before he spoke. But it wasn't always easy to remember, especially in the classroom.

Every morning was devoted to education. and the teachers came to the Villa and Vala enjoyed being just one of three in the class. He was delighted to find Aelia sharing the lessons, he hadn't thought Roman girls did. Maths, a subject he had loathed at Dauntseys, was the easiest to cope with, the principles little changed in two thousand years. On the other hand History, a subject he had loved, was the most difficult; initially because he did not know what year he was living in. He was aware that the Romans successfully invaded Britain around AD40 so it must be after that but then again, he knew few dates. This caused some upset. They were studying Julius Caesar, the tutor troubled by his ignorance, went to speak to Cicero.

"Who is Vala and where exactly did he come from?"

Cicero explained, then asked him what in particular had led to the question.

"Look at this"

Cicero looked up from the tablets he had been reading, and took the tablet the tutor handed him. He scanned it quickly.

"Mmmm, I see what you mean"

Vala, blessed with an almost (and somewhat erratic) photographic memory, (he had once entertained a full carriage on a train from Salisbury to London with a line by line rendition of a film he had seen a few days previously) had culled all the facts from Shakespeare's Julius Caesar.

"How could he know such details or does he have a vivid imagination?"

Cicero, who up to now had been sceptical of Ona's perception of the boy, repeated them to the tutor.

"Well, she may well be right "he said with a smile" but one thing is for sure, he is a special and talented boy. It is our duty to keep an eye on him and keep him safe."

Astronomy was considered an important science. Celestial bodies were a significant part of Roman life. Vala had first taken an interest in astronomy after observing the mass of stars in the night sky at Dauntseys and he had pursued the interest in books and encyclopaedias.

In a class discussion he had mentioned Uranus and the rings around Saturn. In his enthusiasm for the subject he did not stop to think, and therefore did not take into account that it would be another fifteen hundred years or so before they were discovered.

“I do not understand, may I ask, what are you talking about?

Thinking quickly, and taking advantage of his love of Greek Myth he ventured his apologies,” I should have explained. It is a theory of mine, as you know Uranus is the Grandfather of Zeus, I am always dreaming of discovering a new planet and if I did that is what I would call it!”

That seemed to satisfy the curiosity of both Aelia and Marcus, they did not pursue Saturn, which was as well as he had not come up with a plausible explanation. To the adults when his tutor informed Cicero, this was further evidence of his deity

‘Think before you speak’ Vala had once again reminded himself. Thinking of it now, he had a sudden insight. ‘Stop trying to be your Father, it is not clever to seem to be constantly outdoing others.’ This had seemed to pay off, he had learnt to listen first and this seemed to engender a new confidence in him. From then on he had begun to relax and learning became less of a battle, as he stayed with what he was currently being taught..

For Marcus and Vala the final lesson of the day was Military Training. He was delighted when he found out sword fighting was a major part of this activity but this was not the delicate, subtle art of fencing that he had practised all too briefly at Dauntsey's. They ‘fought’ with short stubby heavy wooden swords and leather shields. He and Marcus would attack each other with great fervour, quickly learning that failure to protect yourself resulted in stinging blows. Despite this, the boys loved it. Hot, tired, bruised and sweaty, they would then be marched to the Baths.

With Marcus he could be just a boy, doing what boys have always done, playing board games, playing games with bat and ball, fishing, when Vala would lose no opportunity to tease Marcus, and beg him not to fall in. Marcus, laughing, would say 'but it did you a good turn, my falling in'. At first Aelia had joined in with the games and the joshing, but Ona had her own reasons for persuading her to give up these boyish pursuits.

Vala was aware of Ona's actions, and they troubled him, though he did not know why. There was no one he could ask. Long before, in the beginning, one of the things he asked Helge was for how long he would be away,

"To everything there comes a time; you will know when it is right to return"

His acceptance had been so complete that for much of the time he had forgotten his purpose for being here. Latin was now second nature to him, his education in this was presumably complete, so why was he not back in his own time?

'For everything there comes a time' kept beating in his brain. 'That's all very well' he thought, 'but how am I to know that time has come.'

In an attempt to clear his mind, he walked deep into the woods, a place he often went when he felt the need to be alone, to find solace, to contemplate. Deep in thought he sat down, closed his and searched his mind for an answer, none came. He opened his eyes, then blinked rapidly.

"No it can't be, it's not possible"

There in front of him was The Oak, his Oak and even as he watched, Helge emerged." Had he unknowingly travelled back to the present, was now once again in the school woods?

"What, where, how..."

Helge's smile was benign; as before he seemed to know what troubled the young man before him.

"You have made great progress and yes, you are now fluent in

Latin but ponder this, does it mean that you are ready to return"

"I was hoping you could, would tell me"

"No that I will never do, it is not my role. When the time is right, when fate decides, then will be the time. . But your path is in your hands."

"But how......"

"The choices you make will govern fate.. Do what you believe to be right and all will be well"

Seeing that Sak was still uncertain he continued "You are tempted to stay in this time, you must consider, and decide if that is what you really want; to live a make believe life forever. Was not that the very thing you wanted to escape from. If you follow your present inclinations, you will never know what you might have been or what you might have achieved in your own right, your own world. This is not your world It is unfair of you to expect others to make the decision for you. Only you have the answer. Your future is in your hands" and almost as an afterthought he added "As it always was, so it is, your choice, your future" then he and the oak were there no more, as if they had never been.

Alone in the wood, with no conscious memory of what had occurred, it nonetheless seemed that the problem he had hoped to resolve was less important now.

PAR EST IN CAELIS

When he had first come into their lives Ona had believed the gods had sent him to save Marcus, now, dearly as she loved Marcus, she was not sure of why he would be of such importance.. As she viewed growing friendship between Vala and her daughter, she saw it as something more than the innocent and natural friendship such as might be experienced by brother and sister, or two friends of similar age. If so, this surely was the object of the gods in blessing her family with Vala's presence. A union between them would raise them to divine status, they would become part of Roman mythology, their immortality assured. As she dwelt on this she became impatient for such a union to take place. Most of her days were now taken up in paying homage to all her gods, She made daily trips to the temples, leaving scrolls and lead tablets with supplications, she made sacrifices to them on the altars outside each temple and prayed for signs.

Ona watched for these signs to be made known to her and so saw them in every smile that passed between them, a casual glance, a whispered aside or shared laughter were all interpreted by her as signs of an ever deepening love. She believed it was her duty to encourage the two young lovers, par est Caelis, (a match made in Heaven). She was not a casual observer, who might have construed things differently and seen her "signs" as nothing more than a normal, healthy friendship. Cicero was certainly under no such illusions.

One evening, after her last prayers, Ona joined Cicero in the bed they shared, kissed him fondly and wished him a good night's sleep. She was happy; she could not divine his worries,

"Ona, my dear, we must talk" but even as he said it, he was uncomfortably aware that unless he was very careful he could destroy her happiness, make her question her beliefs and perhaps create an irreparable rift between them. It was a fine line he had to tread

"Ona, you truly believe that Vala was sent by Minerva to form a union between the gods and our family"

"There can be no doubt, he was"

"Can you tell me why you believe this, why our family above all others from across the Empire should be selected for such an accolade?"

"My dearest husband, I cannot answer such a question. I only know that Minerva and Jupiter have answered my prayers with signs that it should be so. Who am I to question them?"

Cicero smiled, sensing his answer, and lifting his head upwards mouthed 'thank you'

"You are very privileged to be favoured in such a manner; I am sure you are much loved on Elysium but I am concerned for you. You are allowing this idea, this belief, if you will, to become an all-consuming passion which overrides all else. Can you not see that it is putting, not just you, but those concerned, our daughter and our beloved Vala, under a great strain. Why do you not let the gods do their own work, their strength after all is infinite. Do you not lessen their glory, are you not attempting to take on their mantle? This could be seen as a lack of faith, rather than, as you intend, evidence of your devotion?"

She turned towards him with a nervous smile.

"Cicero, do you think so? Oh, I thank you for your wisdom. I do get carried away sometimes. I have been blinded by my hopes. I promise from henceforth to leave everything in their hands." She was relieved, a burden she didn't know she was carrying falling from her shoulders. She kissed him, gazing into his dark brown, kindly eyes, and whispered,

"Would a little nudge now and then be wrong, surely it would do no harm".

"Ona, you are incorrigible!" he sighed, then laughed softly. They were still laughing when they fell asleep in each other's arms.

Vala wondered if he was the first to notice the change in Aelia. She was often moody, she seemed impatient, didn't seem to enjoy the company of Vala and Marcus anymore. Maybe, he thought, it is because Ona, for some reason, no longer likes her to spend time with us. In the early days after his arrival they soon became friends, were easy in each other's company. These days conversation was awkward and playing backgammon had lost its charm, at least when it came to playing with him. Returning from the baths one afternoon he had tried to talk to Marcus about this strange new attitude.

"Do you think Aelia is acting oddly?"

"In what way?" After he had explained Marcus broke into laughter

"You are both as bad as one another. We all notice how you look at her and look away if she turns to you. If you ask me I think you are both soft on each other." Vala was taken aback, and slightly embarrassed. Had the things that troubled him about Aelia, troubled her about him? Is that why they now seemed embarrassed in each other's company?

Ona, despite her promise to Cicero, could not leave well alone. She encouraged Marcus to go out more with his friends or she would send him out on spurious errands. Meanwhile she invented tasks for Aelia and Vala to do together. Alone with her daughter she would speak of Vala in glowing terms, praising his good looks, compassion, bravery and intelligence, his kindness, and the fun he was to be with.

For Vala, with his new view of Aelia as a young woman, one whom he admitted to himself he found attractive, this made life difficult. He felt Ona was pushing him into a situation for which he was not yet ready. He wasn't sure how Aelia felt, and certainly wasn't going to ask her. Yet he did like her, how he wished they could go back to the days of easy companionship, without this pressure hanging over them.

Cicero too was concerned; he tried again to reason with Ona.

"There is much of you in our daughter, her determination and resolve amongst others. She doesn't need your encouragement, and it may be unfair to her. Then there is Vala, he is a year younger than Aelia, and we men anyway, are always far behind you women, slow coaches that we are. I feel he is not yet ready for what you so desire and you could harm them both by pushing it too quickly. We must sit back and watch and be there to pick up the pieces should the need arise."

Ona was not to be reasoned with; she felt she knew best and secretly regretted letting Cicero persuade her otherwise. She didn't want to harm them, she wanted what was best for them, in her view..

Until his conversation with Marcus, Vala's opinion of himself had been heavily influenced by the opinion of others, his Father's negativity, the mocking of his physical appearance by his schoolmates, had left him with low esteem. Whilst he had enjoyed the adulation and attention of the past year, it had not really altered his lack of belief in himself. The thought that anyone, let alone Aelia, who seemed to him to be peerless, could find him attractive seemed ludicrous. He felt sure Marcus was wrong. Aelia was a popular girl with numerous friends, he had met many of them, whom she bought home. His ears would have burnt had he been privy to their conversations which now often centred on him, his strikingly good looks, his kindness, even his humility.

"His eyes are so alive" said one, "and that smile" opined another "Oh Aelia, you are so lucky to have him living here. When are you going to do something about it."

"That's what my Mother wants to know!" and with a nervous laugh "but it's really not up to me is it. Anyway, so far he has shown no interest in me in that way thank goodness. We are just good friends"

"You don't believe that! We have seen the way you look at each other and if he won't make the first move, then it is up to you." Aelia looked down at the ground so they could not see her blushes.

They continued to go out on walks together and took many trips into Aquae Sulis, encouraged by Ona. Often these outings were taken in almost complete silence, both deep in thought about the other. Vala thought of taking his hand in hers, but the thought of actually doing it made his heart beat uncomfortably. He always drew back at the last moment. Sometimes their arms or hands would brush up against each other, his heart would miss a beat but the moment would pass. He would search her face, looking for a sign which he did not discern, and so would again become withdrawn. Aelia was also timorous about showing any sign of her feelings yet both of them treasured their moments together. Aelia distanced herself from her girlfriends and now considered him her best friend. She woke each day, impatient to spend time alone with him, but went to bed at night more confused in her feelings than ever.

Vala, who had never before had a close friend, worried about losing her friendship. He thought any show of his feelings might jeopardise this friendship. His fear was not so much being rejected, that he could accept, but how could they continue friends, without embarrassment. What would Ona think, would they want him to leave. How could he do it gracefully, how, in fact, could he leave Aelia, who seemed to him to be everything he wanted in a girlfriend.

In the end it was Aelia who broke through the uncertainty. While walking by the river close to where Vala had saved Marcus, Aelia contrived to stumble. Vala, without thinking, reached out and took her arm, pulling her forwards towards him. In an effort to steady her, put his arms around her. They stood there, it seemed forever, looking into each other's eyes until Vala, without thought, lent forward and kissed her gently on the forehead. The next minute he dropped his arms, muttered an embarrassed, red-faced apology and turned away from her.

In another moment he sensed her closeness, felt the softness of her skin as she slipped her arm through his.

"It's fine and ....I have been waiting, hoping, for so long"

So arm in arm, they walked along the river bank at ease in each other's company, conversation and laughter flowed freely.

When they returned to the villa they were still hand in hand, but reluctantly released each other's grasp before they were seen. But they were too late. Ona had seen, she rushed to tell Cicero the good news.

"My darling wife, the omens are certainly good but now we must be patient, we can do no more, what will be, will be"

"No, no, there is much to be done, so much I must do."

"No! For once, listen to me! They are young; you must let them take time. You promised, of your own volition, to leave it the lap of the gods. So alright, you later added the proviso of a little nudge here and there from you, but no more...."

"But surely......"

"Ona. I forbid you to take any more part. No more interference!"

Never before had Cicero raised his voice with such ferocity. Her lips quivered, tears began to roll down her cheeks, she was shaking.

He was aching with pity for the woman he loved above all else, but he was certain his way was right. Putting his arms around her he did his best to comfort her,

"I know you are doing what you believe to be best, that you love both of them almost above all others. Between yourself and the gods these two young people have been bought together, they seem to have overcome whatever has been troubling them these past weeks, but that is all. We have no way of knowing what has transpired today and we should wait for them to tell us, or not. We must not push them into a situation they may not themselves desire. I admit, they are growing up, though I think myself Vala does not look a day older than the day he came to us, but he is changing. Let us-give them the chance to be young, to find themselves. I say this Ona, out of love for you, as well as for them."

The forcefulness of his first statement and the loving tone of what followed affected her more than the actual words spoken. Recovering from her shock and dismay, she tearfully whispered

"I will try to show patience, I will try"

"I am sure you will. Just don't rush in, think before you speak. Why don't I now summon the servants to bring us some wine and we will make a secret toast to the future happiness, whatever it may be, of our daughter Aelia, and Beatus.?"

"Yes, let us do that."

Aelia felt her love for Vala was for all time, and she believed, hoped, he felt the same. With Ona's encouragement, they were able to for Valae the company of others, to enjoy being alone together. As before, they went for long walks, hand in hand along the river, or picnicked in the woods. On the way back they would find blankets on the ground and food and drink laid out. If they were innocent, the same could not be said of Ona, the instigator of the blankets and the food, who would most times be somewhere around, but out of sight, justifying it in her own mind as "the young lovers could be alone".

It seemed Vala was in an enviable position; he was living in the smartest villa in the area, was in love with the daughter of one of the most important and influential men in Aquae Sulis, and seemingly been given carte blanche to court her. The times he was alone with her were amongst the most carefree and happy he had ever been. Many times, after finishing their picnic they would lie in each other's arms. It was at such times Aelia felt there was something amiss. Vala seemed to be holding back from truly expressing his love. Aelia, in her confusion, tried talking to him but he drew back, seemed to become cool and distant. Yet when they were next alone together the loving Vala was again present, only to retreat again if Aelia appeared to expect more.

Again she would question him, and he would turn aside, embarrassed and worried. How could he explain what troubled him. She would not be able to understand.

He knew that at any moment he might be returned to his own time. It was at these times he would think 'it's all very well Helge saying that my future is in hands but what does that mean. He was puzzling over this, lying apart from Aelia on Ona's carefully spread blanket. She watched him, trying to discern where his mind had gone. He was recalling the words Helge had spoken before he found himself back in the past.

"When you return to your own time you will remember no specifics but you will remember what you have learned. When you return to your time, those with whom you have spent time with will have no memory of you."

Memory is one thing, but what about emotions, would Aelia feel empty, a loss she couldn't identify, if one day he was no longer there, no farewell, no explanation. Would something of their love linger somehow? She might not remember him but would she experience an emptiness she could not explain?.

Some nights he was unable to sleep because of the thoughts that troubled him, his doubts as to what he really wanted from life. He felt it was unfair that he should be called to choose, while he was still so young. He sought an answer to these thoughts, sneaking, as he termed it in his mind, out of the house and into the woods, where he called out to Helge. There was only silence.

He was at a crossroad in his life, he thought, lying awake one night after once more hearing nothing from Helge. Sak, the boy who couldn't make decisions for fear of making the wrong choice, now had to come to a decision, it was time to choose. Aelia or the future? How to make that decision.

THE ICENI

The Iceni were British and ruled over East Anglia. Their King, Prasutagus, had formed an independent alliance with Rome. It had been agreed that on his death the land would be divided equally between his daughters and the Emperor Nero. However, in negation of this agreement, on the death of Prasutagus Rome took all his lands. The Iceni, stripped of their lands and no longer an ally of Rome, had lost everything. When Prasutagus's wife, Boudicca, had protested, she was flogged and her two daughters were raped. She determined on revenge.

Cicero summoned the family to his study. Vala and Aelia stood together holding hands, with Marcus beside them. Ona stood by her husband, they both looked serious and Ona was a little tearful.

"It is with great sadness that I have to tell you that we must leave Aquae Sulis, We are to make for Londinium without delay"

A shocked silence, looks of disbelief followed by

"Why, what for, how long will we be away?"

"I have been tasked with trying to negotiate peace between Rome and the Iceni.........."

"The Iceni, you mean Boudicca!" Vala blurted out, without thinking.

They all stared at him

"How on earth can you know that? I myself had never heard the name until I received this scroll at daybreak this morning and it has not been out of my possession since"

They stared at him in bewilderment, it seemed to him, accusingly..

He dropped Aelia's hand and ran from the room. Aelia went to follow but Cicero gently restrained her by placing a loving hand on her shoulder,

"Let him be, he will come in when ready. I have a strange feeling something is coming to a head. Perchance we are about to find out why he was sent to us"

Of course Sak knew the name of Boudicca, her statue on Westminster Bridge had been familiar to him from a young age, as were the stories of her struggle with the Romans, up to now she had been a heroine in his mind. But he was aware of the savagery of her revenge. If he remembered his history rightly, she stirred up a revolt against Rome and left a number of cities in ruins, including Londinium. Worse, at this moment in Sak's life, she was responsible for slaughtering over eighty thousand Roman citizens.

His mind was in turmoil. He had been warned not to interfere with history yet he could not let this family go to Londinium and face almost certain death; he would be alright, as Helge had assured him that it was impossible for him to be harmed. He had grown to love these people; they had treated him with a kindness beyond even that of Vera and Beram. He wasn't sure why he felt that, but at this moment it certainly seemed so. Surely the saving of one family would not be altering history. Perhaps, a thought occurred to him, that was why he was here, at this particular time. What if the real purpose presence was to save them. In that case, if he did not, then he would be changing history.

Decision taken, choice made, he strode back into Cicero's study with a sudden confidence..

He stood looking at his portrait for a moment. That portrait that had remained leaning against the wall after the abortive attempt to find any one who might know him. Then he turned, bowed to Cicero, and then embraced him. He wanted to take Aelia's hand, but felt it would be wrong. He smiled at her, then spoke.

"What I am about to say may seem impossible to believe but I ask you to hear me out without interruption, or I may lose my courage. I did not lose my memory; I know exactly who I am and where I come from. It was necessary for me to deceive you for if I had not, I would have disappeared and you would have no memory of me. But I feel, like Ona, that I am here for a purpose, not for the saving of Marcus, glad as I am to have been instrumental in that, I think you will discern that that was the catalyst for my coming to you, not the purpose.

"I have not been sent by the gods, nor am I a deity myself. I am a traveller, not from some far off land, but from a far off time, I am a traveller through time. I come from the future. My world is approximately two thousand five hundred years in the future."

He paused to let this sink in. No-one spoke.

"I am called Chris and I was brought back to your time in order to learn your language. Believing me to be lost and homeless you took me in, accepted me for what I am. I love you all dearly."

Again he paused, looked down, then addressed Aelia

"Aelia, you are a truly wonderful person; I have fallen in love with you, your beauty of mind, yes, and your natural beauty as well. I know you have doubted at times, wondering why I have become withdrawn, not taking things forward, or seeking to ratify our situation. It was because I was afraid, afraid that I would be returned to my own time without warning. Those who brought me here said you will have no memory of me once I am gone, yet I was not prepared to risk hurting you."

Aelia started to speak, but Sak hurried on. "I know I did hurt you by my reticence and failure to explain, but how could I explain this to you, until now, when it seems it must be done, was meant to be done. But...." he fingered the three hag stones that she had hung from a leather thong, and put them around his wrist, on a day he wished he would always be able to recall, while knowing it could not be so. "I hope somehow these will travel with me through time."

"Being from the future, I know a lot about the past and thanks to Tacitus, I know all about Boudicca and what is likely to happen if you locate to Londinium. I have been told I cannot interfere with history but I believe I may have been sent to do exactly that, and by not doing it, I am interfering with history. Regardless, because of the love I have for you all, I am going to risk it, either way. I say with all my heart and soul, please do not go to Londinium....."

He began to tell what he knew, seeing it in his mind as he spoke. In a moment he felt as if he was there, in the midst of the fighting. Then something struck him on the back of his neck, dizziness overcame him, his vision blurred and he fell into darkness.

Cicero and his family were gathered in his study. There was much to discuss, Marcus was travelling to Rome to be trained as a Legionnaire. Cicero was proud but Ona was fussing about as mothers do. Aelia was a little distracted. She had discovered an old dusty portrait of a young boy in the corner, dark hair, painfully thin but dark brown eyes that seemed to be laughing. The only thing that marred his beauty was a few blackheads round the bottom of his nose and a large yellow head at the corner of his mouth.

"Pappa, who is this boy"

"I've no idea, been trying to remember how I came by it but keep drawing a blank"

Aelia felt drawn to it, there was something at the back of her mind, but it was very vague.

"Can I have it?"

"Of course, if you want it, though I am not sure why you would."

Nor was she, but it remained with her for the rest of her life.

THE RETURN

Sak lent back against the tree and glanced at his watch, hardly a minute had passed since he had last looked, though it seemed longer. He was no longer crying and the mood of utter despair had lifted, he felt good in himself. He remained sitting under the great oak for quite some time, reluctant to leave and lose the moment. It was some considerable time later that he looked at his watch again and was shocked to see that he had been there for almost two hours! He had to be back in time for tea otherwise there would be trouble. As he headed for the Manor he turned his head in order to get his bearings, so determined was he to be able to return, and maybe again experience that ineffable, inexplicable, sense of all being well. To his disbelief he could see no oak, not a trace, the tree that had dominated the landscape, the tree that had offered him respite from his misery, was simply not there.

Completely bamboozled he had no time to dwell on it, he had to get back to the Manor. By the time he was back at the Manor, all memory of that magnificent oak and everything associated with it had evaporated as if it had never been, he had no memory of it.

After tea he was approached by Goodrich.

"Sak, where have you been, I have been looking for you all over."

"Just out for the Sunday afternoon walk like everybody else."

"Thats all very well but you have not done my Latin homework yet."

"No, and I am not going to....." The words that came out of his mouth surprised him almost as much as they shocked Goodrich.

"But what am I to do....?"

"Same as us all! Do it yourself!"

"But I can't!"

Sak was uncertain why he spoke as he had. True he had wanted to tell Goodrich for some time that he did not want to do his prep but had held back because he had not known how to do it nicely, and now he had said it in a cruel, hurtful and harsh manner. He looked into his friend's eyes and saw the hurt his words had caused.

"Look, what I mean is,I am not doing you any favours by doing your work for you, because you are not learning from that. First of all you must try to do it yourself and if you do that, then of course I will help"

"But what of tonight's prep?"

"Just try, it doesn't matter if you get it all wrong, just make an effort, then we'll sort it."

Sak laughed at himself, where were these words coming from? He was speaking like a teacher who spoke Latin flawlessly, not a fourteen year old who struggled with the language himself.

Back from evensong at the main school and supper out of the way 'prep' was underway. Sak opened his textbook 'Latin for Today' at the designated chapter, Horatio and the Bridge, the story was written in English and their job was to translate it into Latin. The story was about a small town being raided by a horde of Barbarians. There was only one legionnaire to defend it. Luckily the only access was over a single file bridge and the narrative told how this one gallant soldier, Horatio, by holding his ground at one end of the bridge, slayed one raider after another, keeping them at bay all day until reinforcements arrived, and attacking from the rear defeated the enemy, and the town was saved. Sak loved this story but was daunted at the thought of translating it. He sighed, picked up his pen and began to write.

When prep finished an hour and a half later he was still writing. He had written of life in the town before the invasion, he wrote of the growing fatigue of Horatio, of how his resolve and love of the townsfolk had given him strength. He described in detail the swordsmanship and tactics he had employed and much more. On completion he read it through and to him he read it as easily as he would have an English story.

He changed into his pyjamas and was hanging his trousers up when two objects fell out of his pockets onto his foot. Ow! That hurt! What on earth was it? He bent and picked them up, one consisted of three stones, each of which had a hole through which a leather thong had been threaded to form a necklace, the second object was a Roman coin. Puzzled, he held them for a moment. From them both he felt a warmth, a sense of security as well as a feeling of serenity. A third sense was telling him they were special and he felt he needed to keep them safe. He hid them carefully, loathe to let them out of his sight, but not wanting questions from other boys.

Thus Aelia's hag stones and Sak's portrait somehow became touchstones for their lives. Emblems of their love now unknown, surviving the two-way passage of time, and as long as they kept them close they served to guide each other through relationships without getting hurt until each had once again found true love. The coin, a gift from Cicero, surviving the journey through time, was to enhance Sak's prosperity.

Although unaware of all that had befallen him, Sak felt it had been a strange and tiring day and fell asleep easily, unaware that he had travelled, and learnt and this had helped him mature and develop into the person he might always have been, if things had been different..

Jim Hodges lit another cigarette; he was at a loss at what to do. His evening had been spent like many, alone in his study, marking the boys' prep. His Problem now was this work of Saklatvala. His initial reaction on reading Sak's story of Horatio had been one of joy, it was a good piece of writing, it had held his attention grammatically it was perfect. Then it hit him. Jim had a policy of not looking to see whose book he was marking until after he had finished, to ensure no favouritism or bias came into play. He looked to see who had written this mini masterpiece that had so enraptured him,

"Saklatvala!" now that was not possible, a boy who had consistently come bottom of the class for the past three years could not possibly have written this, indeed, he thought, no boy in the school could have written with such deep insight into Roman life, with such accuracy of language, even members of the Classics faculty would struggle. If he had not written it himself, where had Sak got it from? Was it plagiarism, if so who was the original author? Had it been written for him by that ubiquitous Uncle of his that he was always talking about. And why, when the task had been to translate, had he instead written this opus, a much more onerous task. Why do so much uncalled for work? If he had written it, it was as if he had been carried away beyond himself, back to the time of Horatio.

He thought about the boy himself; the general opinion was that he was a pleasant enough boy, always polite but a bit dim, definitely insecure. Jim felt he was always seeking approval; had this longing for acceptance been such that he had found some obscure entry in something like the Encyclopaedia Britannica and simply copied it, believing that nobody would seek it out and so give the boy the benefit of the doubt. It was all very troubling. Jim put the books aside and prepared for bed, he would get to the bottom of it in the morning.

The Masters' Common Room was thick with smoke and the smell of coffee. Jim sought out Mr Reynolds.

"Paul were you on prep duty at the Manor last Sunday?"

"Yes, why, what's up? Evidence of collusion?"

"Did you happen to notice Saklatvala?"

"Funny you should ask, because it was a bit odd. I don't think I have ever seen a student work so hard. After he had opened his textbook he began to write and just did not stop. Even after I had rung the bell signalling the end of prep he continued. His concentration was total"

"What other books did he have around him?" "None"

Having drawn a blank there, he sought out Mr Burgess, the senior Classics Master.

"Andrew, do you have five minutes?

"Sure Jim, what's the problem"

"Read this but don't look at the name on the front of the book, not even after you have finished reading it"

Andrew slouched down into one of the old leather armchairs, I am intrigued."

He read it through once, looked up at Jim quizzically, and read through it again, at times he frowned, sometimes his eyes widened and in the end he smiled.

"Well, I recognise the story obviously but I have never seen it written in such detail, it reads almost like an eyewitness account. It reads well, has a natural flow about it. It's as if a Roman was making a report".

"Now look at the front cover and see whose work it purportedly is."

"No, oh no, no no! There is no way that this is Saklatvala's original work. He must have copied it from somewhere?"

"That's what I thought but from where and any way, his Latin is so bad he would not have not known where to start or finish."

"He must have had some guidance, some help."

"I don't think that's the case either, Paul was on prep duty and swears he just opened 'Latin for Today', then opened his exercise book and began to write and continued to write long after prep had finished."

It was common knowledge that Andrew had served in the Royal Navy prior to taking up his position at Dauntsey's, but nobody knew at that time that he had been involved in Naval Intelligence. During the war he had been seconded to Bletchley Park. In his time he had seen many scams, uncovered many cheats and was much more streetwise than Jim and he came up with a an outlandish theory, but which made some sort of sens.,

"What if he got someone else to do the translation for him earlier and he had written it down in his Latin book on Sunday afternoon when he was meant to be on his afternoon walk. Then come prep time he simply took another book and just wrote a story or just a load of rubbish to look like he was doing his work."

Jim was astonished, it was an intriguing theory but he did not believe Sak was capable of such deviousness. But if he was indeed that devious, the question remained, who did he know who was capable of such work?

To Jim there was only one answer, it must have been his Uncle. The two men had spoken at length on Open Day about Sak; his Uncle expressed his frustration at Sak's inability to grasp the essentials of a language he, Beram, loved and found so easy. Andrew's outlandish thought might just hold water; what had Sherlock Holmes said "Once you eliminate the impossible, whatever remains, no matter how improbable, must be the truth!"

After lunch Sak was summoned to the Headmaster's study. He was puzzled as to why he had been called but unworried as he had done nothing wrong. Mr Forbes sat at his desk, flanked on either side by Messrs. odges and Burgess. Sak's prep book lay open in front of Forbes. The Head was the first to speak,

"I have one question to ask, who wrote this?"

"I did, Sir."

"We do not believe you" was the essence of the message that they, all three, tried to convey, sometimes interrupting each other, explaining why it was impossible and Burgess explained his theory and urged the boy to "tell the truth or there would be dire consequences. Jim Hodges, calmer than the other two said, "Can you explain how last week you could hardly remember one word of latin yet are now fluent in it?"

The truth was he couldn't explain, but his answer astounded both them and him.

"Nescio. Omnia docuit me subito facta est cum sensu. Convenire videbantur"

For a moment there was a stunned silence, then both the Classic Masters burst out laughing. The Head was perplexed,

"He has just told us that he doesn't know how but it had suddenly come to him, and everything seemed to come together. His Latin was flawless. Jim smiled and said "Et loquella tu manifestum est aliquantulus odd" to which Sak replied

"Es vos certus suus non vestrum"

Both Classic Masters again burst out laughing.

"Well Jim you will go down in history as the best Latin teacher of them all. Headmaster. we can't explain it but there can be no doubt, this is the work of Saklatvala."

"Well gentleman, while I am pleased to hear it, will somebody please tell me what just passed between you, I have to confess my Latin is on a par with what we believed Sak's to have been."

"Saklatvala basically said he had no explanation, that it suddenly made sense to him. Jim then told him his accent was a bit odd, to which Saklatvala replied "how could he be sure it was not his, Jim's, pronunciation that was at fault."

Forbes smiled, "Well gentlemen, it seems miracles do happen. Well done Saklatvala, I am pleased." But when they had gone he sat for some time ruminating, trying to come to terms with something he felt was inexplicable.

Sak had thought this was the last of it but there was one more twist; they had failed to tell him that they had phoned his Uncle; the next morning he received a letter.

"Dear Chris,

I was perturbed to receive a telephone call from your classics masters asking if I had colluded with you in an attempt to deceive them into believing that you had suddenly come to grips with your Latin. Before I broach the subject of your obvious cheating I am mortified to have been implicated in your deception and I don't know how long it will take for me to trust you again.

As to your crime, and I use the word advisedl,y no Saklatvala has ever stooped so low and you have brought shame to the family name. You have a choice, you can admit what you did was wrong, apologise to your teachers as well as to me and hope that we have it in our hearts to forgive you or you can continue with your tissue of lies.

I realise you were probably trying to please me but I would rather you were dim witted and honest rather than try to buy my respect by cheating.

Your future at Dauntsey's, indeed your whole future, is at stake.

Beram."

He found the letter hurtful, not only because of the content, but because it was all so impersonal. It had been typed by his secretary and only his name and Beram's signature were handwritten; he could not even keep it in the family. He immediately penned his reply.

"Dear Uncle Beram

I have always respected and believed in your sense of fair play and justice yet in this instant you have acted as judge, juror and executioner without even giving the accused the opportunity of reply.

The truth is I have no explanation as to why everything seemed to make sense and I was able to understand and speak Latin. I did not lie to my teachers nor did infer in any way that you and I were in cahoots.

I am both hurt and offended and feel like the Winslow Boy.

Incidentally the teachers including the Headmaster are satisfied that it was all my own work.

I bear no malice, ask for no apology, just an acceptance that I have been truthful and I trust by penning this reply in Latin makes it easier for you to believe.

Love Chris"

Beram sat in his office, joy, tinged with embarrassment and regret, in his heart as he read Chris's reply. 'I must endeavour not to be so quick to judge in future.'

PART 2 : MOSTLY FANTASY

In Valhalla, the Norse Gods were content. Helge's term of imprisonment had been left for him to determine and they felt that he had chosen well; his judgement in allowing Sak to extend his time in Roman Britain beyond him learning to speak Latin had been, they felt, a master stroke. It had given the boy the opportunity to find his true self, indeed it had allowed him to catch up with his age. Was it time then for Helge to enter the Hallowed Halls of Valhalla?

"No!" Odin made his judgement, "This is just the beginning, we must be patient, watchful, and see what unfolds, for Helge's ultimate fate now rests with Sak; but there is much that pleases us.

Ignorant of the events that had led to his 'Road to Damascus' moment, Sak sensed that his life was changing but was as yet unaware that the change emanated from himself. His success at Latin had given him a new confidence; when the boys had next teased him about his scrawny physique, it no longer bothered him, instead he told himself "well you are scrawny and there is nothing you can do about it, so just live with it!" When the teasers realised there was no reaction the teasing stopped.

One evening in the dormitory the boys were talking about the forthcoming summer holidays and what they would be doing and where they would be going, Sak joined in the conversation,

"Oh you lot, always on about holidays. I just wish I could go on a holiday, instead of which, I will, as usual, be stuck at home with very little to do. We can't afford to go on holidays." They stared at him in amazement, saying nothing, then Murray said

"Oh come off it, Sak, are you trying to tell us that the Managing Director of Kodak can't afford to take his family for a vacation?" "Yes, come off it" joined in some of the others, laughing.

"Well, that's just it, you see. My Father is not Managing Director of Kodak. In fact, far from it. He is a foreman on the factory floor....."

"But why did you say he was?"

"I don't think I actually did. On that first day everything was a bit confusing, when somebody asked, I said that he worked for Kodak. Someone, I didn't know who was who then, jumped to the wrong conclusion. Probably about the kind of jobs your fathers have. It made me feel inferior and ashamed and I didn't have the courage to correct it."

Clang! Clang! Clang! The silence bell rang, and brought the conversation to an end. Sak felt as if a great burden had been lifted from his shoulders.

Over breakfast the following morning, he took the opportunity to continue the conversation from where he had left off the night before, but nobody seemed that interested. Over the next few days one or two of his dormitory asked a few questions and he tried to expand further, but most were unaffected by what he had to say. His friends still liked him, those that didn't, they treated him as they had before, unaware and uncaring of the courage it had taken him to unburden himself of the fiction he had let run on for so long. He was a little surprised, hurt even, by their lack of reaction.

Pondering it in his mind, he wandered down to the weeping willow trees at the bottom of the Manor Valley to try and figure out if it mattered, and why. It wasn't long before the late afternoon sun, which was still warm, lulled him into sleep. When he woke up the answer was in his head, and seemed so obvious. They had always treated him as they perceived him, for what they saw in him. They were unbothered by his background, unimpressed by the uncle he was always boasting about.

It had been his own insecurity, his self-consciousness, his self-absorption, that was the problem. All the teasing that he had endured was because, in their eyes, he was one of them, just another boy and if he had he been less self-absorbed he would have seen other boys being made fun of, just as much, if not more than he himself. They had no way of knowing how he felt, any more than he knew what they were feeling inside; could it be that they, some of them at least, were as insecure as himself. He saw that he had made judgements and assumptions, assessments of people based solely on how they affected him. "Grow up Sak, it's not all about you, start thinking about others and worry less about yourself." Then he asked himself a question "Who are you, Sak? Are you the person you think you are, or are you the person other people perceive you to be?" After some reflection, another question, "Which do you want to be?"

Freed from the emotional baggage he had been carrying, free from the worry that the fiction he had created would be seen through, combined with the confidence of his prowess in Latin, Sak was now free to appreciate and enjoy all that Dauntsey's had to offer. His school reports were no longer something to be dreaded; all the Masters seemed to agree that Sak was at last fulfilling his potential and started to laud his academic achievements. Beram was delighted with his nephew's progress.

"I know you had doubts about taking him away from his family, and I realise it was difficult for you, but surely now you can see it was worth it" Vera smiled, she was also relieved, and very happy, but unlike her husband, she had no desire to claim all the credit.

"I think maybe it was just that he was a late developer. We spent a lot of time together when he was with us and during those times he was a different child, less nervous, more confident and

I felt he was more at ease. There is no doubt that he loved and admired you but he was also nervous of you and was reluctant to voice his own opinions. Surely we must give him some of of the credit"

"Are you saying I wasted my time and money? That had we left him where he was he would have made it anyway?"

"No, of course not. We created an environment that allowed him the opportunity to flourish but all credit to him for grasping it."

"You may be right," he admitted but at the same time he wondered if Vera ever suspected the true reason behind his delight. What hadn't occurred to him was that Sak himself might have suspicions. Even so, maybe he, Beram, did deserve all the credit, after all, it had been his decision to send him to Dauntsey's, which, although he had no way of knowing it, had led to Sak's meeting with Helge; or was it fate that had directed him?.

Sak's new found prowess in Latin aided his understanding of French and he was no longer the butt of the French master's sarcastic humour; he began to excel in other subjects, and was gaining a reputation for original thought. From his first visit to Stonehenge when staying with his aunt in Salisbury the aura of Stonehenge affected him strongly. Now Stonehenge was only some twelve miles away from the school. It was a tradition on Midsummer's Day for some of the senior boys to take the Salisbury bus which stopped by the henge, don their white lab coats and, believing that it really had nothing to do with the Druids, follow and mock the ceremony.

After a history project on Stonehenge, the boys were asked to write an essay on its formation. Sak found it difficult to accept the conventional wisdom that these massive stones had been rolled on the trunks of trees from the Welsh mountains and for some reason erected in what then was the middle of nowhere. To him it just did not make sense. There were other parts of its history that to him did not add up.

"How do we know the date of its construction Sir?"

"Until recently it was pure conjecture, but a new technology called carbon dating carried out on antlers found nearby, put at between eighteen hundred and fifteen hundred years BC."

"What implements were used to shape the stones, especially the ball and socket joints used to keep the lintels in place?"

His teacher obviously had no answers and Sak sensed he was finding his questions tedious so he stopped asking. He felt only an iron or bronze based material could have done the job and besides on a half term visit, Beram had pointed out two daggers carved into one of the stones.

"So does that mean that it was built during or after the iron age then?"

"No," answered Beram "the daggers could have been carved into the stone at any time in the last three thousand years, sadly we shall never know."

He was pondering on his forthcoming essay on his now customary Sunday afternoon walk through the Manor Woods,

"What if, what if those scientists doing the carbon dating had been so engrossed with their new technology, that they had, like him, jumped to the wrong conclusion. Deer after all had roamed freely across Britain for centuries and those antlers may have belonged to an animal that had lived long before Stonehenge existed, or even sometime after Stonehenge was built, as Beram had said about the daggers......." The approach of a somewhat decrepit man interrupted his thoughts.

" Hello Sak, all is well with you? There are no tears today.

"Sorry?" but as he spoke, visions of a different time flashed through his mind, he peered more closely at the figure before him, trying to make sense of the vague sense of recognition, which his eyes denied.

"Sak, we are old friends. We have met before but you have no real memory of it, just as you will not remember this meeting, no, no, don't interrupt, we have been monitoring your.........,"

Sak could not contain his curiosity any longer, "We, who or what is we?"

"Sak, at present this is beyond your comprehension, but one day, if all goes well, you will understand. For the present, you must trust, have faith."

Sak found somewhere deep within him that he did have faith, and his trust was such that he remembered for a moment. As if he was watching a film of himself, he saw a seemingly much young Sak sobbing his heart out under a giant oak, he saw Helge talking to him and images of Marcus, Ona, Cicero and, above all, Aelia flashed before him,

"Helge, Helge is that really you? There is so much I want to ask. What happened to the family, did they go to Londinium......"

Helge was taken aback, he was wrong footed, had somehow made a mistake. This was not meant to happen.

Helge was not alone in his surprise. In Valhalla the Norse Gods were discussing Sak's memories in disbelief

"This cannot be allowed to stand, his remembrance could ruin everything we have planned."

In an unprecedented move time in both ancient and modern worlds stood still, while Helge stood before his gods.

"Helge, you have done well, almost too well. Your decision that this boy would be part of your salvation was a wise choice; his faith and trust in you seems absolute. The depths of his trust is such that it has allowed him to break through barriers we thought impenetrable, we do not hold you responsible. We are pleased with the work you have done thus far but now your task must be to find a way to make him forget."

Helge stood before Sak, but not as Helge, as the gods of ancient Greece and Rome had done so many times before, he took on another guise,

"What are you babbling about boy, what is this talk of Helge? All the other people you were talking about? Your Uncle Beram and his Roman obsession seems to have raddled your mind."

"Father! I am sorry, I did not recognise you."

"Bloody fool"

The shock of seeing his Father here, in his place of sanctuary, so traumatised him, his mind abandoned of all other thoughts. His mind was literally a blank. When Helge reappeared as himself, there was no sense of recognition. All that had gone before was, indeed, gone. Helge was relieved, but at the same time devastated by the effect that it had had on Vala.

Helge spoke and Sak responded politely, no vague memories stirred. In Valhalla the gods smiled in satisfaction.

"Would you like to know if you are right?"

"I'm sorry sir, who are you and what do you mean, would I like to know if I am right?"

The man introduced himself as Helge, and asked "Would you really like to know when and why and Stonehenge was built?"

Sak looked at this strange man and inexplicably had total confidence that he would have the answers to his questions.

"Yes please, and do you also know how and why the stones ended up on the edge of Salisbury Plain? I can't imagine a group of stone age men standing in the middle of a field and thinking, 'I know, let's go to Wales, lob off part of a mountain and bring it back here' any more than a group of Welshmen saying 'oh look at those rocks, I know a field where they would look good!' But how do you know, how did you know I wanted to know? What is going on, I am confused, I...."

Helge laughed delightedly, "trust me, and take my hand." Without consciously considering it, Sak did both. There was darkness all around; Sak sensed a movement unlike anything he had experienced before. In his first adventure through time, Helge had simply placed him in Roman Britain, this was a trickier operation altogether. Taking him back over two and a half million years was fraught with dangers and despite the assurances he had given Sak on his previous trip, Helge did not feel entirely confident that the sub-zero temperatures of the ice-age would not cause Sak irreparable harm. So this time he travelled with him

High above the Welsh mountains Sak felt the chill of the ice covered peaks, despite being wrapped in one of Helge's sheepskin cloaks, He gave no thought to the whys and wherefores of what was happening to him, how was it possible for him to be floating through the heavens. He was captivated by the awesome happenings he could see far below. A creeping, crawling white expanse, Sak had a vague notion that glaciers moved very slowly, perhaps a few feet per year, but below him, moving it seemed at a fantastic speed, was an expanse of white, buckling, changing, flowing, and yet he knew it was ice. It seemed nothing could impede the relentless progress, small mountain peaks fell victim to its power, breaking off, becoming part of this fast moving mass.

Then he was no longer hovering, almost, it seemed, he was standing still, yet he realised that they were flying at the same speed as the glacier was travelling, pushing ahead of itself a mass of huge blueish gray boulders. As they flew, there was a change. Sak could feel the air was getting warmer and below him the ice began to melt. Now the rocks were being pushed along by great walls of water, wave after wave crashing against them. As they watched, following its progress across the country, he saw the great rocks broken up by the sheer power of the water. Then the water began to recede, began to lose its power and the rocks settled where they were, on the edge of Salisbury Plain. Eventually the water disappeared altogether, leaving a group of massive boulders in the middle of an otherwise green and fertile plain; an awesome sight for the ancient Britons who, with no knowledge of their true origin, attributed them to the gods, giving them greater significance than they possibly possessed.

Then, without any sensation of descent, he found himself sitting next to Helge, leaning against some of those self-same rocks they had followed on their journey.

“I had no idea glaciers moved with such speed,” Sak said.

Helge laughed, “They don't, what you have just witnessed was nearly two million years of history compressed into a short time-span, so everything speeded up. You have now seen for yourself how the rocks that became Stonehenge came to be here. Next, to discover how these rocks were transformed into the henge you know today.” Sak for a moment was dumbfounded but somehow, what sounded absurd and impossible in the normal world, when he was in Helge’s presence made perfect sense.

Time seemed out of sequence. It was still daylight, yet he sensed it was dawn. What had happened to the night? Even as he thought this, he found himself enveloped by a shroud of darkness, falling all around him. As he struggled to come to terms with this latest weird event, he was distracted by the sound of someone hammering. Gradually the darkness diminished, not lifting, but dispersing. Turning towards the noise of hammering, he saw the sun had barely risen and seemed to be balancing on the very edge of the earth. Silhouetted against this orb of light was a man, hammering a great stake into the ground. ‘I’d like to paint that’ he thought, irrelevantly. ‘But what is he doing, and why? ‘You could try asking’ he told himself, so intrigued and unafraid, he approached the man.

"Excuse me, may I ask, why are you hammering that stake into the ground?" The man studied this intruder for a while, a puzzled look on his face. After a bit he answered; obviously, he had had no difficulty in understanding Sak, and neither did Sak have any problem in understanding his reply.

"How can you not know, surely you were here when our leader laid out his vision before us?"

"Indeed, no." He reverted to an old ploy. "I am not from these parts; I mistook my way and became lost. I have been travelling many days, living off the land and sought shelter here before darkness fell."

Eyeing him up and down, the stranger found his story believable.

"Looks like you could do with some food, follow me."

They both turned away from the sun and Sak, once his sight had cleared, was amazed by what he saw. The rocks and boulders which had so dominated the landscape before now seemed almost insignificant as he took in the activity going on around them. People were emerging from rough shelters, fires were being lit, the smoke obscuring many of the stones; there was a smell of roasting wild boar and deer which pervaded the atmosphere, making Sak realise just how hungry he was. Men and women alike were filling buckets from a large leather reservoir of fresh water, some, he observed, for washing their faces but the majority used for drinking. Rough wooden tables and benches were scattered all around. Despite the mass of people, Sak was astounded by the sense of order that prevailed.

Having been taught that prehistoric meant before history, which had been defined as before man could record his life, in any way except by speech, he had assumed that prehistoric man was therefore backward in all things. In the first few minutes of being amongst them he realised this was a major misconception. That they could not write was of little consequence, they obviously knew how to communicate! How else could things have proceeded so smoothly, a place for everything, and everyone, and everything and everyone in their place, going about their business, contributing to a communal life.

Enjoying the food he had been given, he looked about him and observed more of what was going on; the fires had died down now the meat was removed, there was less smoke drifting around. The sun, by now much higher in the sky, enabled him to see that some of the stones had been moved, there were huge wooden posts, well weathered, presumably by age, lying around. To Sak his most exciting discovery was the sight of iron tools. 'Ha! I was right; Stonehenge is part of or post Iron Age!' He felt a tap on the shoulder, it was his friend, the hammer man.

Hammer man spoke to the person with him, "this is he of whom I was telling you, the curious stranger who was asking about our work here," and to Sak he said, "This is our leader, the wise one."

Sak looked up and was surprised, he had, for no good reason when he thought about it, been expecting to see an old man with white hair and matching beard, wrinkled dry skin, leathery and bronzed after years in the sun. But the man he saw he estimated to be no more than thirty years old, with jet black hair, bushy black eyebrows guarding the clearest blue eyes he had ever seen, alive, alert and enquiring." Without conscious thought Sak began to rise from his seat and was about to proffer his hand in greeting, but then realised how odd this might look, and he quickly dropped back to the bench.

"So stranger, whither are you from?" Sak was about to say from the west, but, thinking about it, wondered if this would have any meaning to these people.

"I come from the place where the sun goes down at the end of the day" he said, pointing in the opposite direction to where he had seen the sun rise."

"Knoweth you where the sun sleeps?"

"Well yes, in a sort of way."

"Can you take us there?"

"No, that would be impossible. No one can ever get there."

The leader looked at him, his eyebrows came together and Sak was unsure whether it was in anger or in puzzlement.

"You say you come from where the sun sleeps, yet now you say no one can get there, what trickery is this?"

By now all eyes seemed to be upon him, awaiting his answer.

"Each morning you see the sun rise, you know where it is. Have you ever tried walking towards it?"

Many of them nodded, Sak went on, "...and what did you notice, did it become closer, did you ever reach it?"

They conceded that they had tried but that it always seemed the same distance away, they never seemed to get any closer.

"Well it's exactly the same when the sun goes down, what I should have said, what I meant, was that I came from that direction, the direction in which the sun goes down."

The leader seemed satisfied with his answer. As if he was reassured and felt safe, even eagerin talking of his great plan to this stranger.

"The answer to your question goes back a long way, far longer than any of us can remember, but the story has been told and retold many times over the generations and it is our duty to ensure it will continue to be told for many more. This place and these vast stones were very special to those who came before us.

"But why?"

"Listen well, this is the story which is told, and will be told, down through history. Until Our people came to this place they had lived a nomadic life, wandering from place to place, finding food and shelter when and wherever they could. There was no real sense of community, but they felt safer in large numbers, but it was still every man for himself, with no real leader. There came a time when it had been particularly hard for them; seemingly the sun did not shine any more, the sky was grey, it was always drizzling and they were constantly cold, damp and generally miserable. They missed the dawn and seeing the sun appear from below the horizon, the source of their warmth, light and comfort, some speculated that it had fallen off the very edge of the earth and was lost to them forever. Some thought it meant the world was ending. They were miserable, tired and dispirited, many resigned to giving up, letting nature, or whatever it was, do its worst. Then an elder spoke up, 'You have forgotten who you are, what gives us purpose, that we are hunters." The wise man spoke these last words with dramatic pride. He continued, "'when we are short of something, we go hunting. Now we have lost something, surely must we go out hunting. Let us set out to hunt and find our sun.' Thus they set out in a direction of where they believed the sun used to rise."

He paused to drink from a beaker offered to him by a woman, "At that time the days remained overcast, the rain fell heavily, and the dark fell early, but their renewed spirit and resolve was strong as they continued their quest. At long last, after days and days of moving persistently through the damp and gloom the day came when just as the darkness fell the rain stopped. They felt a difference in the atmosphere. The elder declared this was a sign, and they would camp where they were that night, and see what the morning brings."

All through this long telling the people remained crowded around the story-teller. Sak thought it must be a tale they knew well, and yet they seemed as interested as he was, even the children, who sat mostly on the ground, but with their eyes fixed on the wise man.

"And in the morning they were roused by a lad who ran excitedly around the still sleeping hunters, shaking them, rousing them from their slumber,

"Wake up, wake up! Look, look over there we have found it, it has returned!" Barely awake and unhappy at having their sleep disturbed, they did not at first share his excitement but once fully roused their eyes followed the direction in which the boy was pointing and a reverent silence fell over the gathering.

They had approached from the west and in the near dark had not been aware of the great mass of stones lying about them. But what really caused them to look, and rub their eyes was a sight that caused amazement and joy. The sun was rising above the rock furthest away, stark on the horizon, but surrounded by light. Above them was a clear blue sky, the sun was returned to them, they fell to their knees to give thanks."

"So they believed the stones and the rising of the sun were somehow linked" ventured Sak. He immediately realised his gaffe, but there was little he could do.

"Yes, it was a great discovery, they had discovered the doorway through which the sun had to pass each day in order to warm the earth, to give us energy and strength and they were determined that never again would the sun lose its way. From the nearby forests they cut down the tallest and stoutest oak trees and constructed a huge circle of timber around the stones, to echo the shape of the sun and as long as the circle remained the sun would never again be lost. But this, as I have said, was long ago, the wood weathers and has grown old. A decision has been taken to replace them with something that will last for all time, and which we believe was given to us for this purpose."

"You mean the stones?" 'Of course he does, Sak thought, 'you are an idiot sometimes!'

"So it was indeed. The noise you heard will help determine the placement of the doorway. It has been observed that the length of the shadows changes each day, the longer the shadow, the shorter the time the sun stays in the sky. Each day it is getting shorter now, so we mark where it falls each day. The moment it stops getting shorter is where we shall place the centre of the doorway and a corresponding one will be placed to guide the sun to its bed."

He turned towards Sak to see if he had more questions, but to his amazement, he could not see hime. 'Passing strange, maybe the gods sent him, thinking it time that I once again share the story with our people.'

Sak glanced up at the great oak he was resting against. 'Funn,y I don't remember coming here," but he felt at peace with himself and all the world,, and continued his afternoon walk.

As with Horatio and the Bridge, his prep that evening flowed easily from his pen and his resulting essay's originality and evidence of interest impressed the teacher, made him think. Nonetheless, he gave him a lower mark, after all, he had not followed the perceived wisdom of the current time, little knowing that they reflected the time as it was.

This was not Helge's last gift to Vala; there were more adventures in time, each relevant to his school work, and from which, unknowingly, he benefited greatly. This was born out by the biennial review, a school tradition.

Sak's biennial review was conducted by a somewhat bemused Reverend Osborne, School Chaplain, and Master of English and History.

"Well Saklatvala, I don't quite know where to begin, things certainly seem to have turned around for you, and long may it last. But what is your secret? I am sure it is something we'd all like to be able to take advantage of."

"I don't really know Sir, nor understand it myself, but I think it has something to do with truth....."

Osborne raised his eyebrows, "Truth?"

"Well, my truth to be exact, or rather the truth that is me. You see, the idea of boarding school was a complete shock to me. My cousins went but for me, it was never on the horizon, had never been discussed. Having to sit the Dauntsey entrance exam was a complete surprise, I was only told about it the morning I was to sit it and even then I wasn't told what the exam was for. It was only after the letter came saying I had passed I found out I was going to boarding school. There were only two weeks to get everything ready, no time to really think. I felt thrown in at the deep end!"

He went on to relate how, from day one, he had felt out of place, of the fiction he had created about himself, although initially unintended, and how he then felt unable to change things and had to maintain the stories that resulted. He tried to explain how so much of his time had been spent on maintaining the fiction he had created that all else, especially his school work, had suffered. Afraid to form close friendships in case he let his mask slip, he had withdrawn into himself.

Sak looked up at the master, "I think, Sir, that was the Saklatvala you knew. For many reasons I was desperate to succeed at Latin, but my results were poor, there were other reasons for this, to an extent, that I would rather not go into but I was desperately miserable, at my wit's end. I sat in the woods in despair, calling on anyone, anything for help. I think I fell asleep for a while. Then, walking back I felt strangely calm, and at ease with myself and when prep time came everything just seemed to come together. The success of that one piece of work seemed to give me faith in myself and the courage to be able to be honest about who I was. So I suppose my secret is actually having no more secrets, if that makes any sense?"

There was an easy silence between them; Sak had nothing more to say and the Rev. Osborne was studying the boy before him. He had not expected such a deeply personal response from his slightly frivolous question and he was unsure how to proceed. Unaware of the inner torment that had plagued Sak, he, like other members of staff, had been amazed and perplexed by his academic metamorphosis. They hadn't noticed that he had changed in other ways. Saklatvala seemed the same, polite, self-effacing boy, a little reserved and still given to blushing.

"Well, God works in mysterious ways his wonders to perform!"

"Maybe. Do you think that was it, Sir?""

Osborne's throw away line had been close; in Valhalla the gods smiled. In his oak tree Helge rejoiced that his time travelling companion was using the gifts he had been given to such good effect.

"Two years ago your review had been as difficult for me to write as it must have been for you and your parents to read. As in previous years we all felt you were operating under par, not living up to your potential. We felt that you were not really trying, did not care....." Sak tried to interrupt but was cut short as the Rev. Osborne continued "but in the light of all you have just revealed, I begin to understand how the school may, to some extent, have failed you, perhaps there is a lesson for us in there somewhere. But this year your review will be an absolute pleasure to write, you are entitled to be proud of yourself, you have excelled in every aspect of your life here and show great promise of fulfilling your potential."

Sak felt his cheeks reddening, he looked down at the floor to hide his emotions, then looked up with a broad smile, "thank you Sir, so much."

Osborne smiled back at him.

"It's not often that Masters share our pupils' work with each other, there just isn't the time, but there have been three pieces of your work that have excited the Common Room. Your essays on life during the Industrial Revolution, from the mass migration to the new cities, of life in the pits, to the exploitation of women and children in the factories, were written with an understanding and sensitivity that is usually only found in eye witness accounts, but you also tackled the issue of judging history a balanced way, looking at the circumstances of the time.

You managed to not only show the strength of the human spirit but also what it can accept as normal. So the conditions under which they lived and worked might be abhorrent to us, but were their normality, and in that grim reality you showed that there was room for humour, love and compassion. Things did change for the better and you demonstrated that the change that came was led by those who knew and had experienced a better life. It is a perceptive piece of work. Well done"

Sak remembered that essay, how fired up he had felt, but he couldn't now remember where he had found his facts, or what had initially inspired him. But Rev. Osborne still had not yet finished and Sak quite wished that he had; in an odd way he realised the admonishments he'd received in the past were easier to accept than the praises now being heaped upon him, he had never doubted he had deserved those reprimands, but this praise? Had it all been his own work?

Likewise your essay on life in the trenches during the First World War shows an understanding beyond your years. To be honest, we scoured the volumes in the library to see if you had lifted passages from them and, well, if you did we can't find them!"

Sak smiled, here he was sure he knew the source, those volumes he knew so well, he could them see in his mind's eye "The Illustrated History of the Great War." He loved those great volumes, folio size, but landscape, was there a name for that? They had dark red covers and the black legend added to the sombre nature of what lay inside. He had devoured the full page, black and white photographs, showing all aspects of the war, the optimistic faces of the men in 1914, through the horrors of gas attacks and 'going over the top', to the utter despair towards the end of' the war to end all wars'. He thought he might well have been influenced in some way by these books, but the work was all his - or was it, again that uneasy feeling.

What neither Master nor pupil recognised was Helge's role in all this, that due to Helge, Sak had lived his experiences, had been through the horrors and joys of both.

"But," continued Osborne," without doubt the piece de resistance was your work on Shakespeare. Where on earth did that idea come from?"

"From you Sir."

"Me!" Osborne was astounded, "I never taught you Shakespeare."

"No Sir, but during a religious study lesson you told us the King James Authorised Bible, (Old and New Testaments) contained 783,137 words. Coincidentally, I assume, Mr Hodges informed us that in the complete works of Shakespeare there are a total of 884,421 words, some 805,764 more. You said it was believed that the medieval monks spent a lifetime just copying out the Bible. I became intrigued as to how a man who died at the relatively young age of fifty two, had such a prodigious output. Not only did he have to write the plays, he had to research his subjects, conceive the idea, edit and rewrite, as well as sometimes acting in the plays.

I found all this really interesting and wanted to know more of this remarkable man and began to read as much about him as I could. Then a few weeks ago I read a newspaper article saying that an American had decided to copy the Bible out by hand.

There was no information as to what had prompted him, (a Mr Patterson) apart from the fact he was beset by illness. He wrote for fourteen hours a day, seven days a week. Using modern writing implements it took him four years to complete his task. I find it difficult to believe any man, living a normal life, with a young family, could possibly write for fourteen hours per day or even half that, for seven days a week. Scholars like F. R Levis tell us that Shakespeare didn't write his first play until he was 25 years old and his last play was written when he was at 49, so that's 24 years, which means an average of 1.56 plays a year. But apparently, according to Shakespeare experts, Romeo and Juliet took three years to write. During the same period he was not only directing performances of his play but acting in them as well.

So it seemed to me either I was missing something, or there was something else going on. I also read that he collaborated with John Fletcher on his final work, Two Noble Kinsmen, and that led me to wonder if this a one off or was it applicable to others of the plays as well.

“Hmm, interesting! Interesting to note the thirst for knowledge that this has led you to. Your conclusions seem original; I don’t think I’ve come across them before, although of course, I am not a Shakespeare expert. Are you going to pursue this line of research when you leave Dauntsey’s?”

“No Sir I want to study the law”

“Oh, that could be a pity. Still, there’s no reason the study of law should preclude your interest in Shakespeare and his works

MUCH ADO.....

April 1564. If the coach caught anybody's eye it was not because of its grandeur, but quite the opposite. The once fine lacquer was dulled by dirt and grime and was peeling in places. The coat of arms on the door had faded to the point of indistinction and gave no clue as to who was inside. Likewise the livery of the coachmen, tattered, torn with many patches, gave all the indication of a nobleman either down on his luck or out of favour at court. Only two horses pulled this once fine carriage and they were lean and scrawny and their progress was slow, almost sedate and gentle. Nothing here to interest the highwayman, robbers or thieves one might expect to find on the isolated roads along which they were travelling. Nor would they associate the rough wagon following about half a mile behind, with the coach. Had they known of the personage travelling inside, then things might have been different, but the subterfuge seemed to be holding, Nonetheless, most of the occupants were nervy and on edge, apart from the person who had the most to lose. She was a strong, fearless and resolute woman; the journey, the disguise were her ideas. She was heavily pregnant.

After travelling for four days they arrived at their destination. She had no time to appreciate the beauty of one her favourite castles, a place she loved, a place where she had found love and the place where that love had finally been consummated. The journey had been arduous and she felt her time was near. In order to protect her identity and the purpose of her visit, she and her entourage were directed to one of the lodges on the estate; the lady herself, her personal physician, a wet nurse, her lady in waiting, cooks and essential servants, all together in far closer proximity than they were used to and all sworn to secrecy on pain of death.

After bathing she retired to her bed to await the birth of her firstborn. Four days later on the twenty sixth of April she gave birth to a boy. It had not been an easy birth, her labour lasting more than twelve hours. For two days she nursed the boy, never had she felt closer to anybody or anything. Those around her thought her tears were those of joy but they were mistaken, they were tears of anguish, for she knew that never again would she hold the baby, she would not be there to see his first steps, hear his first words; his Mother she might be, but she would never enjoy true motherhood but these few precious moments would remain with her forever.

On the third day he came at last to see her; they were left alone.

"May I see him?"

"Of course, but wouldn't you, rather than just see him, like to hold your son?"

He looked down at the pale face on the pillow, smiled weakly and then embraced her gently, not letting her see the emotions that choked him. Then he picked the child up and held him close,

"He has your eyes you know", he was incapable of saying more.

"Are all the arrangements made?"

"We have found a respectable young childless couple, in a village about sixteen miles hence. He is a glove maker and leatherworker. They know nothing of the child's background other than he comes from a respectable background and they have been led to believe his father died in a hunting accident before the child was born, and his mother died during childbirth."

Feeling the emptiness inside he, she felt like saying 'indeed she did' but kept her thoughts to herself.

"But my dear, isn't there a way in which..........."

"No!" she shook her head sadly, "there is no other way. We have been through it many times. If word ever got out as to his true identity his life would be in constant danger. You know my family as well as I do. No, it must be done now. If it were done when 'tis done, then 'twere well It were done quickly: Now take him, go quickly, for the love of God!!"

Picking the boy up and hiding him under his coat he left. Alone she buried her head in her pillows and wept, wept until she felt she had no more tears left to weep.

Sak was perturbed. He had been researching his subject and found there was a body of thought that held that maybe William Shakespeare was not the author of the plays and poems attributed to him. There seemed to be three main contenders, Sir Francis Bacon, Christopher Marlowe, and the seventeenth Earl of Oxford. Sak felt that this belief was born out of intellectual snobbery, the sort of snobbery that questioned how the son of a glove maker, with very little education, could be capable of writing such great works of literature. He had set out with the idea of proving these doubters wrong, but, unlike many researchers who set out to prove a pet theory, he had an open mind and in so doing found he had stepped into a minefield.

The doubts he had expressed to the Reverend Osborne were growing stronger but there were other factors bothering him for which the English Master had no answer. Why for example, did Shakespeare, knowing that women were forbidden from appearing on the Elizabethan stage, feature women in so many of his plays, making them strong dominant characters? And why were so many of the male characters made to look weak and foolish? Not all, by any means, but enough to make him think and that made him want to have answers.

Once again seeking refuge beneath the oak tree he thought of as his, he found himself listening to Helge. Once again it was as if he was meeting him for the first time and like the first time they'd met, Helge assured him that no real harm would come to him, that time would be suspended while he was travelling, so he would not be missed. And once again, he warned him not to try to change history. Once again (though he didn't know it) Sak had no fear of this strange apparition and found himself trusting him implicitly. Their conversation then, for Sak anyway, took an unexpected turn.

"Well Sak your time at Dauntsey's is nearing its end and I doubt that we shall be meeting again...."

"What do you mean, again? Isn't this the first time we've met? I don't remember......"

Helge smiled kindly, "Shut your eyes."

Sak, without questioning or doubting, did as he was told; he saw an image of a young boy, slumped against an oak tree weeping. He sensed, rather than saw, that boy was himself. Eyes still shut, he 'watched' as Helge emerged from the Oak. This was followed by a parade of faces flashing by, Marcus, Cicero, Ona and Aelia. He knew them! He 'watched' again as the sun rose above the altar stone at Stonehenge, then the acrid smell of mustard gas assaulted his nostrils as for just a second he recalled the horrors of the Great War. For a brief moment he again witnessed the social injustices associated with the Industrial revolution. 'Wrong order', he thought. Then recalled that this was, in fact, the order in which he had experienced the different periods of time. He opened his eyes but said nothing, going over in his mind each of the sequences. He looked up at Helge.

"I remember, I've travelled back in time, sometimes with you, sometimes, on my own I think." Helge nodded.

Sak was trying to take it all in; after a few seconds thought he all of a sudden flushed, and said angrily "But that means all the work I subsequently did was not original, I might just as well have copied it all from a history book, you have cheated me!" The shock and anger shook him. He felt as if all the confidence he had gained over the years was slipping away, had his Father been right, was he just a worthless person?"

Helge, as ever, read his mind. "No Sak you are wrong, mustn't fly off into a tantrum like that without stopping to think, look at the harm it may already have caused you if I weren't here to reassure you. You are so far from worthless and have made such giant strides as a person of worth, that I have chosen now to reveal more of myself to you, and reveal to you our past history and Its purpose. It is no coincidence that I was freed from my prison in order to guide and assist you."

"Prison?"

"Prison indeed! The gods of Valhalla were displeased with me and I was imprisoned within that oak tree many years ago. I was told that the length of my sentence was to be determined by myself. For more than eight hundred years I languished in the darkness not knowing what I had to do to placate the gods I had offended. Then one day I not only heard you when you were in some distress, but I also understood what was troubling you. In that moment I saw daylight, felt the sun on my back and smelled the forest for the first time in nearly a thousand years. In those eight hundred years how many people do you think have passed through these woods? I certainly could not even guess at the number, but you alone were chosen."

He let the import of what he was saying sink in before continuing.

"You did not travel into the past and return knowing what you know without effort. You learnt to speak and write Latin, nobody gifted it to you. I was able to grant you the opportunity and you embraced it. At Stonehenge you saw what you had long believed but had been too timid and unsure of your own intelligence to voice. Likewise with the Industrial Revolution and the

First World War, I, and my gods, observed your empathy with the poor and the downtrodden, we observed you in the Memorial Gardens, overcome, and felt uncomfortable with the words 'Glorious Dead'. To allow you to voice your opinion without causing offence we allowed you to see for yourself the horrors and futility of war but what you articulated well was all your own work, your perspicacity, your depth of feeling.. Sak, you are worthy and deserving of all you have achieved."

"Thank you. I am sorry I reacted so badly. It was a shock, but now you explain it, I can understand better, and I am grateful. But why now, why show me now?"

"This most probably will be the last time I will be sending you on such a journey and I owe you a debt of gratitude. If I simply said thank you, you would have had no idea what I was talking about. But because you have responded, and benefitted, the gods in Valhalla have agreed my rehabilitation is well advanced. I believe my entry to Valhalla is almost certainly guaranteed."

Sak wanted to ask why Helge was not yet certain of his place in Valhalla, but he didn't know how to phrase the question and was scared of causing offence, so he said nothing. At Helge's insistence they embraced, then Helge was gone and Sak's memory of their discussion was blurred. Nonetheless, he was bemused when he found himself not in Stratford Upon Avon as he might have expected, his quest being William Shakespeare, but in the midst of a vast array of troops waiting to board the many ships lining the banks of the Thames obscuring the river altogether.

Something was bothering Sak, there was something strange about this crowd, it took him but a few moments before he realised what it was that was bothering him; it was the sounds he was hearing, he could hear the bird birds as well as the leaves of the trees rustling in the wind but from the gathered masses there was nothing but silence, Sak was reminded of the kind of reverent silence you feel on entering a Cathedral. Then someone started to speak, the voice was sharp, femine yet strong. He looked up, there before him was a great white horse clad in a white armour and astride the horse sat a slender woman, also clad in white, her only colour her mass of long red hair. It was the 9th of August 1588, although he did not know it, he was in Tilbury. He found himself, like the others about him, caught up in the words of the woman on the horse.

"My loving people, we have been persuaded by some that are careful of our safety to take heed of how to commit ourselves to armed multitudes, for fear of treachery. But I assure you, I do not desire to live to distrust my faithful and loving people"

The crowd, so silent a moment before, erupted at these words and were now cheering, some broke into spontaneous applause, Sak was spellbound, not so much by the words, grand as they were, but by the language used and the way it was spoken. ' I'm in Tilbury', he thought, 'and this is Elizabeth the First's famous speech. What a moment!'

"Let tyrants fear . I have always behaved myself that, under God, I have placed my chiefest strength and safeguard in the loyal hearts and good-will of my subjects; and therefore I am come amongst you, as you see, at this time, not for my recreation and disport, but being resolved, in the midst and heat of the battle, to live and die amongst you all; to lay down for my God, and for my Kingdom, and my people, my honour and my blood, even in the dust."

He found himself murmuring along with the next few words, he knew them well. All around her troops and gathered onlookers were in a frenzy of patriotic excitement.

"I know I have the body of a weak and feeble woman; but I have the heart and stomach of a King, and of a King of England too." More wild cheering, almost drowning out her next words,

"And think foul scorn that Parma or Spain, or any Prince of Europe, should dare to invade the borders of my realm: to which rather than any dishonour shall grow by me, I myself will take up arms, I myself

will be your general, judge and rewarder, of every one of your virtues in the field."

Of course Sak was familiar with this part of her speech, and most school children could quote the 'I know I have the body........' but why were they not taught the whole speech? For a moment he seemed to see a bigger picture in his mind, but it faded before he could quite capture it.

"I know already, for your forwardness you have deserved rewards and crowns; and We do assure you on a word of a Prince, they shall be duly paid. In the mean, time my lieutenant general shall be in my stead, than never whom a prince commanded a more noble or worthy subject; not doubting but by your obedience to my general, by your concording the camp, and your valour in the field, we shall shortly have a famous victory over these enemies of my God, my Kingdoms and of my peoples"

Judging by the reaction of her men, Elizabeth had reason to be satisfied that her speech had had the desired effect, the men had been inspired, their hearts a little stouter and their resolve strengthened, but to Sak it suddenly meant much more. He realised how cleverly it had been carefully crafted, its appeal to God, patriotism and the Queen herself was poetic in its nature. He recalled the germ of an idea that had fleetingly entered his head earlier. This speech had reminded him of another time when rousing rhetoric, at the right moment, had helped save Britain from being overrun by a different enemy. Somehow it called to mind Churchill's Blood, Sweat and Tears speech. And of course, his mind sped on, there was Henry V's inspirational speech to his men on the eve of Agincourt as written by Shakespeare. Henry had saved us from the French, Elizabeth saved us from the Spanish, and Churchill from the Nazi's - was there some pattern here, some deeper meaning? Then he laughed at himself, what was he thinking, divine intervention? Was there such a thing? Before he had time to follow this naive schoolboy theory he sensed those around him were stirring at some new happening. There was an excitement in the air. Elizabeth had dismounted from her horse and was walking amongst her troops just as her ancestor had done on the eve of another battle, she smiled at some, nodded at others but there was no exchanged words unti, as she was passing Sak, he heard himself shouting out "Great speech Ma'am; worthy of Sakakespeare himself."

Even as he flushed at his temerity, she had halted and was turning towards him, a look of bewilderment and, was it fear, on her face. The mention of Shakespeare appeared to have unsettled her. She looked at him straight for a moment then asked "Shakespeare young man, and what do you know of Shakespeare?"

Without thinking he replied, "Well I have read his plays, not all of them of course, but enough to know....." he stumbled to a halt, disturbed by the look on her face."

She said nothing, but her brows were furrowed, she stared at him for some minutes, then, turning on her heel, and walked away.

Sak shook his head in dismay. 'What an idiot!' He wasn't even sure of what date Shakespeare had started writing his plays, once again, he just hadn't been thinking, Shakespeare's plays he knew had not been published until 1623, seven years after his death, but when was the first one performed? But then, she must know of Shakespeare, why else had she stopped and questioned him. Was there a mystery here, something he might unravel, not known till now. 'Well, now in the future world, when I am back' he thought, hardly daring to believe it might be so. But for now, that was the least of his concerns.

Here he was , out of time, in a world he didn't know, alone and penniless in Tilbury. For the first time in his time travelling adventures he was at a loss to know what to do next, he felt abandoned by Helge. The dockside and streets were now virtually empty, the troops had embarked on to the many ships and the civil population returned to their homes and places of work. He had no idea what to do next. He wandered down to the riverside and leaning on a railing, he caught a glimpse of his reflection in the water. Until now he had given no thought to how he had fitted into the crowd without arousing undue interest, but now he saw he was clad in a dark blue velvet doublet and matching breeches, and a white ruff. Over this was a dark red cloak and a feathered hat. He looked down at his feet and saw black leather shoes with silver buckles. Momentarily forgetting his immediate worries he took pleasure in his fine clothes. This soon passed as he pondered his predicament. How did a penniless young man make do in this town.

Deep in thought, he was absent mindedly looking at the ships when he was suddenly aware of an approaching group of twittering young ladies. He turned to them, thinking here might be help, only to be overcome with embarrassment when he realised from their remarks they were prostitutes, propositioning him in the hope of making money for themselves. Aware now of the unsuitableness of his costume when he was penniless, and without any desire on his part to partake of what they offered, he stumbled over the attempt to explain that he had no money. He wasn't surprised they didn't believe him, he was horrified when they spat at him and hurled abuse.

He hurried away, scared they would follow him, worried their cat-calls would attract the attention of others. Luckily, at this point, a coach and horses pulled up outside a nearby inn, and the ladies of the night switched their attentions to the group of young bucks now descending. It was late afternoon and he needed to find a place to stay; he was tired, thirsty and hungry. Several times he hesitated outside a tavern, tempted to enter and ask for a glass of water, but each time he turned away, unsure of the custom of the times, whether a glass of water would be freely given. He couldn't risk drawing attention to himself.

Meanwhile Queen Elizabeth was indeed troubled by the young man's mention of Shakespeare. What could he know? How? She had intended to return to Havering Palace, but she wanted, needed to know more.

"I have changed my mind. Inform the Mayor we require a bed for the night."

Though surprised, her courtiers knew better than to question their sovereign and set off to arrange the requested accommodation.

When they were settled, she summoned Dr. Dee,

"Your Majesty, how may I please you?"

"John I am perplexed. I had a short conversation with a young man in the crowd who had shouted something out to me. I am curious. See what your men can find out about him. Do not approach, or speak to him, just observe, then report back to me and I will decide whether to take it further."

"Do you think he represents a danger to you Ma'am?"

"Strangely enough, I don't. I have no logical reason for thinking so, but I would that you do as I have asked!"

"As you know, Ma'am, your wish is my command. I trust that we will find him harmless."

"Do as I have commanded; and ensure no harm comes to him!"

Sak, preoccupied by his immediate needs, was unaware he was being shadowed, that a man dressed all in black had been observing him, had followed his aimless wanderings as he ventured away from the docks to explore the town itself. Then satisfied that there was no more to be gleaned from following him, he reported back to his master.

"It was passing strange, Sir. At first I thought he might be spying for the Spanish as he spent some time looking at our fleet"

"What made you dismiss this notion?"

"I say looking at the fleet, which he was, but I don't think he was seeing anything."

"Forsooth. You are speaking in riddles man."

"Forgive me sir, and hear me out. You yourself have instructed us, when on a mission we are to be alert, make sure we are not followed and ensure we do not stand out. All his actions were the opposite. At first I believed he was looking at our ships so I made it seem as if I was about to board one of the vessels and I turned to look. His eyes were as if lost in thought, he displayed no interest in what I or for that matter, any other person was doing.

When I followed him into town he hovered outside every tavern, would stare through the windows, wipe his lips as if he had just eaten or drunk something and then move on."

"Could he have been looking for someone do you think?"

"Maybe but not, I think, anyone who would be of interest to us. . I believe he is a young man, not yet twenty, from a good family and he has somehow become separated from them. They are probably out looking for him as we speak. Harmless to us I feel"

"Did you hear him speak?"

"No sir"

"Then you cannot be sure he is even English. I am disappointed in you, this is most unsatisfactory we shall speak further on this later!"

"But Sir....."

"Enough has been said. I am not persuaded the conclusions you have reached are necessarily so, but I am obliged to report your findings to her Majesty."

Regretfully he thought, his Monarch would probably side with his agent, but to Dr. John Dee nothing could be that simple, he would get to the bottom of it and protect his Queen from whatever evil was in the air.

As he had feared, Elizabeth was pleased with his agent's report but he felt he had to make his doubts clear.

"Oh John, you and your machinations, not everyone inhabits the murky world you do, by necessity sometimes inhabit. Without you I might well have lost my throne quite some time ago, so I am grateful that you sometimes inhabit that world. I have much reason to be grateful to you, Dr Dee. Now then, I will be more grateful if you would go and find the lad and bring him hither to me. By all means search him for hidden weapons but treat him with kindness and don't be rough."

Grateful as he was for her kind words, he was still a little disgruntled; he was used to the Queen's full attention, used to her following his advice. This deviation from the norm was unsettling, nevertheless he left to do as he was bid.

To his relief Sak had stumbled upon the town well where many had come to get fresh water. He had waited patiently as buckets and other vessels were filled and at long last it was his turn, but just as he was about to reach down and grab the rope he felt a sharp tap on his shoulder. Startled, he dropped the rope as he turned and he cursed as he realised his turn was lost. If he could he would have run from that place as fast as he could but his feet seemed rooted to the ground. He was confronted by three members of the Royal Guard, two of whom were pressing their pikes against his chest while the third patted him down,

"Good grief, I am being searched" he thought and for the first time, when out of his time, he was scared, very scared and the words of assurance Helge had spoken were of no comfort to him.

"You are commanded to come with us,"

"I am commanded by whom?" he asked, sounding bolder than he felt.

"It is not for us to know, we have been so ordered."

Sak found himself between the two armed guards, being marched away, destination unknown. Those gathered around the well had stopped what they were doing to watch. What could this young man have done to be arrested by members of the Royal Guard.

"Headed up river to the Tower" ventured one and Sak, had he heard, would probably have agreed.

The shock of being searched had made him feel guilty, of what he was unsure; it was much like being summoned to the Headmaster's office, one always feared the worst; but as he sank into a seat of the coach he began to think more rationally. The seats were of plush velvet, surely not to be expected if he was thought guilty of some crime or treachery. The guards had been more deferential than rough; they had given him space when they 'marched' him away and it now seemed to Sak that they might have been sent to protect, not arrest, him. Now he thought about it, he was sure there had been some kind of coat of arms painted on the coach. He wished he had taken more notice, but his insides had shrivelled with fear. Maybe all would be well, just as Helge had promised him.

Hesitantly he pulled back the curtain covering the window, but his escort seemed to have no objection. He looked out to see if he could work out where he was or get some idea as to where he was going but it was dark, and there were no street lights. 'And it wouldn't mean anything to you if you could see' he remonstrated with himself, 'you haven't been here before and so how could you recognise anything.' He lay back, feeling more relaxed, whatever would be, would be and there was little he could do about it. He thought back over the long, tiring and perplexing day, wondered if he dared ask for food and drink, not only was he tired, he was hungry and thirsty. Before he could formulate his request the tiredness had taken over and he drifted into a deep sleep.

Her Majesty had again changed her mind; it was not just bloody mindedness, at least, she didn't think so, but she did feel the need to be alone, as much as she ever could be, when she met this youth who had so unsettled her. Of course, she had no need to give explanations to the Mayor but the thought of having to be sociable with him, his family and the many others who would want to pay homage to her, would be not only an unwanted distraction, but would try her patience which could cause offence. She wanted, nay needed, to get to the bottom of that 'worthy of Shakespeare'. What could it mean, what did the youth know? So citing affairs of state. she made her apologies, thanked the Mayor for all he had done to make the day so memorable, unusually, she apologised in case she had caused the household any upset, and then departed,

Sak slept for the rest of the journey waking only when the coach jerked to a stop. he wondered for a moment where he was. He felt wretched, his mouth was dry, his breath, he was sure, was foul, he was desperate for something to drink. He peered out the window and was confused by what appeared to be lights in the sky, coming towards him. He stared as they came closer, and was about to duck, when it hit him! 'Idiot' he told himself, 'they are lanterns'.

And so they were, held aloft by a small group of people, their leader opened the coach door and escorted him from the vehicle. Then he was guided, stumbling a little, up wide steps leading to a portico and a large wooden door, which stood ajar.

In his dazed state his first impression was that he was being ushered into Colditz, a picture of which was on the front cover of the book he had been reading back in his own time-The Colditz Story. He could have laughed with relief when he was led into a vast hall, and given a seat at a long table, on which was food and drink. He ate and drank eagerly and felt somewhat better, but he was still tired, he was not sure what he had eaten and thought the drink might be beer, perhaps that was why he felt so woozy. The myriad candles, seemingly on every surface, and reflected in mirrors and the high uncurtained windows, dazzled and danced before his tired eyes.

He shook himself as he became aware someone was trying to get his attention. "If you could follow me....."

'What now' he wondered, following the man in black. As he entered through the double doors that had been opened for him, he was taken aback by the mass of people that confronted him. The noise was buzzing in his ears, but suddenly, as he caught sight the red-headed figure, things fell into place. Why, he wasn't sure, but for some reason his Shakespeare remark to the queen had piqued her interest. 'How could he have been so stupid?' He wondered once again when the first play had been performed. He ought to know. What year was it now? Shaken by these uncertainties, worried about maybe having to explain himself, unsure of what to do next, he looked about the long and narrow hall and it seemed every member of her court must be in attendance. But why, surely if he had been brought to this place on the instructions of Elizabeth because of what he now understood to be a totally foolish remark, it would make more sense for a private audience with her Majesty. And still the question remained, what did the name of an as yet presumably unknown man from Stratford-on-Avon mean to Queen Elizabeth the First of England?

Groups of people who had been in earnest conversation fell silent as he entered further into the room and he felt every eye upon him,

"Do you not bow before your Queen?"

Sak blushed, all eyes upon him, as he turned towards the shrill voice that had addressed him, such a diminutive figure with a mop of bright red hair. He could feel the sweat running down his neck as he bowed, then disturbed by a sudden thought that more was needed, went down on one knee. and mumbled an apology.

"Well young man, and who is it that stands before us?"
It took him a moment to realise she was still addressing him, and another moment to understand the question. In his confusion he blurted out his real name,

"Christopher, Ma'am."

"Well master Christopher, you think my speech worthy of Mr William Shakespeare, do you?" Embarrassed, he could only nod.

"Explain yourself, who are you and where do you hail from and how is it you are familiar with the works of Mr William Shakespeare?"

Sak had been expecting this question and had decided that the best way of answering would be to tell the truth, no more fake memory loss, no more lies, just the plain and simple truth. Aware that this risky strategy might bring him straight back to his own time he felt he had nothing to lose.

"Ma'am I am a traveller from afar, and the works of Shakespeare are studied at the school I attend."

An intake of breath from those in the room,

"Come sir, what nonsense is this you speak?"

The hint of anger in her voice stung Sak, and warned him that his next words would be critical. It was still his intention to be truthful, but he could not bring himself to answer, not in front of so many people. Praying that his history books were correct, and that she was indeed a linguist of note, he answered her in

Latin. Of course, many others there may also speak Latin, so he lowered his voice, addressing only her, yet speaking with an authority that shocked him, where had it come from. He couldn't imagine that he would have addressed Queen Elizabeth the Second so, nor, he thought, was he ever likely to have the opportunity to do so.

"Madam before I disclose to you that information, I beg that the room be cleared of all people other than yourself, and your closest advisor."

Her reply, as he had hoped, was in Latin.

"Who are you, who dares to give commands to your Queen? This is tantamount to treason. No doubt you are familiar with the penalty that incurs!"

Sak held his nerve, "Ma'am, it is the only way"

"You are either a brave young man or very stupid"

For quite some moments she studied the youth in front of her. He wondered what might be his fate. Yet all must be well, Helge had said it would be so. He must have faith, and hold his nerve. Elizabeth watching him, wondered what to do. Would it be weak to accede to his wishes, wishes, nay, demands more like. Yet it was in her own interests to have whatever was to be said to be said in private. She turned to the imposing elderly man next to her. He had long greying black hair and a face that had lived, tanned and lined, hazel eyes alert and intelligent. His long salt and pepper coloured beard and moustache gave an appearance of mystical wisdom. After a short but animated conversation he addressed those assembled;

"It is Her Majesty's wish that the room be cleared of all but myself and the youth known as Master Christopher. All guards and servants are to depart also."

From the tone in his voice he was not in agreement with Her Majesty's wishes and there was much muttering as the room was cleared, as if the people now dismissed wondered why they were there in the first place.

"Young man, meet my colleague and confidant, Dr. John Dee."

"Dr. Dee, your reputation goes before you, it is an honour to be in your company."

"What impertinence is this, what could you possibly know of me or my reputation."

"Doctor John Dee, Alchemist, Philosopher, Astronomer, Philosopher and Master Spy and..."

"Madam what sorcery is this? I beg you to have nothing more to do with this young man, I see the Devil's hand at work here."

"Hush my dear friend, now even more has my curiosity been piqued. Let him speak".

She nodded to Sak and he, giving a little bow, took his fate into his hands.

"What I am about to tell you must seem incredible, unbelievable, far beyond anything you could even imagine."

Dr John shifted uncomfortably in his seat, how many times had he begun a conversation in this manner when trying to discredit a rival. 'Hmph I recognise a liar when I hear one' he thought.

'Here goes', Sak thought, and took a deep breath, "As I said, I am a traveller, a traveller in time and space. In miles I have travelled a mere hundred miles to reach you, which is nothing remarkable, but in years I have travelled 375. Dr Dee, you queried how I knew so much about you. Three hundred and seventy five years into the future your name is still known," He paused, and smiled at the queen. "As of course, is yours ma'am. You occupy more pages in our history books than Dr. Dee but he is there. And not history books alone, novels are written of him, of you of you both. My knowledge comes from those books."

"Novels, what is this? History books I understand but novels...."

Luckily for Sak, before he could think of an explanation, Dr. Dee intervened.

"If that is true then you must, from our point of view, be able to predict the future. That could prove very useful to us." he mused.

"Indeed you would think so," Sak once again found himself having to explain what his hearers might find inexplicable. "It is true that I could tell you how things turned out, but those who brought me here have forbidden me to interfere with, or alter history..."

"Who are these who sent you?"

Elizabeth and Dr. Dee began to fade and Sak feared that his Elizabethan odyssey was at an end, then Helge stood before him, and he wasn't sure where or when he was.

"Sak, your desire to tell the truth came as a surprise to those occupying the hallowed halls of Valhalla, not to mention myself......"

Sak interrupted him, stirred by the implication as he saw it, of what Helge had said. "Why would I not tell the truth, I have learnt, through your help, that life is better when you don't have to live a lie you yourself have created."

"You didn't let me finish, but I take your meaning and I apologise. However, I feared I would be forced to return you to your own time, having had your last adventure through time. It seems I misjudged not only you, but also those of Valhalla; they applaud your actions and ask that you should tell all, from the very beginning, including what you learnt recently of my story."

"Really? What purpose can it serve to try to make them believe your story. I can't help feeling it makes my job more difficult. I feel I can convey my own experience but..."

"Let me ask you this. Before our paths crossed did you believe Valhalla was real, did you believe it existed at all?"

Sak almost laughed. "But that's my point. Of course I didn't, nobody does, not even in Scandinavia, it is the stuff of myths and legends."

"Ah, what do you think now?"

"What else can I think, but that it is real, when you stand here, when you have allowed me to travel through time, when you have changed my life. I have every reason to trust you and I do, so I believe it is the home of the souls of Viking heroes, of their gods."

"As you say, you are able to say that because you experienced the truth but that makes you a rare person. There are some who do believe, but they are not in the position that you are, to explain this truth. Those of Valhalla are wearied of being seen as mythical figures, of seeing their bravery and suffering being diluted into a 'Boys Own' adventure, and that the gods, Odin and Thor all the others seen as mere figments of imagination."

"So go, take this chance to tell our story as well as yours and make them believe."

"But might not that change history in some way, you said I must not do that."

"You are not, per se, changing history, you are spreading knowledge, what may come of that need not trouble you. This time we have shared, as usual, will not be counted. I return you to the point at which you left."

He was gone and he was back with the Queen and Dr. Dee. The queen's question hung in the air. "Who are these who sent you?"

"I will try and explain. Probably you see me as a young man, confident in himself, bold, knowledgeable even sure of himself. But that has not always been the case," and he began his story.

For three days they listened, some of the time over a meal, or while they walked in the gardens, unattended by any but Dr. Dee, who was their constant companion, as the queen wished it. For Sak it was a strange experience, he found he could read their faces, parts of the story, Helge's subterfuge, for example,

was something they seemed able to relate to, Dr. Dee even nodding in understanding. Telling of modern forms of transport, on the other hand, horseless carriages, machines that could carry people through the air to other continents, made them look at each other, shake their heads in doubt and at one point Dr. Dee definitely harrumphed. Nevertheless, Sak carried on, not stopping his narrative to try to persuade them, and although it was beyond their comprehension, Sak's simple words, told without undue pause for thought, was impressive, they found themselves not only involved in the story but believing him.
Dr Dee wanted to believe, knowing such technology could give him unprecedented power and prestige and his mind focussed on the problem of how to understand it, so that he could utilise it.

For Elizabeth it was different, she found his narrative easy to listen to, and she pondered its truth, taking the opportunity to study him as he spoke. The story had been engaging and told in a matter of fact way but suddenly, for her, it came alive as he was talking about his time in Aquae Sulis.

"....then there was Aelia, how could I let the girl I was in love with and her family suffer at the hands of Boudicca and the Iceni, I had to prevent them from going to London or at least try to, so I began to tell them who I really was and, suddenly, I was back in my own time."

"And you never learnt of their fate?" her usual strident tone was softened, she understood.

Sak was silent, overcome by emotion he was incapable of answering. He fingered the hag stones around his wrist. In that moment Queen Elizabeth saw that he spoke the truth..

She turned to Dr. Dee, "we have no need to hear more, I am convinced. Let Master Christopher enjoy the hospitality of our Court. Master Christopher you are my guest"

But your Majesty, we need more, we need detail, we need to know how these things work. What is the point of it, why is he here, if we can't benefit." He paused, struck by a thought, "unless it is not true, it is some plot to get him into the heart of court, we need proof."

"Proof, proof, what more do you need? Did you not hear his story, nobody surely could imagine such a tragic tale" then, as an afterthought she added "Not even the redoubtable Mr Shakespeare has written of young love with such passion," she stopped, a small smile on her face.

"But Romeo....," realising his error Dr. Dee managed to make it sound like a cough. Howeve, he had more to say.

,
"Madame, well may you have the body of a weak and feeble woman but, so it would seem, is your heart!"

"That is not worthy of you Sir, nor yet of me!" she snapped.

Sak cringed with embarrassment, and the feeling of guilt that crept over him made him hang his head.
"Dr. Dee, are you suggesting that love is a weakness? Do you not know, you poor man, that to recognise, acknowledge and accept love is one of the true strengths of mankind, an emotion that lifts us above the animal kingdom. To sneer at love is the weakness. I pity you, Dr. Dee."

There was no hint of a smile now on the lips of Elizabeth, and Dr. Dee seethed at the interference of this so called traveller in time.

Sak looked from one to the other in the uneasy silence that followed; his feelings getting the better of him, he burst out, "Your Majesty, ma'am, I do not want to come between you. I think Dr. Dee does feel, he feels for you and wants to protect you. But I know you, I have read much about you, you are truly worthy of the position you hold."

"Master Christopher, I marvel at your eloquence and wisdom, in one still young. Maybe you bring the wisdom of your times with you. To leap to the defence of your monarch is most laudable but..."

"If he is to be believed, then you are not his monarch" interruptrd Dr. Dee.

"He is an Englishman in my court and I am indeed his monarch. But come, John, do not be angry or envious of Master Christopher. You heard him; he defended not just my majesty, but yourself also. Does that not give you faith? Your known position in my court is certain, and we know also, thanks to Master Christopher, that it is also in history certain.

Sak decided this was not the moment to reveal some of the more dubious theories about Dr. Dee that he had read.

Dr. Dee was not appeased. "But that is my point, Ma'am, it all rests on this man, or should I say, on this boy, being who he is purporting to be."

"Enough John, I am satisfied. It is my desire that you and Master Christopher should trust each other, and hopefully be friends.

Dr. Dee, with his thirst for knowledge, still had many questions. It would be stupid to alienate this boy if he could enlighten him in any way. He held out his hand to Sak, who shook it willingly.

Some few days later the three of them were strolling through the Palace Gardens.

"You say that your time travelling guide, Helge is it? always seems to sense your needs and takes you to times that will help solve problems or issues you are having difficulties with?"
Sak nodded.

"Why are you here?"

"In truth, Ma'am, I have no idea. There are things about William Shakespeare which to my mind, don't add up, I hoped that I would spend some time with him to learn."

Seeing his queen's unease at the direction the conversation was taking, Dr. Dee hastened to intervene. "What is this preoccupation witht an obscure poet from Stratford upon Avon?"

Sak wanted to laugh, 'obscure poet? Hardly!' Surely Shakespeare hadn't yet had any of his plays performed, and none were published until after his death. Yet not only did Dr. Dee seem to have some knowledge of him, the Queen appeared to know more, after all, he wouldn't be with her now if not for his incautious mention of Shakespeare. He would have thought that the good doctor with his network of agents would have more information on Shakespeare than Elizabeth. Then it struck him that he was learning more about Shakespeare, not as he had expected to, but yes, this could be very rewarding.

Dr. Dee interrupted his thoughts, "Tell me Master Christopher, do you think you are the only traveller in time?"

"I have no way of knowing Sir, but I cannot imagine that I am. I am not that special."

"So, in your opinion anybody could do it?"

"Theoretically I suppose so."

"Ma'am, what say you we do some time travelling?"

The queen laughed, happy at the change of subject from William Shakespeare, so often in her thoughts.

"Do you think then, John, that we can do so. I have a mind to explore the New Elizabethan Age Master Christopher has described. Master Christopher, summon your Viking!"

"I would that I could, ma'am. I have no such power; just as I have no say as to the place in time I am taken to. Ma'am I have only ever travelled backwards in time. I am not sure it is even possible to take a glimpse into the future."

"You are wrong Master Christopher for you have already given is such a glimpse."

"He's got you there." The garden was filled with their laughter as they continued their evening walk.

Elizabeth had sent Dr Dee on a spurious errand to Devon, (to look for an Egyptian cat?) in order that she could spend some time alone with Vala. Her preferred venue was the Gloriana, the

Queen's Royal barge, which she believed offered the most privacy away from prying eyes and ears of any agent Dr. Dee might have planted around the place. It was a warm, balmy summer day, the river calm, perfect for a romantic interlude, which is how some of Dee's agents, whom he had indeed put in place, interpreted it but it was romance of a different kind that was on her mind.

“Master Christopher, whilst you fascinate me with your tales of time travel, you have unsettled me for reasons which I am unsure whether to reveal to you. I have yet to decide. But I do know why your Helge sent you here to my court in your quest to understand William Shakespeare. Can you explain to me why he is so important to you?”

“It's not just me ma'am, he is important to the whole of the English speaking world, no, much more than that., he is the most translated author in history. His works are read and performed in all the countries you could name as well as in countries whose existence you don't even know. He is acknowledged as the greatest playwright of all time. As far as we know he wrote his first play at 24 and his final work when he was 49. That is thirty eight plays in just twenty four years, and as well there are over one hundred and fifty sonnets and countless other poems! When I thought about that it made me curious. How can he have managed it.”

‘Thirty eight plays is it, that's interesting, she thought to herself. Sak noticed a wry smile, and wondered why.

“There are also other aspects that intrigue me, not least his understanding of the human psyche.”

“Psyche, what is that. No, wait, psyche, from the Greek, “the soul, mind, spirit, or invisible animating entity which occupies the physical body. And you find this in Shakespeare?”

“Umm, understanding the human mind at least, how and why we think as we do, what it is that governs our actions.”

“Do all people of your time think as you do, and know so much?”

"There are many who far exceed my knowledge, Ma'am, I just remember what I have been told or have read."
"You talked about his plays being performed in many countries, what is the theatre like in your time?"

"Do you mean the buildings, they are many and varied, and talk is of one being built, the design of which is copied from that of Shakespeare's time. If it is ever built it will be as close to the site of Shakespeare's original as possible. The Globe?" Elizabeth shook her head.

"Ma'am, as to performances, most of his plays are performed as written, although there are a number of differences, most notably being that women are allowed on stage, and have been for over a hundred years, so all his female characters are played by women, so in many plays, such as Viola in Twelfth Night, Viola is played by a woman, masquerading as a man, falling in love with a man rather than a man, who is dressed as a woman pretending to be a man, falling in love with another man."

"That surely alters the dynamics of the drama; I would have thought" she replied, "surely lots of the humour must be lost, I'm not sure I could approve of that!"

Sak felt that much of what he tried to describe was lost on the Queen, mainly, he felt, because of his inability to explain it clearly. To somebody whose only source of artificial light was the candle, the concept of electricity was almost unfathomable though she was excited by and could envisage the lighting which resulted.

"But your Majesty, the one thing that cannot be changed or bettered are the words, the poetry, the rhythm. That is the glory of Shakespeare,' that nature might stand up and say to all the world, this was a man!'" He couldn't resist declaiming those last words.

"So history has treated him kindly then?" she almost purred, then again the wry smile. 'For what do I want to be remembered?' she questioned herself, 'to have been a great monarch, remembered through the ages, or for...' she shook her head and listened to Sak's reply.

"On the whole yes, but there are a few doubters."

She frowned, "doubters, In what sense?"

Sak wondered about her response, why should it matter so much to her?

"As I mentioned, there are some people who don't think he wrote the plays, that someone else did."

She shifted uneasily in her seat, "and who are these doubters?" "People who have studied English, and Shakespeare in particular, who consider themselves experts. Mostly men, and some women, those from privileged backgrounds who have had the best of educations, they think to themselves, 'I couldn't have written these plays, maybe the poetry, but how could a country boy from a humble background and little education, in the narrower Tudor age, forgive me Ma'am, but so it seems in our century, how could he write such plays, have so much knowledge of a wider world."

"They think then that our world is narrow; how is this? Do those history books of yours not tell you of great doings, exploration, travel? They know nothing then, are ignorant of the facts..."

Sak, seeing her agitation, worried he had upset her. "But most reject the idea, see it as nothing more than intellectual snobbery"

"Hmph! So if not William, whom then do they consider the true author?"

Sak again wondered why she seemed so concerned, why did it matter so much to her?

"Christoper Marlowe has quite a few adherents....."

"Nothing but a ruffian" she interrupted, "he had some talent and showed promise, but was killed in a tavern brawl I believe. Any other contenders?" her voice again strong and resolute and her face regained its colour."

"It is also thought that he was one of your spies, Ma'am" Sak said slyly, watching her face. She looked amused, but said only "and who else, pray?"

Sak paused, as he sought to remember exactly who else, whose names would mean something to her. "The Earl of Oxford is one, and Francis Bacon, Ma'am"

"Interesting suspects that I can understand. Intelligent men both, and both write well, but with little imagination" she damned with faint praise. "And who else, pray?"

Another name dangled in front of his eyes, but he dared not speak it, who knew how she would react.

"None ma'am, not that I can think of, not names that would mean anything to you."

"Don't be so sure of that.". She stared at him intently for some moments, sure that he was holding something back; 'leave it for now' she thought, 'I will return to it later if it seems necessary.' They had been on the river for a couple of hours and there had been little conversation for the latter part of their journey, both lost in their own thoughts but finding time to enjoy the water, the sights and the occasional wildlife. Sak was recalled from his thoughts when the rhythm of the oarsmen slowed and then ceased altogether.

"Lift oars off thwarts!" At the shouted command of the coxswain he turned his head and his attention was caught as the eighteen oarsmen raised their oars to the vertical and allowed the vessel to drift towards the river bank where men on shore grabbed the ropes thrown to them in order to secure the barge.

"Hungry, Master Christopher?" He had almost forgotten about his companion, so lost in the moment he had been, but he instantly realised he was hungry, hot and thirsty.

"Indeed I am Your Majesty"

"Shall we then enjoy a picnic"?

Sak's heart sank; he had visions of tramping over Hampstead Heath with his parents and sisters, of a tatty table cloth spread on the grass and trying not to gag on the roast beef sandwiches his mother had prepared, which seemed to be made up of pure gristle. He could see and hear as his Father, open mouthed, chewed lustily on his sandwich, (of lean meat) while shouting at Sak for being so ungrateful, 'you would never have survived the war if you had been that fussy back then' his father's voice echoed in his mind. He remembered the flies and wasps.... Please God, let it be better than that, was his silent prayer as he stepped gingerly from the boat, then raised his eyes and looked about him.

He almost laughed with joy when he took in the sight before his eyes. This was no picnic as he knew it, this was an open air banquet, just for the two of them. There were footmen in full livery there to greet them. A refectory table had been brought especially from the nearby Hampton Court. Sak had a mental image of the footmen manhandling it across the meadows. It was laden with foods of all kinds, venison, partridge, pheasant, chicken and duck, there were breads, butter and cheeses, (those last three alone would have sufficed, mused Vala) along with assorted vegetables and fruits. Again, he had an unwarranted vision of the table being manhandled, this time already spread with the repast, oh, how he wished it had been so and he could have seen it.

A selection of wines had been prepared but Sak was relieved to see jugs of water on the table, much to Beram's disappointment Sak had no liking for wine, but Beram considered water to be the drink of monkeys, goats and apes!

Sak was ushered into a seat opposite the Queen. The servants were unobtrusive, almost invisible, but no sooner one plate was cleared or a glass emptied it was immediately replaced by another.

Conversation seemed to flow more freely than hitherto. More, thought Sak, like two friends chatting, joy and laughter were in the air. It was an idyllic, carefree afternoon and Sak felt that for the first time he was seeing the real Elizabeth, not Elizabeth the Queen but Elizabeth the person. Similar things seemed to make them laugh and Sak felt emboldened to share his vision of the laden table chuntering across the meadow.

"Do you want to see it so?" said Elizabeth, obviously prepared to order that it should be done. Sak burst out laughing, and so did she. So the afternoon progressed. Sak had eaten of his fill, but every now and again would take another small bunch of grapes or some cheese. At the queen's insistence he tried a small glass of wine but secretly found it more even less enjoyable than the wines of his own times, and after a swallow or two he choked, and resorted to his glass of water. The queen laughed at him, "you are but a lad, in truth" she said, "but a game one. Drink your 'wine'; they call it Adam's ale, after all."

Towards evening she suggested they take a walk and as they strolled along the banks of the Thames, Sak was surprised to feel her arm slip through his,

"So tell me, Master Christopher how does history treat me?"

"History treats you well, ma'am, we look back on your reign as a golden era, an age of discovery, of power and wealth. If you were to ask people in my time to name three English monarchs, your name would always be one of those three. You are seen as the greatest Tudor of them all, surpassing even your Father."

"That's all very well and gratifying to hear, but it's not what I wanted to hear." She turned to face him, her eyes searching his, her voice softened, "what I really want to know is what they think of me, when they hear my name, what do they think, what do you think. How am I remembered?"

Sak looked at her, 'she may be a queen,' he thought, 'but she's just like other people, she's vulnerable, she wants to be admired, but maybe also liked.' He started his answer "Elizabeth, the Virgin Queen........"

She pulled away from him and started to laugh, a low laugh rising to a higher pitch as her shoulders drooped; she began to shake and her laughter turned to tears.

"That's it? All I have done for England, all the sacrifices I have made, all the difficulties I have overcome that would have daunted so many, and I am immortalised for being a virgin, a failure as a woman. Master Christopher, you have darkened my mood." Before he could say more, enlarge on his statement, she turned from him and summoned a servant to accompany her to Hampton Court, leaving Sak alone on the river bank.

Sak was desolate, what had he said to cause such a response. He had fully intended to continue, to say how men rallied to her, but she had interrupted him, What was he to do now? It was evening, and once again he had no roof over his head. Momentarily, he wished he had stuffed his pockets with some of that food that was now being hurriedly packed away. Embarrassed in the presence of the busy servants, he turned idly and walked away beside the darkening river.

Back in the Palace Elizabeth was reconsidering her abrupt response to the idea of herself being mainly remembered as a virgin, feeling perhaps she had been too harsh on the young man, she had interrupted him not giving him a chance to expand on his statement. After all he was, as she had, said earlier, still just a lad, obviously not totally unschooled in the ways of love, there was, after all, his account of Aelia but his experience was narrow, how could he know that the thought of being known as unfulfilled as a woman had cut her to the quick. Young Master Christopher was probably bewildered by her actions.

Sak was sitting in the dark of the evening, under one of the many weeping willows growing along the river bank, his back against the trunk. Reverting to his old self, he felt he had probably just messed things up once again. His knowledge of Shakespeare was just as it had been when he had found himself in Tilbury, he was no further ahead and no doubt had wasted this opportunity, no doubt he would soon find himself back in his own time.

As he sat there waiting he was overcome by a sense of deja vu. There were three orange coloured balls of light dancing in the sky. Where had he seen that before? Oh yes, it seemed so long ago, from the coach as he first arrived at the palace. And they had turned out to be lanterns, and rescue. As he watched they slowly increased in size and yes, his heart rejoiced, they were lanterns, was it possible they were looking for him? Quite close now he saw the form of three figures, thought he heard his name called and shouted an answer. The lights came to a standstill and he could discern the three bearers, apparently in earnest conversation. Two of them were gesticulating, sending shadows flying out across the ground, 'shadow puppet' thought Sak, before they turned and walked away, leaving the third man, who now approached him

"Master Christopher." He was overcome, the Queen herself had come to find him. Together they returned to the Palace.

Morning found her walking alone in the Palace Gardens. She had been perturbed and had little sleep. Should she unburden herself, reveal the secret she had kept so long. Could she, should she, trust him?
"Be assured, madame, you can!"

Amazed and alarmed by the voice that had answered her thoughts, she turned and saw there before her a stranger.

"I would not have brought him to you if he was not trustworthy."

She studied him for some time. "You are Helge?" she ventured."

"I am he, Madam."

"An unexpected pleasure, Sir."

He gestured to her and she sat with him on a wooden bench under a large oak. Helge looked up into the leaves, and thought many thoughts. Then he turned to the Queen and asked how he could be of service to her. They sat and talked long into the afternoon until Helge had managed to assure Elizabeth she could trust Master Christopher, as she called him, totally. It was when Helge was about to take his leave when she asked Helge if it was true, as Master Christopher had told it, that Helge's final freedom lay in his hands.

"Simply put, yes, that is so."

Then you are more fortunate than I, for there is no release for me. I may be ruler of all I survey but there is no freedom from the prison that is my life. I will reveal my secrets to Master Christopher, as we have agreed, but I beg of you, are you able, will you, give me a taste of the freedom my heart desires? Is it possible you can enable me to experience the new Elizabethan Age of which Master Christopher speaks."

"On that I will need to consult" and with those words he was gone.

OBVERSE

At dinner one night Beram brought his atlas to the table and pushed it in front of Christopher, the British Isles stared him in the face, "What country is that?" Beram demanded, trying not to laugh.

"I've been here before" Christopher thought, but that was long ago, what's going on now?"

He laughed along with Vera and Beram, but the moment felt uneasy in some way.

"It's been a long journey for you and not always an easy one, we realise that, but as this part of the journey ends, we just want to say well done, we are proud of you."

It was 1963 and Chris had just completed his penultimate term at Dauntsey's and was spending the final part of his holidays at the flat. Until Beram had mentioned 'this part of the journey ends', he had not had any idea that this might be his final holiday there, he thought it had been a slip of the tongue, until Vera had said to him, "Would you like to put your things in the spare room?"

His memory went back to his first day, his joy at being given his own room. Rightly or wrongly, he had come to consider that this was where he belonged, he had been, still was, proud to be seen as part of these two people whom he loved beyond all others. Now, suddenly, without notice, it seemed he was again just another nephew. He silently rebuked himself for having thought otherwise. But then, why shouldn't he? No one had told him anything, he was given no choice, how could he judge. So, no more excuses, time to face up to facts! Now he knew.

What, he wondered of the friendships he had formed, the Crichtons in the next door flat, especially Elizabeth, then there was

Christopher Swain and Ruth Barns who lived in the top floor flat, what a quartet they made sharing many adventures, fishing on Hampstead Heath, swimming together, going for bicycle rides, as well as some memorable birthday parties, were these friendships destined to end also?

"......So what do you think of that ?"

Vera's question jolted him back to the present.

"I'm sorry, I didn't catch what you were saying, I was miles away."

"Do I still need to pull your ears to make you concentrate?" More laughter and again Chris joined in, although hethought it unwarranted, and not in the least funny.

"I was just saying the Crichton's have decided to live in Greece; Gordon, Catherine and Ian are there now looking at houses, leaving Elizabeth to mind things here."

He was a few weeks shy of his eighteenth birthday and it alreadt seemed to him life as he knew it had just ended. All the things he cared about were being stripped away.

"It would be good to see her, Liz,I might go round after dinner."

Beram and Vera exchanged looks.

"What? Why are you both looking like that?".

"There's something rather odd going on, at least, it seems so to us." Vera went on to explain that Liz had a distant relative staying with her, she seems rather, rather, I guess odd about describes it."

"In what way odd?"

"It was a few days after the others had left; Liz answered the door to this woman, a complete stranger to her, asking for Gordon, at least, Mr. Crichton, saying she was a distant cousin. She claimed she was from Foula..."

"Foula, where is that? I've never heard of it"

"Not surprising, neither had we."

"Not even you, Uncle Beram?" asked Chris, surprised there was something that Beram didn't know.

"I know now. No point in loading your brain with information you don't need. Once you have a need for it, seek it out. Which is what I did. It turns out Foula is part of the Shetland Isles, the most western of the islands and possibly the most remote part of Britain, end of the world some say. Liz told this woman her father was away and to come back in a few weeks. Apparently she became quite agitated, said she had no money and no documentation to prove who she was. Liz was about to call the police but then this so called cousin started talking about the family in a most familiar way, mentioning episodes, knowledgeable of some of their most intimate details. The really surprising thing is, at least to us, she also knows about you!"

"Me!, what could she know about me? I certainly don't know her."

"To be more precise, she knew of you and how close you and Liz were, growing up, which Liz reasoned could only have come from her father so, as she said, it seemed easiest to let her stay."

"How long has she been there then?"

"Just a few days, but Liz tells us that her behaviour is very strange, verging on the bizarre. She seems very unworldly, spends most of the day looking out of the window at the traffic on Highgate Road muttering to herself, seems frightened of electricity, not daring to touch the switches and the first time Liz put the television on she could not take her eyes away asking 'what magic is this?'"

"Most odd. Do they have electricity on Foula?"

"I believe not, nor I think has the motor car yet arrived on the Island, which would go a long way in explaining her behaviour but the most bizarre thing of all, she says she has no memory of how she got here, according to her story her only memory is finding herself at Liz's front door."

But that doesn't make sense; she remembered she was a member of the family you
said."

"Well" said Vera, "You can make your own mind up, she has expressed a wish to see you, (a wish that Vera had felt was more of a command!) so they are coming for dinner tomorrow night."

Chris spent much of that morning in the kitchen with Vera as she made preparations for dinner; time alone in the kitchen with her had been such a central part of his life prior to Dauntsey's and memories of happy times filled his mind. Oddly, he thought one of his happiest moments had been when something, he could not remember what, had upset him. Vera, sitting in front of the open range, bade him sit on her knee and pour his heart out. Why he was unsure but he cherished that moment as one of his happiest moments. For the present it was as if time stood still and yesterday's conversation, which had made him feel cut off, had never happened.

His main focus was on Vera and the meal she was putting together - coq au vin, his favourite, but he also spent much time at the kitchen window which looked directly into the Crichton's flat. He wanted to catch a glimpse of the strange woman next door.

"What do you suppose this woman wants with me? She can't possibly know me, I have never been to Scotland..."

"We are all curious, but be patient, I am sure all will be made clear this evening. Now stop gazing out that window and make yourself useful, peel the potatoes and then shell some peas!"

But all was not made clear, if anything her visit muddied the waters. Chris answered the door to Elizabeth's knock and they greeted each other warmly,

"Chris this is...." She got no further as the figure behind her pushed her rudely out of the way and swept into the hallway,

"I am Elizabeth's cousin Bessie, you I presume are her friend Chris," she looked at him for a few moments, "hmm, you appear younger than I had thought, Master Christopher."

"But nobody has called me that since I was ten years old!" Even as he said it, he had a weird feeling that it was not so, but he shrugged it off.

"Never mind that, from now on, to me, you are Master Christopher!"

Dumbfounded, he could think of nothing more to say. He ushered them both into the sitting room and watched her obliquely as Beram offered them drinks. Physically she was a diminutive figure not much over five feet tall, he reckoned, with auburn hair piled high on her head to give the illusion of height, yet she didn't need that to give her a presence; there was a confidence about her that for some reason he had not expected. She was not quite the batty woman Beram and Vera had described. He could see what Vera had meant about her issuing commandments rather than asking or making suggestions.

He had, as Beram had advised, looked up Foula in the Encyclopaedia Britannica. He discovered it had a population of about 36; was she perhaps the Grande Dame, like that woman on Sark, which might account for her somewhat imperious manner. It didn't, though, account for the state of her teeth, which horrified him. They were yellow and black and appeared rotten. Uneasily he turned away and made to close the curtains to shut out the night, as well as to muffle the sound of the rain. She restrained him, a hand on his arm.

As tactfully as he could he withdrew his arm and asked "Would you like a drink?" She did not answer, she seemed distracted by the reflected patterns the vehicle lights were making on the road. Eventually an uneasy silence was brought to an end by Beram summoning them to the dining table.

Yet that was no relief. It was surreal, rather like a farce. Beram, in his role of genial host, accustomed to holding forth and bringing everyone into the conversation, found it difficult to engage his guest in any meaningful conversation. Elizabeth too tried her best, bringing up subjects of conversation relating to her family, to things she and Chris had done in the past, and suggesting he should visit them in Greece when they were settled. Bessie appeared to remained oblivious, she seemed to lack the most rudimentary of social skills, or even manners. She was apparently fixated on Chris, staring intently at him, looking to no one else. Out of the blue and apropos of nothing that anyone else could see she said "Master Christopher, I believe the nearby heath has some pleasant walks."

"Yes indeed, it is one of my favourite places in London. Liz and I go there a lot when we are both home….."

"We will go walking there tomorrow morning."

A bare statement, an order, but one he couldn't see how to refuse without sounding rude and he wasn't prepared to be rude, despite her behaviour. When it was time for Liz and her guest to leave, somewhat earlier than was usual, Liz thanked Vera for the dinner, 'delicious as always' but Bessie said nothing, stalking away, unaware of how ridicu;ous she seemed.

Early the next morning Chris and his odd companion were seated on a bench by one of the three large ponds; Chris thought he had detected a change in Bessie, she seemed somehow softer, less domineering, older and a little shrunken. For some moments they just sat there in silence. Then another of those abrupt commands "Look into my eyes!"

Taken by surprise, he turned and stared at her. A change was taking place. Her poise became more assured, her eyes were alive, practically shooting sparks and the ill-fitting clothes miraculously, were something befitting royalty. His recognition was immediate, initially not as someone he knew personally, but from pictures from history. Then, like a mist lifting to reveal what had been hidden, his mind began to clear,

"Your Majesty!"

"Yes Master Christopher, it is I. Let me tell you of the strange event that led to this masquerade." 'No beating about the bush then' thought Chris, even as she continued "The morning after our picnic, do you remember it? I was up early and taking a stroll in the gardens when I was confronted by a stranger. A stranger and yet I knew him, yes I knew him because you had described him so well, it was your Helge..."

His head was spinning, this was all too much, this was not as it was meant to be. But then, what was it meant to be. He had no idea. The queen was still speaking.

"You see, he understood and sympathised, empathised even, with my plight. Whether you know it or not, you, by being you, are Helge's salvation, his ultimate freedom rests with you. I have no such saviour here on earth, in my life there is no hope of respite, my life is damned by duty, it will never be my own. I was overcome with curiosity about the new Elizabethan Age of which you spoke, and I longed for something just for myself, Helge and the gods of Valhalla have granted my request so long as you are my guide. For just a short while I have the opportunity to be myself."

"Ma'am, I apologise for asking, but is your true self really the rather, er, obnoxious woman I met yesterday?"

"I do sincerely hope not; I am more somewhat disappointed that you should entertain such thoughts. No, that was Helge's idea, a subterfuge. He explained that taking someone into the future, especially a notable figure from history, is fraught with various dangers. For instance, Helge told me your Uncle Beram is a highly educated and very intelligent man, a poet of note as well as an artist, but more than that he is a student of history and that gives him an insight others don't necessarily have. Helge also informed me he is a man my friend John Dee would have been proud to know, as he too worked in intelligence. During the last great European conflict he interrogated foreign agents.."

"Are you sure? I never knew that."

"Fearing there was a possibility that Beram would unearth the truth, Helge suggested the persona you saw, so weird a character that Beram would be distracted until I had the opportunity to make myself known to you."

"Calling me Master Christopher was not so clever then, was it?"

"Oh, but I could not resist it. Anyway, you did not discern it. In our, or rather, in my time, you came over as an assured, confident young man, but yesterday you seemed more a callow youth."

"So where do we go from here?"

"Show me your world, Master Christopher, if you would. It is what I have come for."

"Indeed ma'am, willingly. But before that, I feel there are amends that need to be made. I am sure you would wish to make some apology for your rudeness of yesterday evening, I assure you, whatever the rationale you had, your behaviour was unacceptable."

"It worked though, didn't it. Nevertheless, if that is what you advise, but how?"

They walked and talked, enjoying all the heath had to offer, from children flying kites on the top of the hill to the abandoned dairy. It was early evening when they arrived back at the flat. Beram had just returned from work and the atmosphere was understandably frosty, the more so when Sak left her alone with them while he went to fetch Elizabeth.

"Why didn't you bring her back here? The way she treated your aunt was totally unacceptable, you shouldn't subject her to that again."

"Trust me Liz, just come to our flat, I promise it will be alright."

She looked at him in some surprise, but went with him. When they were all together he looked around, wondering quite how to say what he had to say. "I think last night was a bit uncomfortable and out of place for all of us. I have discussed it with Bessie, and she would like to say something, so if you could all give her another chance. Bessie, the floor is yours.."

Beram smiled to himself in satisfaction. Maybe his ambitions for Sak may yet be realised.

Everyone turned to look at Bessie, who suddenly seemed to shrink before them, she looked uncertain and vulnerable, but then she pulled herself upright. "My behaviour these past few days has been most regrettable and I am genuinely sorry for that. I make no excuse for there is none that you could understand, nor should you be expected to. Elizabeth, you took me into your home on my word alone and made me welcome, yet I showed no gratitude and was concerned only with myself." She smiled at Elizabeth, slightly shaking her head. Elizabeth smiled back at her. How had Chris produced this miracle?

Bessie turned to Vera. "This afternoon Master Christopher has spoken much about you, your generosity of spirit and generosity of time you have for anyone in need. He obviously values you most highly. So I hurt not only you but him also when last night I virtually ignored you and treated you little better than a servant, and made no thanks for the delicious meal you laid before me. He tells me any good in him comes from you. And Beram.." she looked over at him, "Beram, there is so much to admire, you tried valiantly to remain the genial host and yet I was rude and dismissive. I admired your patience, though you could not know it. I have said there is no excuse and yet I want to try and explain why I behaved in such a manner."

Chris looked askance, she had already said there was no excuse they could understand, where was she going with this?

"My life on Foula bares no resemblance to the way life is lived here. I suppose it's as if time travel was possible and someone from the Elizabethan age was suddenly transported to the modern age, how alien they would feel..."

Chris shook his head at her, this was off script, not what had been agreed on.

Bessie continued. "Well that's exactly what it feels like to me, everything is new to me, our source of light is candles, we cook over open fires, there are so few people on our island. No ship brings newspapers, we travel by horse, donkey or bullock, no horseless carriages. I did not know such another world as this existed and then something happened, I found myself here, alone, frightened and lost...."

"So how did Gordon get in contact?"

"He didn't Elizabeth, I lied, another thing for which I can only apologise. Do you remember you once wrote about your family, about your love for Master Christopher and put it in a bottle?"

looked guiltily at the others, blushing at the memory. "It sounds so foolish now. I was very young."

"I found that bottle and reading your message, I wanted your life, and to know Master Christopher. Luckily for me, though not for you, you had included your address, no doubt hoping for a reply from whoever found the letter in the bottle. Here I am, I am the reply, I am sorry..."

There was a silence, then everyone began to talk at once, questioning Bessie about her life on Voula, about her journey, questions she managed to cope with very well.

Later that night as they lay in bed Vera turned to Beram, "Well what did you make of Bessie's latest story?"

"Didn't believe a word of it. But when you come to think of it, she does have a remarkable resemblance to Elizabeth 1st. Perhaps she really is a traveller in time."

They laughed at the absurdity of the idea.

Chris had just three weeks to introduce Good Queen Bess to the life lived under the reign of her cousin, (albeit fourteen times removed) and one who bore her name, before he returned to school for the last time. Something he hadn't expected and which amazed him was her easy acceptance of much of modern life, the horseless carriage which that first night had so intrigued her, in all its forms delighted her. Somewhat annoyed at having to queue for her first bus journey, once on board she positively bounded up the stairs to the top deck and crowed at getting the front seat, delighting in the views. Until she thought they had come too near a bus in front, and would crash into it. But she was soon diverted by being able to peek into someone's bedroom. Chris was only thankful that the person was fully dressed. The Tube was an exception, the noise, the speed and the crowds seemed to terrify, and one trip was more than enough for them both.

Chris had the bright idea, he thought, of taking her to see some familiar landmarks and they went to the Tower of London and Hampton Court. But she hated them. They are dead" she exclaimed, "they have no life, and are devoid of any purpose, horrible, horrible." Chris was touched when the sight of her father's armour did seem to move her, and she ceased talking and commenting for a while.

For many years Vera would, every Thursday drive south of the river to visit her Mother in Croydon; visits Chris had always enjoyed when he was able to go too. So he was pleased when Vera asked "Why don't you ask Bessie if she would like to accompany us today. She seems about the same age as my mother, they might enjoy each other's company."

'Grandma Matthews' greeted Bessie warmly, and behaved as a graceful hostess, to the manner born. Bessie, to do her justice, tried hard but they found very little in common so conversation was strained. The afternoon tea was delicious, and Bessie was effusive in her thanks, so all ended more or less well. It was as they were approaching Westminster Bridge that Vera, as she had often done in the past, suggested on impulse a visit to the theatre.

"I wonder what's on at the Old Vic, it's close by and I thought if Bessie liked the idea, I know you do Chris, we could stop by.

What do you think, Bessie, would you like to see a play? They are known for their Shakespeare productions."

Bessie responded with obvious excitement, "that would be lovely, thank you."

But she was taken aback, used to the rowdiness of the Globe audience she felt ill at ease in the dignified, respectful atmosphere of the Old Vic. 'Were these people not here to enjoy themselves?' she wondered to herself. As they were making their way to their seats she was amused by the snippets of conversations she overheard, some dissecting the play, discussing Shakespeare's motives for writing it, others questioning the the choice of an an Italian director

"Who is Franco Zeffirelli anyway?"
"Oh, I hear he is a film man can't think what the management were thinking."

She laughed inwardly, 'who better to direct a play set in Italy than an Italian, give him a chance' but she kept this thought to herself.

"I've heard that an unknown actress is to play Juliet, Judi Dench, or something, apparently, she's very young."

This was too much for Bessie; she could not. "Juliet wasvery young, just fourteen!" she snapped, as she swept by them in her most imperial manner and took her seat.

"This Judi Dench is too old then, isn't she?" was the woman's injured response.

Bessie ignored her; any misgivings she might have had dissolved the moment the lights went out and the curtains raised, she was transfixed, her eyes not moving from the stage for even a moment, she was oblivious to all else. Chris, sitting next to her, was initially fascinated by the young actress playing Juliet; she was, he thought, the most beautiful girl he had ever seen. To his annoyance, he found himself distracted by Bessie silently mouthing the words being spoken and at times it seemed she was pre-empting the actors' words. He watched and listened throughout the first half and realised she was word-perfect.

At the Interval Vera offered to get them all a drink, they both declined but Bessie walked with her to the Bar and waited patiently as she got her drink. "Vera, I want to thank you for one of the most wonderful evenings of my life. Never ever have I ever seen such a performance, it seems perfect. When the curtain went up it was as if we had been transported to Verona itself, so realistic was the set and I marvelled how they gave the sky such depth, brilliant, brilliant. As to the acting it was as if we had crashed into the lives of two young people, it is unlike any performance I have ever seen..."

"I am so pleased you are enjoying it. What I like most of all is the sheer joy and happiness of their love with no sense at all of their impending doom.."

"I should hope not, but indeed, this performance is as it was written." She caught herself, then continued "....I am sure." Then, in order to deflect attention away from her near slip, she added, "I am somewhat taken with the actor playing Romeo. Do you know of him?"

Vera consulted her program, "A young actor called John Stride, I've not heard of him before. According to the notes he is an up and coming star on television, but I wouldn't know of him as Beram won't have a television in the house!" At that moment the bell rang and the Interval was over.

In the car on the way home Bessie was unusually chatty, finding in Vera an intelligence equal to her own, but she could not find a way to discuss the one thing that had impressed her the most, women playing women, so much more effective than men. She embraced Vera warmly when they got home, "Thank you again, you have made my stay so memorable, I doubt that we shall meet again" and on that cryptic note was gone from Vera's life.

Television caught her interest when it showed footage of Elizabeth the Second's visit to Australia. "Australia, where is that? I don't think I am familiar with it."

With the aid of a small Globe which he had been given as a child, Chris showed her where it was and gave a potted history in so far as he knew it.

"So a land inhabited by criminals, not a place suitable for royalty." she snorted.

"That was a long time ago ma'am," he protested, "It is now a land of opportunity, the desired destination for many and a leading member of the Commonwealth......" More explanations were demanded and a response given.

"Oh this is all too much, you are making my head ache."

Despite which, she almost insisted, but remembered in time to ask nicely, that Elizabeth put the television news on each night so she could follow the Royal couple arounf Australia and New Zealand.

"A very comely man, that Phillip," she remarked.

"Yes, it is a true love match. The Queen fell for him the first time they met, she was only fourteen at the time. The Establishment did all they could to discourage her, to keep them apart. Serving in the Royal Navy Philip was at sea much of the time, as well as being posted overseas. But the Princess, as she then was, remained adamant and waited thirteen years before eventually marrying him in 1947."

Chris was unsure if she had heard anything of what he had been saying. Her face was vacant, a distant look in her eyes. She didn't want to go out the next day, she said, preferring to be alone in her room. There She stayed for four days, before asking Liz if she would ask Chris to visit her in her room.

"Master Christopher I wish to explain my perhaps uncouth behaviour. I allowed myself to be overcome with envy of your Queen. It seemed she was free to marry for love. I am a Queen with absolute power, but with little personal freedom. Your Queen has no real power, (a constitutional monarch I think you called it) but more freedom than I, or so it seemed to me. I was jealous but in the last few days I have been reflecting on this and I have come to the realisation that I am happier in my role. I can make a difference, have a purpose in life, which I don't think my namesake has. I feel for her, even though with purpose comes responsibility which sometimes weighs heavily upon me. I have been forced into decisions which have broken my heart..." There was silence between them, Chris sensing that there were some memories too painful to share. Eventually she looked up at him, smiled wistfully, "Master Christopher, thank you for sharing your world, it has been a privilege but I feel a desire to return to my time, to be in a world I know and understand but I do have one final request. "Please, take me to Kenilworth."

He thought of her reaction to the Tower and Hampton Court and wondered if it was wise. He was fearful of taking her to what was little more than a ruin, "Are you sure that would be a good idea. Remember Hampton Court..."

She was adamant " I desire to be taken to Kenilworth."

So a few days later found them at Victoria Coach Station. When Chris first mentioned they would be travelling by coach she was taken aback,"coach'?" she exclaimed, 'they still have coaches?" Chris hadn't given the matter a second thought and was taken aback by her confusion. All was explained when they went to board. "Oh you mean we are travelling by single decker bus," she exclaimed with some relief.

"Yes, why, what did you think?" Even as he said it, he realised she had been expecting a coach and horses, but why should that distress her so?

She laughed, "nothing much, a simple misunderstanding on my part."

Feigning sleep, she relived the last time she had made this journey by coach to Warwickshire. A very different kind of coach, and much slower. She remembered every moment, every second of that journey and wondered why she wanted to return. When they eventually arrived Chris expected her to express dismay at the the castle ruins, but he need not have worried.

She ignored the state of the castle and made directly for the remains of the great window. She beckoned Chris to sit beside her,

“Master Christopher, you have been puzzled when, researching Will Shakespeare you were sent to my court. Helge made a very wise decision and I owe it to him to now reveal to you his reasons.

It was almost dusk Chris shook himself, Bessie, Elizabeth, had been talking for hours, talking, explaining, excusing, and sometimes weeping. Now he took her hands in his and held them tightly. They sat there for a few moments looking at each other until she said “Well Master Christopher, the time has come for us to go our separate ways, I to my time and you to remain in yours. It's mostly been a fun ride Master Christopher, and I do thank you.....

With that she was gone.

A QUEEN'S SECRETS

And this is the story the Queen told.

"Master Christopher, your history books have treated me with kindness, more kindness than possibly I deserve. I think Dr. Dee would have been amused to hear me described as 'Good Queen Bess', and to hear that the age in which I ruled was a golden era. To me that seems somewhat fanciful, but what I find most ludicrous of all is the notion of the Virgin Queen! You listened to my Tilbury speech and heard me say I had the body of a weak and feeble woman but the heart and stomach of a king..... but that, my dear friend, was mere rhetoric, something that needed to be said to inspire those sent to fight in my name to save England from the Spanish. It was not what I felt in my heart."

"But surely...." not letting him finish, she continued, "Don't get me wrong, I love my country and will continue to make whatever sacrifices necessary for the good of England. What I mean is that in my heart I consider myself to be a weak and feeble woman..."

"But that is not how others perceive you....."

"Exactly, that is the point I am trying to make. Who are we? Are we the person we feel inside or are we the person other people perceive. When people see me I think they tend not to see the person, but to see the Queen and their judgments are based on that. Think for a moment of Shylock, 'Hath not a Jew eyes? Hath not a Jew hands, organs, dimensions, passions? Fed with the same food, hurt with the same weapons, subject to the same diseases, healed by the same means, warmed and cooled by the same winter as and summer as a Christian is? If you prick us do we not bleed? If you tickle us do we not laugh?.........'

Do I need to go on? Substitute Queen for Jew and I am sure you get the point. I am, like you, a mere mortal, with the same passions and feelings as anyone else. I have strengths and weaknesses and like all others, I craved love and like many before me I found love, but unlike your own Queen, I was unable to let my subjects share my joy, instead I had to allow myself to be courted by the royal Princes of Europe and by many other suitors and like Scheherazade before me, I had to let them leave with hope of a liaison. This was time that I would rather have spent with the man I truly loved, but no, for the good of my country I had to play this game! That's why I feel a weak and feeble woman and because of my weakness, I made the greatest sacrifice of all, a sacrifice that perhaps only another woman can understand."

Chris wanted to reach out and offer her comfort but did not know how. He wanted also to explain that maybe it hadn't been roses all the way for the present Elizabeth either, that she had responsibilities; that many had tried to prevent her marriage, that she was the cynosure of all eyes, across a world much bigger than that Bessie knew. Instead he said "I will try to understand."

"I know you will try, I have faith you will understand. I hope you won't mind, but before Helge allowed me to travel forward in time, he felt it necessary to reveal something about my would-be travelling companion. He told me of the cruelty of your father, of how you yearned for his love and respect, how hard you tried and how, despite your efforts he, in your eyes, rejected you. You do not understand his reasons, though I am sure he thought them good. I too had a cruel father, I was but three years old when he divorced my mother, and he had her executed that same year. Later, under the Succession Act, he, my father, disinherited me. I too know what it is like to feel worthless."

"I think perhaps my father's cruelty should not be compared to that you suffered....."

"Perhaps not, but we have both had to subjugate our true feelings and do what was expected of us. You found solace in the fantasy life you created for yourself until it all became too much for you. Fate stepped in in the form of Helge..."

"I think he saved me, saved me from myself I mean."

"No, that is where you are wrong! He helped you fulfil your potential, gave you the confidence to become the person you are today, the person you would have become had your upbringing been, um, been somewhat different, shall we say."

"Thank you, I wish I could believe that. I'm sorry, I interrupted your story, I wasn't thinking, do please go on."

"We were, apparently, fated to meet, to be of help to each other. I am rambling on, because I find it difficult to say what I have to say. Though neither you nor I are destined to remember meeting, the fact that we have will enrich our lives and the lives of those around us in ways we may not truly understand."

Chris nodded, thinking back to the time his Latin had so improved, wondering had he perhaps. .. No, don't think about that now. What is it she is trying to tell me?

"Did you hear what I was saying, you seemed in a dream world", her words jolted him back to the here and now. I was asking how much you know of the history of Kenilworth."

"Of Kenilworth?"

"The castle anyway, yes"

"Not a lot I'm afraid, although it has always been one of my favourite castles."

She sighed, "Mine too. Do you know to whom it belonged in my time?"

"I think it was Robert Dudley, Earl Of Leicester," he said, thinking, 'I know it was really'. He had been about to tell of the scandal surrounding the Earl but stopped just in time as he remembered some of the scandal involved her.

She heard the hesitancy in his voice, "Why do you falter, tell me what else you know."

He glanced up at what was left of the great window which had once overlooked the grand staircase,

"They say that his wife died falling from the grand staircase, indeed some say that she was pushed by the Earl......"

They! They say! Who pray are they?"

"Some historians for a start."

"And do these 'historians' give any reason as to why he would have pushed her?"

"So he could be with the woman he loved"

"Do they say who this woman may have been?"

"Ma-am, there is some speculation it may have been you"

She sat there with her eyes closed for what seemed an eternity, leaving Chris on tenterhooks.

"Master Christopher, thank you for telling me the truth, it cannot have been easy for you, although I cannot, I think, have your head chopped off if you displeased me. This brings me to what I want to say. Amy, Robert's wife, did sadly die when she fell down the stairs but I can assure you, hand on heart, it was an accident. Robin, my Robin, would not, could not, have harmed her. In his own way Robert loved Amy and she him, but they were not, after the first few years lovers..." A lengthy pause, then "but we were!" Another long pause.

"Robert was the love of my life, a fine man, a passionate and caring lover. It was I who granted him this castle and he turned it into the one of the finest palaces in the land. His marital status, in many ways, and I realise how this might sound, acted as a cover to our affair and after Amy's death, we had to be more discreet, it became more difficult, and quite soon after that it ended. Do not, I pray you, judge me, it was a different age; Amy knew of and accepted our liaison. So good Queen Bess, Virgin Queen, I am not."

Chris wondered if he was meant to say something, but what? He felt his inexperience and was afraid he was blushing. Before he had thought of any appropriate words, Elizabeth, no longer Bessie, continued.

"But there is more. I gave birth to his son, here in one of the Hunting Lodges on the estate........" and she told him of the journey in that nondescript coach, of the birth, of holding that baby for just a few hours, before giving him up.

"But why give him up? Surely as Queen..? He blurted.

"Think, Master Christopher, much as your naivety endears you to me, do you really think the bastard son of the Queen of England would have gone down well? I know, believe me, I know how many kings have had children outside of their marriage, but a queen? No, I think not, and further, I feared for his welfare. This mother wanted her son to live. Was that wrong?"

He shook his head.

"Robin found a childless couple living in a village some fifteen miles away who consented to adopt him. Far enough to be brought up independently, but close enough for him to be able to keep an eye on him and report back to me."

Chris's mind was suddenly working overtime, for he knew that fifteen or so miles from Kenilworth lay the village of Stratford Upon Avon! He wondered if he was beginning to see why Helge had sent him to the court of Elizabeth. Maybe he was overthinking things. Nonetheless, taking courage in both hands he asked, "Ma-am, forgive me, are you perhaps saying then that your son became William Shakespeare? That if he had not survived, the world would never have known the works of William Shakespeare?"

She looked amused, "you are leaping to conclusions but I confess, mark though, with regards to your last point, I would say rather that the world would not have *heard* of William Shakespeare!"

His heart began to beat a little faster, his mind once again working overtime, he hardly heard what she was saying, so eager was he to put further questions to her, "Are you saying then that your son William Shakespeare was not the playwright and poet William Sakespeare? That there is another.?"

She laughed and gently chided him, "calm down and listen more carefully, Master Christopher, you are acting like an excited schoolboy."

'But that is exactly what I am' he thought'

"There is but one William Shakespeare, however the true author and poet used the alias William Shakespeare...."

Unable to contain himself he blurted out, "But why and what made him pick on that name? Was he or his family beholden to the Shakespeare family in some way."

She smiled, looking down at her feet, then lifted her head and looked directly into his eyes, "Him. Him! Why do you suppose it was a man?"

He made to answer, but paused, unsure if he should mention yet another conspiracy theory he had come across. 'Oh well' he thought, 'nothing ventured, nothing gained.' He drew a deep breath and ventured "There are a group of people who believe Shakespeare was not, shall we say the contented family man as portrayed. Their reasoning is that some of his love poems are apparently written to men, from this they believe that he may have been bi-sexual. You know what I mean by that?" He looked at her uncertainly.

"Really boy, if I didn't know, I could work it out! But I find these theorists tedious; of course they were aimed at men or at least, one man in particular, because they were written by a woman!"

She paused and when her anger had died down continued "It seemed to me the greatest gift his Mother could bestow on him....."

"Mother! Wou mean Mary Ar...." he stopped himselfjust in time, disappointed at his own reactions. He was afraid it might seem that he had not been listening as she had shared some of the most intimate details of her life and he realised he had just assumed that if Stratford William was not the author of the plays and poems that bore his name, then the true author must be a man! Elizabeth as author had not occurred to him. His mind in a whirl of confusion, he was afraid she might feel he was not a worthy listener and would clam up and the unique opportunity he was being offered might be lost forever.

"Master Christopher, forgive me, all this must be very confusing for you and hard to take in. I must confess I am toying with you a little. Who knows how much time we have left together and in that time I am turning much of what you have thought you knew on its head. I have probably been talking far too quickly, in an effort not to leave even the smallest detail out. I am speaking to you as I have never spoken to any other person. I have been revealing to you some of the darkest parts of my soul, parts that have been hidden until now. .Thank you Master Christopher for letting me unburden my soul."

"But why me?"

"Because you, unwittingly, seemed to be coming close to discovering the truth anyway."

"In what way? I'm not sure I quite understand. I did have some thoughts but..."

"You were asking how any man could write so many works in such a short time span. Had you continued with your research, you would have concluded that it was not possible and would have searched for an answer. You listen to the theorists and come up with better conclusions than they seem able to perceive. Then Helge sent you to Tilbury; you shook me to the core when you shouted out 'Worthy of Shakespeare, Ma'am' and I having no idea who you were, or where you came from, feared you had somehow discovered the truth. Twas a very unsettling moment."

This time he let her words sink in before making any reply and then he could only manage "But why?"

"I will not bore you with details of my life that can be found in the myriad of books that seem to have been written about me, historically factual or not, they are mostly irrelevant to my tale. I was a child of three when my mother was executed. although, at the time, I was unaware of it, although I did wonder why people around me who had previously addressed me as my Lady Princess, now called me merely my Lady Elizabeth. Even at three I was somehow aware of the demotion. I found out much later that my father had me declared illegitimate, and I was considered as nothing more than the 'bastard child of a whore!'"

"There was little wealth in our household, which necessitated my governess having to beg the court for money. Is it surprising I had little self-worth and believed that our reduced circumstances was somehow my fault. A tutor was found for me, thanks be to God, and he changed my life and is much responsible for the woman I am today. Robert Ascham made me strong, his belief in me allowed me to believe in myself, and his greatest gift was to teach me to read and I began to devour books of all description, they were my escape from loneliness and misery. I begged to learn more and others were brought in to teach me, Latin, Greek, French and Italian. By my twelfth year I was fluent in all four and that allowed me to discover new lands in their native languages. Italy became almost as familiar to me as England. This in turn led me to the joy of writing. At first I was content to translate the works of others. At a young age I translated my Mother's prayer book into Latin and some of Ovid's love poems into English, then came the joy of creating and I began to write my own, mainly religious to begin with."

Chris recalled the latest Shakespearian theory to hit the news.. "Did you by any chance write any religious poetry, psalms for example?

"Psalms? Why do you ask? There is something more here I think. Your question is not random."

"There is a theory doing the rounds that Shakespeare wrote many of the Psalms contained in the standard Bible we now use." He was struck by a thought, it was the King James' bible, and King James came after Elizabeth. Once again he had let his enthusiasm mislead him. 'Oh well, too late now, carry on regardless, Christopher, you idiot.' So he did. "It is said that he left clues. The forty sixth word in Psalm 46 is 'shake', and the forty sixth letter from the end is 'spear."

She roared with laughter, "Preposterous! Give me some credit, I have never been shy of acknowledging my works, although as you now know, not always in my own name. What a tortuous and far stretched piece of logic. Do the people of your time really have nothing better to do?"

"It's called research Ma-am."

"To what purpose? I merely venture to ask, to understand why time is spent pursuing odd notions when there is so much real work to be done."

"Pseudo intellectualism I think it is called, something like that. Coming up with a theory and then trying to prove it, they think it makes them look intelligent."

"Poor deluded fools, may they one day see the light. It may seem a little hard on you though Master Christopher, the only one in the land who knows it is nonsense yet you must keep silent. After all, you can hardly say 'I know because Queen Elizabeth herself told me', I suspect they would lock you up."

"Then I shall have to come up with a theory of my own!"

"So you too can be a pseudo intellectual?" she teased him, then seemed to go off at a tangent. "Occasionally I would be taken to the court to see my father but he always seemed remote, uninterested, although I have been told he was impressed by my intellectual prowess, but if that is true, he never told me, much like your father methinks. There was one saving grace in those visits however, my latest stepmother at the time of which I speak, Catherine. In truth she was not yet twenty years old, not unusual in our times, but somehow she seemed much younger. I was nearly ten, we became very close, good friends, so I looked forward to visits I might otherwise have dreaded. Then suddenly she was not there, gone, and nobody would tell me why or wherefore. Eventually after much badgering from myself my governess broke down and revealed the awful truth. My Father, her husband, had had her arrested, taken to the Tower and summarily executed. My world was shattered, in pieces. I was nine years old, Master Christopher, with no family to turn to for comfort. There and then I vowed I would never marry, never trust a man again, never let another man hurt me. My only solace was my books, as I have already told you. I read voraciously, anything I could lay my hands on, they were my escape from the cruel and harsh world I inhabited. However the escape that reading gave was not enough for when a book was finished the same world was still around me, the memories were still with me. There had to be a way to exorcise the demons that were haunting me. I began by writing letters to my father, not only expressing my hatred of his abhorrent actions but wanting him to realise what I was going through, to understand my emotions. Of course the letters never reached him, as I destroyed them almost as soon as they were written, but the very act of writing them made me feel better about myself. And an idea was forming in my mind."

"A few moments ago you acquainted me with a conspiracy theory concerning Psalm 46 which I dismissed as the nonsense that it is. I am surprised however that none of your so-called scholars really understand what the truth is behind my plays, how they allowed me to unburden myself..."

'Hmm' Chris wondered, 'how could they, the scholars, realise what was behind the plays when they didn't know the truth of their begetter?' He decided not to raise the point then, but to raise another, "But when we went to see Romeo and Juliet I heard you admonish an audience member by saying 'it's just a play."

She smiled, "You are quite right. A number of my plays have two levels, the story/plot can be enjoyed as just that, but they are also allegorical, conveying hidden messages."

"Forgive me, but to me this does not make sense. If I understand you correctly you are saying you started writing these plays when you were little more than a child and yet earlier you admitted using the alias William Shakespeare, how so? He was not even a twinkle in his mother's, I mean your eye."

She sighed in exasperation, "You must learn to listen properly, and see the whole of what I am saying and not pick things in isolation."

Embarrassed once again by his own inability to absorb without questioning, he asked her to pardon him, and continue her tale, vowing to hold his tongue.

"Initially the plays were written to help me, acting as a catharsis, they were never meant for publication. After writing, I hid them away, fearful lest anyone discover, read, and worse, understand what lay behind them. Like the letters I considered destroying them, they had after all served their purpose. Why I did not? I am unsure. To my relief they remained undiscovered even as their number grew. Writing had become a source of great joy, I loved writing and gradually the tone of my writing changed, as the need to purge myself was no longer the defining reason to write. Years passed, I ascended the throne and, despite the vow I had made on Catherine's death, I fell in love, well, you know the rest." Here she paused and looked away.

Then, as if she felt time fleeting, she hurried on "Through Dr. Dee's secret network I received regular reports from Stratford, enabling me to share my son's childhood and growth to manhood. The most difficult thing was not to interfere, to give advice. I had just to be a bystander in my son's life. I heard of his love of the theatre and his attempts at writing poetry, his struggle to become a playwright. Dr Dee managed to obtain some of his works...," again she paused, then, giving a rueful sigh, continued "... in all honesty, they were somewhat woeful, needing a lot of work, although, it seemed he had a penchant for producing plays. I am his Mother, I longed to aid him. It suddenly seemed obvious. With my Father no longer alive and my place on the English throne secure, I could let my plays be seen and my poetry be heard."

"Through the owner of the Globe, William was brought to London, and given humble lodgings south of the river quite close to Greenwich. In the evening he was accosted by a rather coarse and vulgar woman." She laughed suddenly "Remember Bessie? But this was worse. Revolted by both her appearance and smell, he was giving her a wide berth but the sound of her shrill, witch-like voce uttering his name compelled him to stop; forcing a package on him she said 'this is for you, inside is something to your advantage.' Then she was gone. That Master Christopher, was my finest acting performance and the closest I ever came to my son again." She fell silent.

After a while Chris felt the need to break the silence, "And in that package?"

"Three plays by William Shakespeare, an anonymous letter from me and a little money to tide him over."

"May I ask what was in that letter?"

"Simply put, select what he thought was the best of the plays, persuade the management to have his choice produced. To take the credit for the writing of it and if it went well, more plays would be forthcoming. Finally, never, ever, divulge to anybody that he was not the true author."

"And he never questioned those terms or queried who his benefactor might be?"

"How could he, what leads did he have? Besides, would you have looked such a gift horse in the mouth? Remember also, he was twenty five years old, thus far had led a rather mundane and uninspiring life, and was often in debt. So there you have it, the true origin of William Shakespeare, playwright and poet.

"And the play he chose?"

"The story of the two star crossed lovers, ,Romeo and Juliet."

"But Romeo and Juliet was not one of his early plays......"

"Master Christopher, is that what your scholars, these Shakespeare experts tell you. They have no idea when any of my works were written, I have already told you the majority of my works were written long before William was born. Your experts can only tell you when they were first published or performed, NOT written. Do you doubt my word!?"

"I wouldn't dare."

She smiled at his temerity. "I left the world a somewhat cryptic clue that there might be more to William Shakespeare than meets the eye. Towards the end of my life I sent William a deliberately unfinished manuscript, Timon of Athens, with the suggestion that he add his own ending. I never lived to see the play completed despite his many attempted collaborations, most notably with one Thomas Middleton. Let your experts figure that one out."

"I meant no offence, I'm sorry. I am grateful to you for sharing so much with me. When we part I wonder how much of what you have told me might be believed. Of our meeting I will say nothing. You need not fear your secrets will be revealed but I fear I will be labelled as just another conspiracy theorist."

"I feel sure you will write a compelling tale."

"Thank you, one last question if I may. Now that you have witnessed how your works have endured and been judged by history to be the finest works of literature ever written in the English language, do you regret they are in William's name?"

"In a long life of ups and downs, twists and turns and intrigues, there are many things I regret. I have had to be hard, at times seeming cruel and uncaring. Oh, the execution of Mary! It tore my soul apart. I regret not being able to bring up my son; I regret not being free to love. Giving up authorship of a few plays seems but a mere trifle, and what mother would not sacrifice all for her first born. Perhaps, perhaps I have overcompensated; my Mother never had the opportunity to demonstrate such a love."

They sat in silence, each lost their own thoughts. Then, prompted by some vague feeling that maybe things were at an end, Elizabeth turned to Chris and asked "You said 'one last question' and I answered it, but tempus fugit, is there more you would know?"

"One thing, I didn't mention it, because it is after your time, but maybe you know. A printer published your sonnets with a dedication, it is seen as a great mystery and many have questioned its meaning, and many thought they have divined to whom it is addressed. It's something along the lines of 'To the only begetter of these ensuing sonnets, Mr WH.'"

She burst out laughing "Oh, poor Will."

"Poor Will?"

"Yes, who else begot the sonnets. As you now know, it was me, but to the world it was Will. I don't see the mystery."

"Why, W. H. of course. Who was W. H.?"

She shook her head, "Maybe it is not so in your day, but it is plain enough in our times. It is implying that Will, the begetter of the sonnets, is under his wife's thumb. Do you not see, W. H, Will Hathaway, his wife's surname, saying she is the head of the household."

"Ah, we say the wife wears the trousers, maybe other things as well. What a story I will have to tell. You don't mind, do you?"

"It's quite funny really, I wrote Will's plays and poetry, and you will write my truths, and no-one will know for sure what to believe. I find it satisfying."

They smiled at each other, and somehow, in the moment, they each knew their time together was at an end. Chris felt in his pocket and pulled out his fountain pen. It was one of his prized possessions, bought with the first money he had ever earned, "Ma-am this pen......"

"That is a pen? It looks like no pen I have ever seen!"

"Please. I spent part of the Summer holidays picking fruit, blackcurrants for which I received threepence a pound, I managed to save enough to buy this pen. Look, I'll show you how it works."

She watched, fascinated, "It must make writing much easier..."

"Much quicker as well. You love writing and will write more than I ever will, it is my gift to you, I would be honoured if you would accept it."

She almost choked on her words "It will surely intrigue Dr. Dee" and then she was gone.

Sak stretched, glanced at his watch and was surprised to see how little time had passed. He got up, brushing off the autumn leaves that had fallen and as he did so he saw his fountain pen lying on the ground. How did that get there? Relieved he had noticed it, he picked the pen up and continued on his Sunday walk.

EMERGENCE OF KELSEY

Jim Hodges looked up from Sak's exercise book and smiled, "Genius or lunacy? I am not sure but it is certainly original. Queen Elizabeth the First, the true author of the works attributed to Shakespeare. It might almost be believable, but Shakespeare's Mother is taking it a little too far....". He shook his head, "How on earth do you dream up these outlandish ideas.?"

"I really don't know Sir, where do any ideas come from? I think about things, and ideas come into my head. I like to write them down and see if they make any sense. It's odd though. Do you recall the day when Latin suddenly made sense to me?"

"I certainly remember the event, though not the day"

"I do. It was a Sunday; I had been for a walk in the Manor Woods, nothing extraordinary had occurred but I was fretting over the prep you had set us. I had always enjoyed your lessons and was desperate to demonstrate that I was better than you thought and not lazy, but was hindered by Goodrich."

"What's he got to do with it?"

He told of how he had somehow found himself obliged to do Goodrich's homework, how he, Sak put his best efforts into the other's boy's work to the detriment of his own, as he realised that they must look different when being marked.

"I assume you now feel free to mention this, Goodrich having left?"

"Yes, but he did accept it when we discussed it, and I was able to help him. But that evening, for some reason I decided to do my work first and everything seemed to fall into place, and somehow I was better at Latin than I had been before. It was weird really, but the point I am trying to make, it happened on a Sunday."

"I don't see the relevance"

"I can't explain it, but when I was on those Sunday afternoon walks I used to make up stories in my head, then I would write them down later but they never looked the same on paper, alas. The odd thing is that many times the stories were beyond my imagination, totally outside anything I have experienced and Sir, this is the point, it only occurred to me recently, it was always on my Sunday afternoon walk in the woods, every original idea I have had come to me on a Sunday, while walking in the woods. I just wonder if there is a connection."

"Perhaps you had better stop those walks then." He laughed as he said it, but Sak thought, 'no, those walks have saved my life, made a difference, no way will I stop them. Who knows what else may strike me.' He was recalled to the present by the teacher's voice.

"Now to your piece on King Lear. Taken on its own, as you presented it to me, it seemed to make no sense. That Lear represented Elizabeth's father, Henry VIII, and that Goneri, Regan and Cordelia were three expressions of herself and the ambivalent feelings she had for her father, would seem to be a nonsense, but if we accept your proposition that Elizabeth was Will's Mother, as well as the author, then your work has a certain logic to it. But how to mark it? That is the question."

"I am not sure I understand Sir"

"If I mark it according to conventional wisdom then it would be a low mark, if I mark it on original thought it shows, then the mark would be at least a Distinction, but, and here is my dilemma, you are about to sit your A levels. I have to take into consideration that your future is at stake. You must see that if you follow this route in writing your 'A' level essays, an unimaginative examiner may mark you down, may fail to follow your logic. By awarding you a Distinction I would be giving you possibly unreal expectations. it's too big a risk to take"

"Sir!" he protested half-seriously. "I never put you down as being a Mr Gradgrind or Mr McChoakumchild."

The image of children being nothing more than empty vessels having facts, facts, facts, nothing but facts poured into them had made a lasting impression on him when he first read "*Hard Times*". Whilst there were some teachers who seemed to follow this adage, Jim Hodges, he felt, had never been one of them.

Mr. Hodges smiled, "Point well made and taken, Saklatvala. I explained the position as I saw it. I don't want to unduly influence you, but when you need to make a judgement, it's your call as they say, but consider, if there is no question concerning King Lear, might that not leave you up in the air."

"Oh no Sir. I have thoughts on a number of his, or do I mean 'her' plays. Think about "*Romeo and Juliet*". Don't you think this might represent her frustration that she was not free to love as others in her kingdom were, the suicides being a metaphor for the death of her feelings and those of the man she loved. There are other indications that Elizabeth might have been the true author, not only are many of the strongest characters female and the men made to look weak and foolish. Could it, as I believe, be her way of paying homage to Catherine Howard and somehow an affirmation of her vow never to let a man dominate or hurt her again. At least make people think, isn't that what education is about, not just facts."

"The Reverend Osborne tells me you intend studying law, I think I can see why, but In promoting your theories you make it sound as if you are defending an old friend rather than putting forward a reasoned argument. You need to be impartial."

Sak shook his head, "not if I'm a defence lawyer, surely. Though I don't know yet what branch I am going to follow. I must admit that lately the subject seems to have taken over my mind, and though this might sound silly, it feels as if I am somehow inside her head and need...."

The teacher felt uncomfortable at the direction the conversation was taking and issued a jokey warning, "Careful Saklatvala. Joan of Arc heard voices in her head and we both know how she ended up!"

They both laughed, Sak somewhat embarrassedly, he felt that the teacher had misunderstood what he was trying to explain. As if he too was uncertain, Mr. Hodges changed the conversation to a discussion of the subjects Sak would be taking in the upcoming 'A' level exams.

Sometime later, exams over and the results known, Mr. Hodges was holding 'one to one's with each of his pupils. Sak felt relaxed about it, was even looking forward to his turn.

"So Sak, I understand your first choice is Magdalen College, any particular reason?"

"I looked it up and many of our leading Law Lords went there. Although some people consider Brasenose to be the 'Law College'. I haven't really made up my mind, and of course, it now depends on what the colleges think of my results ."

"Do we look forward to Lord Saklatvala then?"

"Oh that will never happen!"

"You never know"

"I do though, because soon Christopher Saklatvala will be no more, I've applied to change my name"

""You carry an honourable name. Why would you want to change it?""

"That's just it. I am proud of my name and my family history, but whenever I meet people for the first time my name is an embarrassment, where did it come from, how do I pronounce it, how is it spelt. I have been at Dauntsey's eight years and there are still Masters who can't pronounce properly; I will be entering a profession where I will be meeting new people on a daily basis so need a name easy to say and easy to remember"

"So what is the name to look out for?"

"Kelsey, Simon Angus Kelsey, I want those initials. S A K, it's the name Dauntsey's gave me."

"Ah well, a rose by any other name.... I will follow your chosen career with interest, but let's not get ahead of ourselves here. Your A Levels were reasonable, a distinction in Latin as we expected, A plus in English may have let you down a little, I think you were hoping for more there, which would have helped, as your passes in History, Geography and Classical Literature were average, nothing to write home about, so I have to caution you that you have no guarantee of a place at Oxford, or even elsewhere. Unlike America we have relatively few Universities, about twenty I believe, so there is a lot of competition. It is a good idea to be prepared for a disappointment. This is not to say that we, Dauntsey's, aren't proud of you for what you have achieved here, it was well done, whether you gain a place or not."

Sak smiled wryly, remembering the advice Mr. Hodges had given him before the English exam.

"Work hard. If you choose to pursue the unconventional route, then refine and polish your arguments in such a way that after the examiner has finished reading your papers he might say 'I have learnt something today' or 'I have never looked at it like that before. Make them think. We have done our best, now it is up to you."

Oh the rashness of youth, he recalled how he had gone into the examination hall full of confidence, but doubts were now beginning to creep in. Maybe he should have taken the safe route.

"Maybe I was somewhat arrogant, (a family trait I am afraid), being so sure I had all the answers, it might have been better if I had followed your advice and been a bit more circumspect."

"Ah, I wondered about that. So you stayed with your convictions. Sak, I'm pleased to hear that you chose to follow your own line. A good teacher, as you had the temerity to point out to me, should encourage original thought; stimulate those new ideas without which the world will never move on."

"Thank you Sir. I shan't despair. If I fail to get into law school, I can always teach! You know what Shaw said, 'those who can do, those who can't...."

"Teach! Thanks a bunch Sak, now I know what you think of me?"

Sak felt the colour rising in his cheeks as he tried to formulate an apology, it had been meant as a joke. He was then relieved as he realised this was how it had been taken, when he saw Jim Hodges laughing.

"My advice to you is to relax and enjoy this final term, come what may."

So enjoy it he did, comfortable with his friends and other people in his year, and seeing the staff in a different light, as they treated him like a young man, rather than a pupil for whom they were responsible. He came to see them as adults, with their own lives and concerns.

The las Sunday arrived, and he wnet for a nostalgic walk in the woods; maybe he was expecting to meet Helge one last time. If so, he weas not disappointed.

"We are ordained to meet for the last time; I leave you with one last gift, uset it wisely, how you use it will determine both our destinies."

"But ..."

Before he could say more Helge was gone. So how was he to use a gift wisely, when he had no idea what it was, what it entailed. Trust Helge, enigmatic to the last.

Then came his last School Assembly; the final hymn, sung at the end of every term, brought Sak's life at Dauntsey's to an end.

> *"Lord, thou hast brought us to our journey's end:*
> *Once more to thee our evening prayers ascend;*

Once more we stand to praise thee for the past;
Grant prayer and praise be honest at the last."

Sak exited the main gates for the last time, singing the words of this hymn over in his mind. Simon Angus Kelsey walked down the Poplar lined driveway, musing on how different his life might be at University – if he was accepted!.

LIVING THE LEGAL LIFE

Academically, he had justified his place at Brasenose, Magdalen, he thought ruefully, hadn't wanted him. Ah well, maybe that was there loss in the end. He had much to thank Brasenose for. He felt he was worthy of his place there, academically but socially it was a little different. Even now, in his seventies, he felt much the same about himself as he had as a teenager. Many of his personal insecurities had besieged him throughout his life. Even when people assured him otherwise, he found himself doubting. He thought back to the time when his secretary had found him almost weeping over a letter. Too upset to reply when she asked what had upset him so, he silently handed her the letter. It read

"Dear Sir,
I doubt that you will remember me, but you changed my life, all I have achieved is because you made me tell the truth. In 1971 I was charged with grievous bodily harm. My Defence lawyer, appointed by the court, and to whom you had been articled, was clever, streetwise, and slick. I was guilty of the charge, there was no doubt about that, but the evidence was slim, the witnesses nervous, and the defence lawyer took advantage of this. He charmed the Jury, twisted the truth and gave me every chance of being found not guilty. Then fate stepped in, on the final day of my trial, when he was due to sum up, he had a car accident and couldn't make it to court in time. The judge offered to postpone the trial but you insisted you were capable of carrying on. You asked him for "time to consult with your client."

Recalling this, Sak smiled, his career was nearly ended before it had begun.

"I will never forget the face of the judge and the jurors when the case resumed and you stood up and said, 'M'lord, my client wishes to change his plea to guilty.'
I am sure you remember the ensuing mayhem. The judge asked me

himself if I now wanted to plead guilty and despite the chance to dodge the bullet, I stuck to my guns. Why did I do that? When you said "I will defend you, give you the best defence possible, but only if you tell the truth!." I thought what sort of defence lawyer is this clown, there was no way I could do that. Then you surprised me by saying 'here is what I believe happened'. Uncannily, you seemed to know exactly what had occurred as if you had been an eye witness, you seemed to know what had been in my head. You made me see that if I was found not guilty, the victim and those close to him would not get any closure, that I would not be able to live with myself and would never do anything worthwhile. You advised me to change my plea, show remorse and apologise.

I received a custodial sentence but the minimum allowed by law, the victim's family came to see me to thank me for my honesty and to offer forgiveness, and, for me the greatest blessing, my wife did not abandon me.

Anyway Sir, I served my sentence, and have since devoted my life to helping guide young offenders. I just want to say, your legacy lives on, thank you."

"And you still doubt your ability?" Lesley was a good, loyal secretary but he did exasperate her from time to time.

He had never forgotten that court case, or the furore that followed. Word had reached the office before he reached Chambers. He entered to silence and angry stares; a junior broke the silence, "Mr Proctor asks you to go directly to his office". The door had barely opened when the torrent of abuse started. This was a side of the Senior Partner that Sak had not seen before, the sleek, calm, sophisticated charm persona of the courtroom had given way to a shouted tirade of anger.

"Never, never, never in all my experience have I heard of anything so stupid, so foolhardy. On the verge of winning a case, you, a junior member of this firm, for some perverse reason decided it was your duty to side with the prosecution!"

His face was getting redder as he struggled to get his words out quickly enough,

"..... regret the day we agreed to take you on. In one action you have ruined the reputation of this firm, I doubt anybody will use our services again, we are ruined, and I tell you now, I will use whatever reputation I have left to ensure that you never, ever practice law. You are a disgrace."

Sak had given a nervous smile. "Even a person pleading guilty is given the opportunity to state his case, may I please explain?"

"Explain, explain! It had better be good!"

"The law requires a guilty person to have the right to a good defence and.........."

"That is right and that is exactly what I was giving him!"

Believing his career was in tatters anyway emboldened Sak to continue. "Does the law demand a good defence twist the truth, tell lies even, where does the law state that a good defence means a guilty person is found innocent and allowed to go free? If the law means that, then I want no part of it...."

"Then you will get your wish, now get out of here and never set foot in here again."

Sak almost smiled, it sounded so much like 'and never darken this doorway again. For some reason he felt quite optimistic. "Before I go, let me just ask, is it true that you had a road accident this morning........"

"Yes it bloody is, as you damn well know, else we wouldn't be having this stupid conversation, but maybe it is an opportunity in disguise, having allowed me to see that you are not worthy....."

"Forgive me interrupting," why should I worry, Sak wondered, I have already been dismissed, "so, the road accident meant a trip to the hospital and that made it impossible for you to attend court on time?"

"Yes, and I had someone ring the court and the judge said he would have the case suspended until I could get there. Which you somehow, and don't ask me how, a mere snivelling junior, managed to overturn that. So what are you getting at?"

"Would you say the accident was your fault Mr. Proctor?"

"No it bloody wasn't and although it is none of your business, I have already instituted legal proceedings."

"And how would you feel if the other person engages an unscrupulous defence team who deny the accusation, twist the facts and you are found guilty. Would you feel justice had been served? Or perhaps you would prefer that his defence lawyer encourages him to plead guilty to the charge in order that the matter be settled quickly and fairly?"

"I understand what you are saying but it is not the same."

"Could you explain the difference please?"

Proctor sat there for some time, gradually his colour dropped, disappearing from his face. As he resumed his normal demeanour, a small smile appeared on his lips.

"They said you were a clever bugger, with a slippery tongue. So tell me, you young jackanapes, what happened in court today will be all over the papers tomorrow. Do you see any way to stop this firm becoming a laughing stock?"

"Actually, I think I can see a way. But why should I? You have made it quite clear that this firm has no more to do with me, nor I with it."

"Alright, my temper got the better of my judgement. Expound, and if I like what you have to say, well, we shall see."

Proctor had been right about the press. Thanks in the main to a junior in the outer office, who had seen an opportunity, and seized it, the newspapers had been alerted to an apparent schism in the offices of one of the leading law firms in the country; for 'thirty pieces of silver' the gutter press had been given an almost word for word account of the shouted exchange.

The office was besieged by both press and television reporters. When Sak, whom they all supposed had been sacked and left the premises in high dudgeon, made an unexpected appearance, it caused even more chaos. But despite having microphones shoved in his face, a myriad of shouted questions thrown at him, being jostled, pushed first this way and then that, he managed to keep his cool.

Amongst the sea of faces there was one that he recognised, if his mop of thinning red hair and a scraggy beard were not enough to make him stand out, he also stood head and shoulders above the rest, Fyfe Robinson, roving reporter from the "Tonight' show if I am not mistaken. Mr Robinson, if you would like a few words, please follow me into the office."

The protestations of the other journalists were ignored as best as possible, as Sak led the way inside. The meeting was short and to the point, there was no interview as such at this point, but Ian Proctor and Sak Kelsey agreed to appear on the Tonight program with Cliff Mitchelmore that evening.

As usual, the program started with Cy Grant's satirical calypso on news stories that had peaked the public's interest.

De judge was very cross,
Cross, cross
He was at a loss, cos
De lawyer not make no show
He rang to say he was going slow,
Slow, slow
Cos he was down in the hospital
Woe, woe, woe.
But de junior, a young lad called Sak
Upped and said
He did not lack
The words to take the case on
Dat judge was cross
And at a loss
He say,

What's your notion,
Show me your motion
Tra la la la la
Come on tell me your notion
Tra la la la la la
Show me your motion
Tra la la la la

"Thank you Cy, that leads us rather nicely into our lfirst story, I must say gentlemen, for two people who were allegedly at loggerheads yesterday, everything seems remarkably equitable between you now."

Proctor was the first to speak, "Perhaps you shouldn't listen to careless gossip Mr. Mitchelmore. Only joking, Cliff. When news reached me of young Kelsey's actions I was gobsmacked. I think it is understandable. Who was this viper I had nurtured in my bosom, was this how he was going to repay my interest and my support, by undermining my authority. First there was shock, followed by disbelief and then anger. It took a while for Sak,..."

"If I may interrupt, for the benefit of our audience, who is this Sak?"

"That is how we refer to Kelsey, get him to show you his briefcase."

Sak, smiling sheepishly, held aloft his briefcase for all to see. 'Lucky I had it with me,' he thought. Proctor continued "anyway, it took him some time to return to the office and I let my anger fester, become all consuming, possibly clouding my judgement. The moment he walked into my office I exploded. If I might just say in my defence, I had suffered a traffic accident in the morning, hence my lack of show in court. So I was not at my best. That explosion of fury resounded round the office where previously no-one had even heard me raise my voice. If I may say so, I am an equitable man. Known for my coolness and judgement, and love of fair play."

"Indeed, Mr. Proctor, I would have to say that is how you have been portrayed in the press until now, but then, I can see you did have provocation. Do you know how this explosion became public knowledge, surely it was better pursued behind closed doors?"

Proctor growled. "Some junior in the firm heard the altercation and took it upon himself to make a killing, in more than one sense of the phrase, if I may say so! Apparently he made the decision to contact the media and well,.... You know the rest. It is important that my office is virtually soundproof to protect client confidentiality, so whoever the Judas is, soon to be ex-Judas when I discover his identity, did not hear what followed, but by then the damage had been done."

"So will you tell us what did occur between you two?"

"Sak asked to be allowed to state his case and eventually I stopped fuming and listened, and realised that possibly he was going to be even more successful than I had originally envisaged."

"That is a little oblique. What was actually said?" Cliff Mitchelmore wondered if they were ever going to get to the point. Still, that was his job, to draw out the truth. He turned to Sak, "Mr. Kelsey, would you like to give us your side of the story?"

Before Sak could pull his thoughts together, Mr. Proctor leapt in. "What happened is not that easy to explain. There are certain professions that we follow for idealistic reasons, like teaching, the law and may I say journalism. I am sure every school teacher sets out to teach with kindness, understanding and love, never to lose his temper, to be diligent and fair; every journalist sets out to tell the truth, to report truthfully, fairly without bias, and every lawyer sets out to be fair and just. But as we get older, more experienced, we tend to drift away from the ideals of our chosen profession. Teachers, faced with the realities of life, pressured to deliver good exam results, coping, or trying to cope, with children he or she may find it difficult to manage, lose their confidence and end up doing what it takes to survive. Not all, of course, but many I am sure." He paused to take a breath, and consider his next point, he didn't want to offend anyone, anymore than he may have done already..

"Journalism can become more about selling newspapers, or in the case of television, winning over viewers, rather than remaining impartial and presenting the truth for the public to judge for themselves. The old adage about not letting the truth get in the way of a good story is not really funny. Though I practice it myself, only.with friends though, where it is understood. Which brings me to lawyers, or to this lawyer anyway. I started off with the highest ideals. I achieved early success, I started to win cases and I enjoyed winning, still do!. I enjoyed the theatre of the courts and, to put it crudely, had the gift of the gab and began to see that juries were influenced by the singer rather than the song. Although he did not say it in as many words, Sak led me to ponder if I was selling my soul to the Devil!"

"So no controversy, no sackings, (pun not intended) no story?" Cliff sounded disappointed"

"No sackings, that is certain, Sak has a good future, of that I am also certain...." ever the good lawyer, he paused dramatically.

Cliff filled the pause, "Could you elucidate?"

"I have discussed this with my partners and, as from tomorrow, the Company will be known as Proctor, Young, Wheeler and Sak. There, Cliff, is your story. A Tonight exclusive."

The cameras were now all focused on Sak,

Cliff turned to him enquiringly "Don't you feel you are a little young and inexperienced for this appointment?"

Sak's voicewas trembling ashe ventured to reply. "I am overwhelmed. Just twenty four hours ago I thought my career was over but now, well I just can't think straight, not good, I suspect for a partner in a law firm. This is too much to take in and........." he could find no words to continue, shook his head and abruptly stood up and left the studio.

Cliff, looking bemused, closed the show, "that's all for tonight, the next 'Tonight' will be tomorrow night. Until then, good night!"

Looking back now, Sak smiled; much to Proctor's surprise and perhaps relief, in the morning, after a night to think it over, Sak had turned down the offer of a partnership. "I have very little experience in life let alone the business world, and am not worthy of being a partner." Smiling slightly, he had added "well, not just yet anyway."

"Oh so you at least intend staying on then, do you! I suppose I should be grateful for small mercies." Proctor had clapped him on the shoulder, and somewhat surprisingly, offered him a glass of whisky, in what was to become the first of many.

Sak, stirred by the memory, took a sip from the glass of whisky on his desk, looking once more round the office he had occupied for so long. Tomorrow, if things went well, would be his last day in court; in the evening he would return for one last glass, clear his desk and make his farewells. Like Proctor before him, and the original partners before that, his name would be removed from the letterheads, the firm's signage, obliterated from history, he would be forgotten.

KELSEY'S LAST CASE

The final day of the trial was a fitting end to the career of Lord Chief Justice Simon Kelsey, epitomising many of the hallmarks for which he had become famous. It involved a famous crime, dubbed by the press 'the Frankenstein Diamond'. The robbery of the world's largest black diamond, the Karloff Noir, 421 Carats, valued at some forty million pounds, was a worldwide headline grabbing event. It had been stolen from Hatton Gardens in London, where it had been sent for cleaning. The man responsible for cleaning the diamond was an Alfred Martel, who was working late, when he was attacked from behind, drugged and tied up. He had seen no-one. Security had been high, featuring, among other security measures, cameras that could not, allegedly, be bypassed. And nor were they.

The police were baffled then stunned, not so much by the crime, but by what they saw when they viewed the security tapes. As Inspector Barrat put it at the first press briefing, "It was like an old time reunion of all the major jewel thieves of the last twenty years all Challenor's old friends. It seems, despite the headlines, they were unaware of the security cameras or totally unconcerned and we have clear pictures of them all. Arrests all over London were made early this morning. We are confident of a quick recovery of the diamond."

But the diamond had not been recovered.

Barrat was surprised to learn all those arrested in the dawn raids appeared to have hangovers, all said they had been at a birthday party for the leading London gangster, Bobby Challenor, at the '*Anne Boleyn*' pub in Eastham the night before, something the Landlord was able to confirm. Although there were no security cameras at the '*Anne Boleyn*', footage on many mobile phones showed a rowdy, drunken party with many, if not all, the suspects in attendance.

The poor quality of the phone images made positive identification difficult, but nonetheless, in the end, the case was brought to Court. It was too high profile to be dismissed for lack of convincing evidence. Judge Simon Kelsey was in attendance.

The Defence lawyer was effective, using laughter to good effect in getting the jurors on side. And he had plenty of material! Latex masks of the accused were found in a skip in an alley close to Hatton Gardens, it seemed obvious what had happened. There was no case against his clients.

"M'Lord and members of the jury, why exactly are we here? I put it to you that my clients could hardly be in two places at the same time, whatever the cameras may say. Contrary to belief, the camera can lie, and here is the proof. It would appear the robbery was perpetrated by persons unknown, disguised as my clients."

The prosecuting counsel called an expert "You examined the masks?"

"Yes Sir"

"And what did you find?"

"Nothing,"

"Nothing, what do you mean by nothing!"

"Just that, there was absolutely nothing to be found on those masks, no evidence they had been worn, no evidence that there had been an attempt to clean them."

"Anything else?"

"Just one thing. We requested the police to go back and research the area, the skip where the masks were found and adjacent skips." He paused, milking his moment in the spotlight. "They found the boxes that contained the masks. I'm not quite sure why they weren't found by the police in the first place."

"Your conclusion?"

"That's not my job, but I could venture a guess that those boxes were discarded at a later date, to further confuse the issue."

Arguments went backwards and forwards for several days. It seemed certain the suspects must be acquitted. The prosecution's parting shot was that he had never been involved in a case where the accused were all able to give each other an alibi, and he felt distinctly uneasy about it.

It was time for the judge to consider his summing up. He returned to his chambers, leant back in his chair, then, as was his wont, he closed his eyes. Opening them moments later he was in no doubt as to what had happened, and how he was to proceed.

"The court will rise."

Sak entered the courtroom, but before taking his seat and addressing the jury he beckoned the Clerk of the Court and handed him a note. The clerk left the courtroom, returning moments later to general bewilderment, with Challenor's wife, who had been seated in the Public Gallery. The Judge indicated she should take a seat in the main body of the court.

"Ladies and Gentlemen of the Jury, it has been a long and at times tedious, trial and I commend you for your attention and patience. You might take the view that this case is clear cut, the accused are clearly visible on the security video and a verdict of guilty would seem reasonable. However, you may take the view that the discovery of the masks in the skip casts doubt on their guilt. You have to take into account that the masks were never used, what was their purpose? If it was to confuse the issue, they've clearly succeeded."

Raising his eyebrows, he posed the possibility that it was nothing more than an unhappy coincidence, causing a ripple of laughter. "Then there is the mobile phone evidence showing the accused enjoying a birthday party at the 'Anne Boleyn' Public House in Eastham. One thing is sure, the Defence lawyer is right, they could not possibly in both places at the same time. You must consider which you think is the more credible, not an easy task. You should also bear in mind that the accused were identified from the video tapes, and arrested within hours of the robbery being discovered, yet despite an exhaustive search, the diamond has not been found. In delivering your verdict you must be certain of the facts and justice must be seen to be served, if you have any doubts then you must express them, bring in a not guilty verdict."

In the dock the accused breathed a collective sigh of relief, believing he was guiding the jury to a not guilty verdict. Challenor himself breathed more easily, the sight of his wife being brought into the court had momentarily unsettled him, but now his idea of using two sets of masks seemed to have paid off, there had to be 'reasonable doubt'. 'Stroke of genius' he thought to himself, one set of masks to be worn by those at the birthday party and carefully disposed of, and the unused masks to be left in plain sight, to cause confusion. Surely their acquittal was all but assured.'

"There is however another possibility."

The Defence bristled, thee Lord Chief Justice's summings up were legendary, what was he going to come up with now?

"Magicians are familiar with the term 'smoke and mirrors' and use a technique known as mis-direction, making you see what they want you to see. It is my belief..."

The Defence team jumped to their feet, aghast at the direction the judge's words seemed to be taking.

"My Lord, I object, I strongly object. This is not, cannot be, right. Your conjecture or beliefs are entirely irrelevant, you can only comment on evidence already presented to this court and your task is to direct the jury's attention to the law and how it is applied."

"Thank you for teaching me my responsibilities." The judge's tone was friendly, and the court laughed. "My learned friend, you are right in what you say, but there are many ways of looking, and that is pertinent to this case. Throughout my long career I have been bound by one thing only, to seek the truth and ensure justice is done. I ask for your patience and if at the end I have not satisfied you or the jury, you can call for it to be called a mis-trial in which case a new judge will be appointed to hear it. But I don't believe it will come to that, I will show you the evidence in a new light which I believe will satisfy you."

"It is your court My Lord, but it is not your place, do you want to go down in history as the judge whose last trial was declared as a mistrial, which is what it would be, whatever happens. But it is your court, so do I have a choice?"

"I don't intend to break the rules, I apologise if I have given that impression." Turning once again to the jury he continued. "As my young friend said, look at the evidence, which is all I am asking of you. Clear pictures of the suspects at the scene of the crime, less clear pictures of them at another place. Latex masks in a skip behind the premises, masks which have never been worn. Baffling, I agree. Is it not possible all this evidence was planted to deflect you into thinking the suspects had to be innocent of the crime, while all along it was a double bluff. Is it possible two sets of masks were made, but only one set was used, by those at the '*Anne Boleyn*', to create an alibi for the others and to fool the police, the public and you, the jurors." He paused, to let his words sink in.

"I see my young friend is about to burst at the seams, ready to shred my theory to pieces, so I will not keep you much longer. Proof is what you need and proof is what you shall have. So far all attempts at locating the diamond have failed, yet its whereabouts is close at hand, in fact I believe it is here in court."

A collective gasp echoed around the court. "What better way to hide the diamond than have it in the open for everyone to see and you have all seen it, in fact I am looking at it right now........ am I not, Mrs Challenor?"

Letting out a low moan, without thinking ,her hand tried to

cover the tawdry looking brooch on her lapel. She was shaking as she muttered, rather too loudly, "No, no it's not possible, there is no way you can know that..."

"Shut up, you stupid bitch," screamed Challenor from the dock, " keep your stupid mouth shut".

"Why should I? You use me when it suits you, but it's too late, you must see, he knows, but it is you who gave it away, yelling at me like that, I am not covering for you no more, he knows everything," she shouted back.

"He knows nothing!" But it was too late, the damage had been done.

The court was in chaos, the media were torn between being the first to let their offices know the latest events, and staying to see what happened next. As was his usual practice, the honourable judge had banned mobiles and other means of electronic communication from his courtroom. It seemed Challenor could not be silenced and he had to be forcibly removed, as was his wife. Kelsey called for a short recess and retired to his Chambers. Lesley, his long suffering secretary, asked if he was in need of a coffee and when she returned with it remarked "What an end to your career, very appropriate really. The first case ended in mayhem because of you, and now your final case is ending the same way."

"Well, it shows consistency at least. Is that such a bad thing?"

She shook her head, "Not in your case, Sak."

"Once more into the breach dear friend, let's see if we can wrap this thing up."

Order had been restored and his Lordship, after thanking the jury for their patience, continued with his 'summing up'. "The Court has shown sympathy for Alfred Martel but was it, I wonder, warranted.."

A shocked silence, then the Prosecution rose, "M'lord, methinks perhaps you have gone a little too far this time, Alfred Martel is a victim"

"Is he though? I am not convinced. According to his evidence, he had trouble removing the stone from its setting, which meant he was running behind schedule. He would have us believe he made an impromptu decision to work late that night to complete his work. According to his testimony it was a balmy summer evening so he left the door ajar in order to enjoy the breeze".

The jury remembered.

"In these somewhat unusual circumstances, I recall Mr. Martel to the stand." Martel was seen to look momentarily to the door, then reluctantly made his way to the front.

"Was it normal practice for you to work overtime on the spur of the moment?"

"Not normal practice, no, but it was not unheard of."

"Ladies and gentlemen of the jury, could it be mere coincidence that this was the very night that Mr. Challenor had planned to rob the premises? If that is your belief, then Mr Martel is innocent of any wrongdoing. However we should consider whether a share of twenty eight million pounds is enough to turn the head, yet alone the head of someone who has spent years cutting some of the world's finest diamonds. Might it not have left him bitter at what he considered a lack of due recognition of his skills, resentful at his relatively low salary. Could this not make him an easy mark for Challenor? Was this why he had agreed to be the inside man?"

"M'lord I must object, not only is all this totally out of order, it is now descending into farce. This is pure guesswork on your part"

"Is it?" and looking him directly in the eyes, "Mr. Martel?"

Alfred's normal pallor changed to a deathly white, his eyes barely left the floor, his voice just a whisper, "No Sir, it happened just as you say, the break in was staged."

“Can you explain why you chose to hide the diamond by not hiding it? It was your idea, was it not?”

“Yes Sir”, his colour had returned and his voice was almost tinged with pride as he explained, “Very few people are familiar with black diamonds and, in my experience, see them as having the same qualities as white diamonds, sparkling as do rubies and sapphires. But it is not so! The black diamond is a different animal altogether. They have no translucency, having the appearance of a black shiny stone. In many cases there is a white mist running through them, giving an effect not dissimilar to marble. I, we rather, took a gamble that a cheap rather gaudy setting for the diamond would fool everybody and it did, everyone apart from you. I’m still surprised you even noticed it.”

“Ingenious, and as you say, nobody else gave the cheap looking brooch on Mrs Challenor’s coat a second glance.” He turned back to the jury “As I said before, a simple case of smoke, mirrors and mis-direction.”

The Defence team consulted with their clients, which now seemed to include Mrs Challenor, and Alfred Martel. After a relatively brief consultation the Defence rose to announce that all wished to change their plea to guilty. Challenor asked permission to address Judge Kelsey.

“Just one question m’lord, how did you know, how could you possibly know?”

Sak smiled, “In truth Mr Challenor, I am not really sure. I listen, I observe and at some point in every trial with which I have been associated, I know what has happened. Despite the opinion of the Defence, I have not abused my position, I listened to exactly the same as all here in the court heard. I summed up what we all heard, long years of practice may have sharpened my gifts, but would I be doing my job if I ignored what I have divined from what we have all heard, I think not.”

Challenor almost smiled, “Just my luck, I plan the almost perfect crime and am thwarted by a judge who, against all the odds, has a gift for hearing the truth!" He looked around the court, making sure of his moment in the spotlight, "It's a fair cop!"

"It is indeed Mr. Challenor, I have done my job, I have summarised what we heard and directed the jury as to their duty." With that he passed sentence, and swiftly left his courtroom for the very last time.

Case over, justice done once more, Sak returned to his office for the very last time. He was tired, no, more than that, he was worn out, exhausted even. After more than forty years on the bench he had known it was time to call it a day. He looked at his wig thrown idly on to his desk, his initials S.A.K. barely visible after years of use. He smiled to himself, he had changed his name to Kelsey to make life easier for himself, but from his very first days at Brasenose he had put his initials on almost everything he owned so fellow students and lecturers alike all came to call him Sak; only a few remembered the surname he had chosen with such care. There were times when he wondered why he had bothered to change his name in the first place and on occasions he had toyed with the idea of changing it back, 'Now I am retiring I might change it back' he thought. 'It would certainly confuse people, and give me anonymity in my dotage, in the unlikely event of anyone wishing to document my career, they'd suddenly come to a halt, reach a dead end.' The idea tickled his fancy.

He took a photo from the desk and wrapped it carefully in bubble wrap, then laid it aside. He idly picked up his wig and twirled it on his finger; he would take his wig, his gown, and what else? He looked around, of course, his briefcase and whatever bore his initials, other than that, he didn't think there was anything he wanted.

What a life it had been, what a curious adventure. His rather odd upbringing, maybe everybody thought their upbringing rather odd, but surely all fathers didn't resent their children, as his father had seemed to resent him. Why had his mother let him be taken away? Why had his uncle and aunt wanted him, only to seem to abandon him later, as if it had all been too much trouble? Maybe he had been too much trouble, to everybody. He would never know the answers to these questions now. His father was dead, but he could remember vividly the time he had himself lain in hospital at death's door, and his father appeared and beckoned him to follow him. To where? He was convinced that had he followed him, he would now be dead. He had had no intention of doing so, Then a voice spoke to him, a voice from his present life, and he chose to follow that voice.

Stirred by memories, he picked up the photo he had wrapped so carefully a short time ago, and unwrapped it. He slumped back in his chair, holding the treasured picture on his knee. It brought it all back, the memories and the miracle, as he saw it, of his courtship.

AELIA'S PROMISE FULFILLED

Celia opened the front door before Kelsey had time to take his keys from his pocket, "I have been watching for you, I hope your last day went well, but you must tell me later because you have a visitor."

Kelsey was surprised, and slightly disappointed, he had looked forward to discussing his day with Celia. It was rare for visitors to come to the house without an appointment, other than family of course, and unusual for Celia to admit a stranger into the house.

"Who is it, male or female, a client?"

"No, he just said his name as Paul and that you were his fashion guru at uni!"

"Oh, come on now. Me a fashion guru, you've seen the photos! The poor student who owned only two black turtleneck sweaters and a dark green V-neck pullover to go on top. Heavens! They were rarely even washed, two or three times a semester! I can't think I was ever anyone's fashion guru!."

"I don't think you ever mentioned before about the lack of laundry. It seems strange now, when you are so fastidious, and insist on clean and fresh clothes every day."

"I wouldn't like you to get the wrong idea, I did shower every day. But let's leave it for the moment, we are keeping my mystery visitor waiting."

The mystery visitor set aside a glass of whisky as he rose from his chair to greet his old friend, "Sak my old mate, it's been a long time."

'It must have been a long time' thought Kelsey, he had no recollection of the person before him, but was mildly amused to see his guest wore a black turtleneck sweater over which he had a V-necked pullover. ‘Whoever he is, it appears my fashion sense lives on’, he thought wryly’. They shook hands, but Kelsey said nothing, waiting for enlightenment.

“You have no idea who I am, do you?”

Kelsey shook his head, laughed, and apologised, “I’m sorry, I meet so many people in my work and...”

“Paul, Paul Tankman, Brasenose 1964.”

He remembered the name and looked thoughtfully at the man before him. His mousy brown hair was mussed up, and his face was lined, though no more than Sak’s own. It was the impish face and engaging smile that eventually brought recognition.

“Good heavens Paul, what on earth are you doing here and what's all this fashion guru nonsense? That really confused me.”

“ I once asked where you bought your jumpers and you took me shopping at CWA.”

“Really, I have no memory of that, but it looks like you're still wearing a dedicated follower of that particular fashion!”

“Good taste never goes out of fashion, Sak.”

Sak shook his head, asking “but what brings you here now, it must be nigh on fifty years.”

“I know. I have been meaning to congratulate you ever since you were elevated to the peerage but I didn’t want it to appear that I was social climbing. Today I found myself in the area, and thought I would take advantage of it. I have to confess it was partly curiosity, I wanted to meet your wife, the woman who finally snared Sak!”

“What are you on about. Give me a moment to pour myself a whisky and then you can explain yourself.”

As Sak poured his drink Paul delved into his briefcase. He grinned, “perhaps this will help explain.”

Sak turned to see his friend on his knees as he unrolled an old and yellowing black and white panoramic photograph," the final photograph, young lawyers all, optimistic that the future of the legal profession was safe in their hands."

Sak, whisky in hand, joined Paul on the floor, staring at the myriad of faces staring up at him as long forgotten memories came to the fore, memories of innocent love, of heartache and loneliness, not to mention laughter and joy.

" I wonder where they are now? Are you still in touch with any of them, Sak?"

"I come across the occasional one in the course of work but we tend to stay remote lest we allow personal feelings top get in the way of sound judgement. How about you?"

"None at all, other than Annie"

"Annie?"

"You will remember her as Annie Tucker,-see if you can pick her out."

He had a mental image, blonde, plumpish, never stopped talking. He soon found her, remembering at the same time that she had the most wonderful voice worthy of any opera company,

"Spot on, Sak. Annie and I continued seeing each other after graduation and nearly married, we are still friends. But in 1972 I married a girl called Trudie, loveliest girl you ever did see. She was my best friend then and remains so to this day. Wife, mother of my children, mistress and lover. I consider myself to have very fortunate."

As Paul continued, Sak smiled to himself, memories of Paul at college were comimg back to him.

"No, my heart was never in the law, family pressure, expectations etc left me little choice initially, but my real affinity was with the arts, theatre, film, and music ...."

As Paul spoke, Sak's memories became clearer, he could see Paul, guitar in hand entertaining his fellow students, not only with traditional folk songs but also with the satirical songs of Tom Lehrer. It had been Paul who organised the dances, who managed to persuade such diverse artists to visit and play, Georgie Fame, the Bonzo Dog Doo Dah Band, as well introducing the intoxicating music of the West Indian Steele band. He had both acted in and directed many of the University's productions and his knowledge of films was legendary. And yes, Sak remembered , Paul had been quite a ladies' man.

Paul went on "the law was too restricting for me, so I decided to go into teaching, which offered me the opportunities to indulge my passions whilst inspiring my students to think and fulfil their potential, those that had any. I think I made the right choice," he paused, smiled, and looking again at the photograph he started pointing at various faces. "You went out with her, and her, wasn't she one of yours, oh and the dark girl, I rather envied you her. You went out with so many girls, not just from our year. From what I heard many more would have been happy to go out with you. . Most of the rest of us blokes were rather envious, we tended to stick with just the one, fearful we might lose even her to you."

Sak rocked back on his heels dumbfounded, if only they had known, those other blokes. For all the confidence his new found academic prowess had given him, there was one influence from the start of his time at Dauntsey's that still haunted him, Spindleshanks! At college he had still seen himself to be the 'nine stone weakling' mocked so mercilessly in the Charles Atlas' advertisements. The skinny social misfit doing nothing while a muscular figure threw sand all over him. He could see no reason why anybody would want to go out with him, yet apparently they did, Paul was right, he had been out with all those girls.

"You really have no idea Paul, really have no idea and I suppose, neither did anyone else. You may not believe me, but at Uni I felt I was the loneliest person there."

"Come on, Sak, is the famous judge's memory failing him. I was there, remember."

"I couldn't confess then how I felt. It's true I went out with loads of girls but when that relationship was over, did you never wonder how I remained friendly and on good terms with all of them." He paused as he considered, "well anyway, almost all of them. I suppose there were one or two..... But in general, there was never anything more, just friendship! Don't get me wrong, I valued each and every one of those friendships, but I think I was immature, naive even."

"Aha! Little wonder the girls viewed you as the most unobtainable man in the place, even some of the married lecturers were considered an easier catch than you! My heavens, Sak you wasted your time there, so many opportunities."

"I didn't think so."

There was another reason why Sak had been unwilling to move his relationships to what many would have thought the ultimate goal and it was one that even now he would never divulge, it was not that he had high morals, it was not even his shyness, although they all played a part. The true reason somehow lay in his bracelet of stones and how could he explain that to anyone. Although he had no memory of how he had come by the hag stone bracelet he was aware that it had come into his possession when he was a young boy. Much teasing and mocking, "ooh look at Sak, he wears a bracelet", and his father's cruel mocking about "my effeminate son" were not enough to make him remove it. Unaware of the day Aelia had slipped it over his wrist he nonetheless believed the stones not only spoke to him but also protected him. Time again when his father raged against him and Sak was in despair, he was aware that the bracelet tightened a little, rather like a gentle hug and the stones gave off a comforting warmth which both calmed him and gave him the strength to bear with his father's jibes.

But it was in matters of love that the stones appeared to be at their most active.

The 1960's are portrayed as the summers of free love, the beginning of the permissive society, but many, Sak included, were still immersed in the values and uncertainties of the fifties; was it right to hold hands on your first date, how long should you be dating before your first kiss? He remembered a girl who was keen on him inviting him to the cinema, he spent the whole time wondering whether or not to put his arm around her, he was almost sure she was giving him encouragement but not sure enough to do anything about it, he didn't even hold her hand. She had dropped him after that. This uncertainty had dominated his first attempts at romance - until, as he thought of it, he had started to listen to the stones.

Once, attending Evensong at Christ Church Cathedral, he had found himself sitting behind a tall girl with long flowing blonde hair; he recognized her as a fellow student but hadn't found the courage to speak to her. Towards the end of the service the stones began to warm his wrist, but as he turned to exit the Cathedral they began to grow cooler again. He paused, and as she got closer they started to warm again. Aware of this strange happening but with no idea of its significance, he continued on his way. The stones cooled and then seemed to rattle against his wrist. The girl, was her name Paula, caught up with him and somehow struck up a conversation. They agreed to go for coffee and thus the first of his 'romances' began.

Sak believed he was in love and things started off well enough; they enjoyed each other's company, going for walks, dinners at the local Indian restaurant, and the occasional chaste kiss goodnight, then as Sak began to feel more passionate, that the time had come to move things on, the stones began to cool whenever Paula was close; it took him a little while to accept the message of the stones but in the end he accepted what seemed to him the inevitable and by mutual consent it seemed, they had agreed to be no more than friends. That set the trend for him throughout the rest of his time at university, many platonic relationships but nothing more. But aware of how bizarre this must sound, there was no way he would say any of this to Paul.

Sak was brought back to the present by Celia entering the room, surprised to see both her husband and his friend on the floor on all fours, pouring over an old photograph

“I thought you might like some coffee. Can I just ask, what on earth are you two doing down there on the floor?”

“Reliving our past, but more importantly, Paul says he wanted to meet, and I quote, the ‘girl who finally snared the heart of Sak.”

Celia laughed, “hello Paul, pleased to meet you properly. But you asked the wrong question. What you should be asking is ‘who is the man who captured the heart of Celia Russo’?”

“She is right you know Paul, that really is the question you should be asking.”

Paul studied Celia a little more closely. Tall, Paul estimated at just under six feet, slim and elegant, long hair now greying but with a few remaining black strands, olive skin and deep brown, questioning eyes. He could imagine how captivating she must have been when young, but wondered if age had given her something more, she was still a ‘head-turner’ in his estimation.

Sak, as if reading his mind, said “Yes, she was quite a beauty and by the time I met her, had many suitors.”

“Where, how, did you meet?”

An innocent enough question, one that Sak had heard often enough and dreaded. He couldn't tell anybody the truth of the matter, and although he had a well-rehearsed answer it couldn’t convey what he privately saw as the almost magical nature of their courtship. Paul, like others before him, found the tale he told convincing, romantic and satisfying but truth is always better than fiction and only Sak knew the truth. Oblivious to the others for the moment, he closed his eyes as he remembered.

Legal Aid had been in its infancy and because of the reputation he was building up, aided by his appearance on the BBC Tonight show, his services were in great demand. He had spent little time in the office and liked to call himself a peripatetic lawyer. On this occasion it had been the last night of a fairly long tour of the West Country and he had intended returning to London, but the trial had finished late, so he had booked into the County Hotel in Yeovilton. As he was settling into his room after a heavy dinner the internal phone rang,

"Mr. Kelsey?"

"Yes, that's me."

"There is a lady in reception, a Miss Russo whom wishes to speak with you"

"I do not know Miss Russo and have no wish to speak with her at this time of night. If she would like to ring my office and make an appointment...."

"She says would it help if you knew she was one of the jurors on your final case today?"

He was on the verge of insisting that he be left in peace when something changed his mind. "Please tell her I will be down momentarily." 'Now why did I say that, must be losing my mind'. As he thought this, he was aware of the warmth of the stones on his wrist.

He recognised her as soon as he stepped out of the lift. He had noticed her from the start, attracted by her looks and bearing. Later he had observed her watching him intently but had taken her attention to be a sign she was concentrating on the proceedings.

"Miss Russo I presume?"

"Judge Kelsey! Thank you for agreeing to see me, especially so late. Please, I would find it easier if you could call me Celia."

He guided her to the lobby lounge where he ordered coffee, after asking for her preference. "Celia then, what's this all about, is there something about the trial verdict that bothers you?"

"I must apologise if I gave that impression. It has nothing to do with the trial. I was desperate to make you see me. As you will perhaps now guess, it is a personal matter, I am afraid"

"I am intrigued." 'What a prig I sound', he thought.

"Well, that's it; I mean I am intrigued too. This must sound strange but I am sure I know you; there is something very familiar about you, I have this very strong feeling ....."

"Celia," he interrupted, "I am sure I would remember you if we had ever met...."

She interrupted in her turn, "no, no. I didn't say we had met, I said your face was familiar to me and I want, I feel I need, to understand. I promise, it is no mere whim...."

Tired and now once again annoyed at being disturbed he interrupted once more "Miss Russo, Celia I really feel this conversation can go nowhere. How can I explain what I do not know? I am tired and if you'll forgive I will return to my room." He rose to his feet but almost before he moved the stone 'spoke' once again, warm and jingling against his wrist they seemed to be trying to convey an urgent message. Bemused, both at himself and events, he sank back down again and thought to change the direction of the conversation.

"Russo, that's not an English name, is it?"

"No, it's Italian"

"I rather thought it might be. Where are you actually from?"

Laughingly she replied "England! I was born in Bath and I still live there."

Of course, he should have recognised the West Country accent from his time at Dauntsey's and his judicial tours of the West Country. It was an accent he had always liked. "Did your family come here after the war, like so many Italians?"

"Oh we can trace our family in England back to Roman times...."

"In all that time the name never changed, became anglicised? Isn't that a bit unusual? My paternal grandfather only arrived in this country in nineteen o one and the spelling and pronunciation seems to have changed almost immediately."

He felt ill at ease, unsure how to proceed and, but for the stones, he would have found an excuse to return to his room. Unwillingly he returned to the original subject. "Can you say what it is about me that seems familiar to you,"

She answered immediately, "there's something about your eyes, I feel as if you have been looking back at me all my life."

"Or maybe you have been looking at me, or my eyes rather. They say I have my grandfather's eyes, and he was quite famous, so you may have seen photos? Myself, I have only visited Bath about three times in my life and those were all very brief visits. I doubt very much that these eyes ever set sight on you, now, if you will excuse me, I am returning to my room. I have to make an early start. Celia, I am sorry not to have been of any help but I would advise you to put this out of your mind, it's just one of those things. Goodnight now." Despite a harsh jangling and the icy coldness of the stones, he returned to his room.

Sleep did not come easily as he tossed and turned. In the early hours of the morning he gave up the attempt, his wrist seemed to be burning where the bracelet had pressed against it. He switched on the light and saw that his bracket was gone, but on his wrist letters burned red, as if he had been tattooed.. He blinked, and looked again. C-E-L-I-A!

'Oh, this is absurd. It can't be happening, I must be dreaming' he thought, 'it makes no sense'. He turned over and tried to get comfortable, but something seemed to be caught up on his right foot. He reached down to free whatever it was, and felt the familiar stones of the bracelet. With some relief, he returned it to his wrist. Later that morning he returned to London in a somewhat distressed state, distracted, feeling unable to concentrate on his work. This was so unusual that it came to the attention of one of the senior partnesr. "Sak, you don't seem yourself this morning. Did something happen in the West Country? Or are you sickening for something? I've checked, and it has been some time since you took any time off. Maybe you should take a few days now. The calendar seem seems okay, so perhaps you should take advantage, hmm?"

Relieved, he packed up his briefcase and left. Wandering down the street he found himself thinking, 'Celia, it was all about Celia, why would the stones not let him forget about Celia? No, that was ridiculous, admit it, it was not the stones! From the first there had been something about Celia, a strong feeling of attraction he hadn't wanted to acknowledge, not for any very good reason, he had thought it was unprofessional. But the case was over, that no longer applied. He regretted the curt way in which he had ended their meeting, for not admitting but that he too had felt something, he couldn't put his finger on precisely what it was, but he was aware of a void, something missing. Face it, he wanted to be with Celia again, to watch her face as she tried to explain the inexplicable, to see the intelligence in her eyes, the little smiles. Could he really be smitten? He couldn't even claim to really know her, No, but maybe that at least could be put right. Using the court network, thinking wryly to himself that this act alone was unprofessional, he found a phone number; a little nervous and feeling sick in the pit of his stomach he dialled the number. He waited nervously, he thought of hanging up, before they eventually answered, "Bath 4579"

"Hello, I was wondering, is Celia there"

"Not at the moment, this is her Mother, can I take a message"

"Thank you yes, can you tell her Simon Kelsey called, and I would be grateful if you could get her to call me." He left his number.

The three hours he had to wait before her call came through were sheer agony. He had no idea whether she would respond and he had only himself to blame if she didn't. He tried sitting down and reading but was unable to concentrate, he resorted to pacing the floor, when that proved ineffective he stared at the phone, willing it to ring. The dull ache in his head, and the pain in his stomach grew more acute, he shouted at the phone, "ring damn you, RING."

He knew he was being absurd. Perhaps Celia was at work and hadn't yet got his message. What did she do, anyway? Maybe she had the message but wasn't able to ring at this time, or maybe she just didn't want to talk to him. What a mess! He leant back in his chair, feeling exhausted, closed his eyes and sleep overcame him.

RING RING, RING RING, RING... He woke with a start and lunged at the phone lest it rang off before he got to it,

"Hello, Celia?" (Oh hell, what if it wasn't?)

"Yes," her voice was soft and she sounded nervous. "I'm sorry about last night, I don't know what I was thinking! Why did you call me, I thought your dismissal of me was pretty final."

"Yes, and I regretted it almost immediately, so please accept my apologies..."

"Accepted - is it my turn to dismiss you now?"

Oblivious to the soft laugh which followed, he hastened to say "No, please don't do that. Look Celia, this might sound strange, given our first meeting but I have this feeling that it is important that I see you, and as soon as possible."

"Feeling, hmm? But why, you didn't seem to think feelings were important last night."

"I can't blame you for being bitter but just as you can't explain the feeling of familiarity with me I can't really explain my feeling. Only that it feels, sorry, that word again, seems imperative that we meet."

"I could argue with that, but it happens I don't want to, I'd love to see you again."

Kelsey felt a calmness, a rightness, and the warmth of the stones on his wrist seemed to confirm his feelings.

He left for Paddington Station early the next morning in time to catch the first train to Bath and arrived in the city at about ten fifteen. As they'd arranged, she was there to meet him, looking, he was sure, even more beautiful than he remembered. 'Not pretty,' he thought, 'stronger than that, definitely beautiful.'

They were glad to see each other, but a little uncertain. The drive to Celia's family home was feeling a little awkward, so Celia talked about her home, "I think I told you we can trace our family back to Roman times and legend has it that one of our ancestors had a position of some importance, but that is probably apocryphal and can't be substantiated, but what is true is that my great-great-great Grandfather built our house in the grounds of an old, derelict villa, using many of the old materials in its construction, no planning laws or preservation orders in those days, so it is a mish-mash of building materials, ancient and modern you might say. We are still discovering bits and pieces in the grounds, many of which we have kept in a sort of private museum, you might find it interesting. I hope you will."

Sak thought how pleased Beram would be if this, what was it, relationship? worked out.

Her mother turned out to be an older version of her daughter, retaining her own beauty and elegance. As they sat enjoying freshly brewed coffee she stared intently at him and eventually turning to her daughter, "I do see what you mean darling."

"Why don't you show Simon round while I prepare lunch, I am sure our little museum will interest him"

Sak started, Simon? Oh yes, that was his name. The museum, in reality a repurposed double garage was awash with Roman artefacts, there were coins, bits of broken pottery, ceramic oil lamps, complete Samian bowls, all of which suddenly lost Sak's interest. He stood stock still, staring in disbelief, his face was pale and his legs were shaking. He turned to Celia, grabbed her hand and rushed her out of the building and back into the kitchen. To Celia's mother he said "I am so sorry, Celia and I must leave for London immediately."

There was a shocked silence, Sak tried to explain, "when you first saw me you stared in much the same way Celia had when she first laid eyes on me. I believe I now know why, but we have to go. We'll be back tomorrow in time for lunch, and hopefully I can explain, not evderything, but a bit. But I need to make sure."

Yet another awkward journey. He begged her to be patient, to trust him, and she spoke kindly, but in a bewildered way. His hands were shaking when he inserted his key into his front door, 'what if I am wrong?' He led Celia to the door of the sitting room, "one more instruction, the last I promise you. Please close your eyes."

He opened the door, "Ok you may open them."

The colour drained from her face, her legs turned to jelly. Luckily when she fainted, he caught her before she fell to the floor. He glanced again at the picture above his mantelpiece. A portrait of himself at fourteen years old painted by his sister. Facially it was identical to the faded picture he had seen in Celia's museum.

"How can that be?" she whispered as she came round.

She rose from the chair to study the picture more closely, it was not just similar to the painting she had lived with all her life, it was in essence the same boy, which must mean..., but how could it be?.

"So I was right, wasn't I? You have been with me all life, I just never knew."

She turned to face him, then they were hugging each other and their lips met for the first time.

Back in Bath the following day they were seated around the kitchen table. Her mother had been amazed when the portrait had been revealed to her. She clutched her rosary and muttered Hail Marys under her breath.

"I don't understand what is happening, it must be God's will, all this done to bring you together. I need to be alone to give thanks, why not go for a walk, I'll have lunch ready when you return.

Hand in hand they strolled along the banks of the river Avon. Unaware that they had reached the spot where Aelia had first slipped her hand into his, he stopped, turned to Celia, dropped to his knees and proposed.

"Get up you old softie, surely you don't need to ask. It is how it is meant to be. I can't argue with fate, even if I don't understand it.

Unnoticed, the bracelet slipped from his wrist.

Sak came to with a start, how long had he been lost in his memories? Not that it seemed to matter; Celia and Paul seemed almost not to have noticed, and were chatting happily away. Celia, aware he had come back from wherever he had gone, touched his hand and smiled at him.

TIME OF THE OAK

Sak slipped down from Helge's shoulders, and stood before him, feeling unable to speak, barely able to think, overwhelmed by things forgotten, memories that had now returned to him. Helge smile, "You have remembered." Sak leant forward and put his arms round him, hugging him with genuine warmth, while his mind worked busily, trying to sort what to say, and how to say it. He was recalling, now he'd remembered, how Helge had taken him on a journey, a journey through history, through his history. He somehow felt he had been an invisible intruder in his own life.

Unwillingly, he had watched while on Helge's shoulders. as an overbearing father bullied and mocked his young son. Then he was uplifted when that passed and he 'saw'his aunt and uncle coming to his rescue. But he still didn't know why that had happened, why his parents had agreed.

"Can I go back and witness that moment?" he asked, confident Helge would know to what he was referring.

"What purpose would it serve now? Those years are long passed. You are what you have become, the sum of all your experiences."

Sak shook his head, for a moment he'd forgotten what he had become, despite of, or perhaps because of all that had happened. In that moment he laid to rest the spectre of his father.

He had a fleeting sense of himself when young and in despair, leaning against the oak tree. He saw himself again in Stonehenge, in Aqua Sulis and during Elizabethan times. He was aware of the hag stones warm against his wrist, and for some reason his mind turned again to Aqua Sulis. Once more he stood before Aelia, as at their parting, he felt the old sadness and regret. In a moment it passed, and as in a revelation, he murmured wonderingly, “Aelia - Celia?”

He looked towards Helge and saw him smile, almost he looked smug. That first meeting with Celia, and his thought at the time that it had happened because of the stones. But Celia had not been Aelia, yet something tugged at his mind, there was something there, a sense of the rightness of it all. Aelia’s gift maybe? No, he was being foolish, he was turning into a silly old fool.” He had not spoken his thoughts out loud but now Helge spoke.

“It doesn’t really matter, does it? Not now. You have come here to save an oak tree, not knowing why, but realising it was important. Tomorrow will be what in days of old we called the Time of the Oak. it has fulfilled its purpose. For almost two thousand years that Oak has been my prison”

Oh yes, I remember you told me something of that before.

“My prison”, he looked up into the branches of the oak, a look Sak found hard to interpret. Helge was speaking again, “my life on earth ended in the year 840.AD. As I told you, I had expected to be received in Valhalla, but it turned out this was not to be. After years of faithful service I was judged to have abandoned my people, betrayed the Viking code. I could not argue, I felt I deserved to be punished. Odin and Thor determined the length of my imprisonment in the oak was dependent on my subsequent actions. Darkness descended upon me and I languished in that blackness for many years having no idea of how to proceed. I reached a point where I despaired. I did not see how I might earn remission. It seemed absurd, a cruel joke. What actions could I perform, locked inside the darkness. I had to accept that my treachery had been such that there would be no end, just darkness and despair.

The thought of never seeing daylight again, of not hearing birdsong, of never seeing sunshine and shadow, of not being aware of rain falling on leaves and grass, never smell again the scents of the forest. I felt the gods had abandoned me just as they believedI had them. I understood their anger and resigned myself to my fate, I gave up. Then one day I sensed the tears of a young boy and heard his sobs, For some reason it was those tears that released me from my prison, or perhaps more accurately, they granted me a form of day release. I found I was freed whenever you needed me but afterwards was returned to the confines of the oak."

"I am so sorry, I had no idea." To himself he thought 'am I really sitting here, listening to this absurd story." Yet he knew it made a kind of sense, even explained things that sometimes puzzled him.

"Well of course you didn't. As you've now remembered, we had many adventures in time which allowed you to become your own person, and determine your own destiny. Then, before you left Dauntsey's, I gave you a gift. I knew that how you used that gift would determine my fate. I had to have faith that you would do so wisely, I could no longer guide or influence you. I had been given my chance, and while I knew that, in many ways you were more important to me than my own fate. You have used that gift well and now you are retired and have no need for it. Odin and Thor are of one mind, I have earned my release, for which I thank you. My release will happen the moment the oak falls."

"This gift? I was not aware..., what form did it take?"

"It was from the beginning the same gift, the ability to travel in time."

"No, that can't be. It didn't happen after I left Dauntsey's."

"Did it not? Before we set out on your first adventure in time I explained that life in your time will be suspended. Tell me, what has been your routine always, before you interview a client, or when you are about to sum up a case?"

He thought back, it was strange, he hadn't realised before, although probably his secretary had. "I close my eyes for a few seconds in order to clear my mind."

"Ah! To you it seemed but a few moments, because of that suspension of time. In reality, if that is the right word to use in the circumstance, you are taken back in time to witness the very root of the crime, understand the reasons for it ....."

"You mean to say I have no real ability, my insight, which has made my career, for which I am famed, this has been no more than a conjuring trick." He realised he was angry, hr feltbhe'd been made a fool of yet again; he had nothing of which to be proud.

"There you go again, the little boy feeling sorry for himself, for all your famed intuition, you can be obtuse sometimes."

Sak bit back "Not surprising, is it? I need those little jaunts in time to tell me everything! If they don't happen, I revert to my usual, obtuse self, obviously. Evidently even!"

"The knowledge my gift gave you could have been used for your personal gain, not for justice. You could have made a lot of money helping criminals t o get off, framing the innocent, blackmailing people. But that never occurred to you. You saw the truth and used it to ensure justice was done, even when it sometimes caused you problems. You dispensed justice not just with mercy and compassion, but with understanding. You have changed many lives for the better. And from my point of view of course, your actions have brought about my release. I hope you will be here tomorrow, when this mighty oak, the tree of heaven, also comes to rest."

Sak arrived at the oak to the sound of chainsaws and strimmers, clearing the area around the great tree and preparing the ground where they wanted her to fall. He was minded of his time as a member of the forestry group, clearing ground with scythes, and when a tree, through necessity, was felled, the clear, clean sound of the axes as they made contact with the tree to be felled. There was something noble, or was it only romantic, about man against the tree. He recalled with fondness the aroma of freshly cut timber but now it was different. There seemed to be noise and smoke, the smell of hot oil, he felt for the tree in the midst of all this mayhem.

He was pulled from his thoughts by a lad asking him to move back, 'health and safety you know!' Then the executioner, (as Sak thought of the tree feller) donned his hard hat, goggles and ear-muffs, revved up his machine and started to cut into the tree that had given Sak so much comfort as a boy. Wood chips and sawdust flew in all directions.

He slowly became aware that he could hear a voice, chanting, from the heart of the oak, it seemed.

How to kill the mighty oak tree,
How to fell the tree majestic
How to lop its hundred branches
Is there not some mighty hero
That can fell the mighty oak tree
That can lop its mighty branches.....

The men and the noise had faded into the background, Sak seemed to see a mighty Norseman, bearing a huge hatchet, stride towards the oak. The mighty hatchet was born aloft. Now two voices were chanting in unison:

Yields the oak with hundred branches,
Shaking earth and heaven in falling,
Eastward far the trunk extending,
Far to westward flew the tree-tops,
To the South the leaves were scattered,
To the North the hundred branches.....

For a moment the mighty oak seemed to resist the attack. It seemed she groaned, exhaled her final breath and began to fall. Of those there only Sak saw Helge standing proud in the prow of his long boat for one final voyage, the Valkyries emerging from behind the clouds, guiding the boat and Helge to his final destination.
The voices faded. The once mighty oak crashed to the ground, as it did so something hit Sak on the head then fell to the ground. It seemed as if Helge turned, and there was that voice once more:

On each twig an acorn growing
Golden balls upon each acorn
On each ball a cuckoo singing....

The voice faded away.

Sak bent down to discover what had hit him; it was a twig, bearing an acorn. He picked it up, in the sunlight from above it seemed to have a golden sheen. He put it in his pocket. Then he heard it, 'Cuckoo! Cuckoo!' Smiling, he walked away. He felt no loss, rather that all was as it was supposed to be.

He emerged from the Manor Woods, knowing it had been the oak's time to fall. With no memory of Helge, or his adventures through time, he felt Celia calling to him, and huttied on his way.

THE END

[The lines are from The Kalevala]

Printed in Great Britain
by Amazon

50745396R00153